Advance praise for Charles W. Rath's

In Lieu of Flowers

D1320322

"*In Lieu of Flowers* is a murd...love story in disguise. Growing up in a small town in the 1950's, I could relate to much of the human dynamics in a uniquely personal way. Brilliantly told—only the way Rath could tell it. You will reminisce, laugh, cheer, and mourn as you read—then you will want to re-read it."

-Emil J. Brolick, Former President and CEO
of Wendy's Company

"*In Lieu of Flowers*—set in the heartland of central Ohio—recounts a much simpler time, with the modern-day issues and complexities of the most fascinating characters. The narrative of Billy's guardian angel not only provides a perspective on Billy's life, his exceptional musical talents, and the life of his immigrant parents—but also paints a rich portrait of Anäel's heavenly world. What a wonderfully well-researched, fascinating tale, elegantly written by a great storyteller."

-Tim Busch, President of Nexstar Broadcasting, Inc.

"Imaginative storytelling and endearing characters! The author vividly portrays life in America in the 1950's, an exhilarating era with many forces in play. Get set for a journey down memory lane in the presence of good and evil."

-Matt Dee, Creative Writer, Editor, and Former Director of Advertising
Production for Wendy's Restaurants

"*In Lieu of Flowers* is both mystery and autobiography. Its detailed descriptions reveal the insights and experiences of its author, whose 'coming of age' in rural Bellefontaine, Ohio was affected by his emerging love and knowledge of jazz and his perceptive awareness of the local gypsy culture, the disturbing mafia, and the realities of social injustices impacting the good people of his community."

-Mabel G. Freeman, Ph.D., Retired University Administrator

"I've always pictured 'the fifties' in black and white, like the TV reruns I watched growing up in the sixties. Families were charming and moral. The good guys always wore white hats and came out on top. *In Lieu of Flowers* is a coming-of-age story, set in the fifties, presented in vivid Technicolor. Billy Barnes lives and dies in a world rich with incidents, accidents, and colorful characters. Gypsies, mobsters, and an aging burlesque dancer add unexpected texture to a love story wrapped in jazz and tied up with a dark rainbow ribbon of the cultural truths of the times. The visible spectrum of this story spans religion to racism, but the most enjoyable elements are invisible—the dreams of a young musician, the music drifting through each chapter, and a guardian angel narrator who, if we're lucky, will tell us more stories in future works by Charlie Rath."

-Michael Ivey, Broadcast Director, Storyteller, and Former Commentator on NPR's *All Things Considered*

"The author creates a perfect escape for us complete with youth, the promise of talent, a benevolent and worldly guardian angel, food you can smell and taste, music you want to hear again and again, and complex, interesting humans living out their lives. I wish I could live in the world the author creates, but I have to settle for a long, deeply rewarding visit each time I pick up this charming, memorable book."

-Theresa Loar, Lecturer on International Affairs and Former Diplomat

"Charles Rath is a gifted storyteller. With *In Lieu of Flowers*, he has created a tapestry of fully developed characters, and exposed a slice of our national DNA which touches on the celestial hierarchy, ancient history, poetry, gypsy culture, race, mob influences, and an encyclopedia of the distinctive styles of our jazz and blues legends. Charles understands the soul of a musician and what it takes to develop a timeless classic. He has also provided a wonderful love story, with all of the complex elements that true love must resolve. The story takes place in locales and during a period that I know quite well, and Charles is giving us a most enjoyable reading experience."

-David J. Shanahan, Author, Raconteur, and Former Theater Critic

"Centered around Ohio's Million Dollar Playground during our 1950's childhood, Charlie Rath's *In Lieu of Flowers* is an intimate blend of drama, humor, trial, and triumph. Recalling those exciting, pleasurable times, we have enjoyed many lengthy conversations reflecting on those wonderful, crazy escapades at the Park's arcade—the carnival rides (such as the Dodgem, which our family owned), water skiing, boating, swimming, and Danceland's two venues: Stardust Ballroom and Moonlight Terrace Gardens. Each mention of a place, a person, or a happening reawakens those golden years, which unfortunately were tarnished by the intrusion of an unsavory element which prematurely ended our family restaurant—and, for that matter, signaled the imminent decline of that grand era. Thank you, Charlie, for this special memento."

-Bernard and Pat Sweeney, Sandy Beach
Amusement Park Restaurateurs

In Lieu of Flowers

A Novel

by

Charles W. Rath

To Lou i Tew and my great ND friends! Best Wishes Charlie '58

The author gratefully acknowledges permission to reprint lyrics to "Skylark" by Johnny Mercer (words) and Hoagy Carmichael (music). Copyright © 1941 (renewed) by The Johnny Mercer Foundation and Songs of Peer, LTD. All rights for The Johnny Mercer Foundation administered by WB Music Corp (all rights reserved). Used by permission of Alfred Music.

The author also wishes to acknowledge the *Bellefontaine Examiner*, whose contemporaneous original reporting on the July Fourth riots on Indian Lake serves as the basis for the news article that appears in Chapter 3 of this novel.

The author is also grateful to the Logan County Historical Society, which served as the source for a number of locations, dates, times, and photographs related to Sandy Beach Amusement Park and the surrounding area.

ISBN-13: 978-1-7333182-0-4

Front and back cover design by Alan Gregory

To my wife, Susie;

to Annie and Tom, Katie and Bill, and Charlie and Michele;

and to our nine real-life grand-characters: Zach, Evelyn,

Henry, Gigi, Will, Charlie, Amelia, Ian, and Madeline

Logan County Coroner's Office

Abstract: Postmortem Examination

Of the Body of

Willis (Billy) Barnes

Full report on file: Case # FLC – 668 – Autopsy Office, 2nd

Floor

8:43 a.m., 4 July 1961: A postmortem examination of the body of a 24-year-old Caucasian male identified as Willis (Billy) Barnes is performed at the Logan County Medical Examiner's Office, Bellefontaine, Ohio. Examination conducted by Coroner Samuel H. Brown, M.D.

ATTENDANCE:

In the performance of their usual and customary duties, Autopsy Assistants Sissy Auberger and Chuck Slicer and Photographer Myron Clark are present during the autopsy. Also present during the autopsy is Russells Point Police Department Chief of Police, Joseph Kuldau.

CLOTHING:

The body of the deceased is received clad in black pants, print t-shirt, white briefs, and black sandals on bare feet.

PROPERTY:

A yellow metal band ring is on the left ring finger.

EXTERNAL EXAMINATION:

The body is that of a well-developed, well-nourished, adult Caucasian male 166 pounds and 73.3 inches, whose appearance is appropriate for the stated age of 24 years. The body is cold. Rigor mortis is present. Livor mortis is purple, posterior, and blanches with pressure.

GROSS:

See report on file.

MICROSCOPIC:

1. Positive microscopic findings discussed are limited to those that are patho-physiologically significant. Sections from the cardiac apex reveal diffuse hemorrhage and marked tissue disruption, consistent with fatal injury resulting in immediate or nearly immediate death.

2. Routine microscopic examinations of tissue sections from the following organs are normal: liver, kidneys, spleen,

pancreas, and stomach.

PATHOLOGIC DIAGNOSES:

A. Penetrating gunshot wound of the anterior chest, intermediate-to-distant range

B. Perforation of heart with internal bleeding

C. Recovery of 145-grain bullet – dull aluminum jacket

D. Trajectory: Front to back without significant lateral or vertical deviation

OPINION:

This 24-year-old male, Willis (Billy) Barnes, died of a gunshot wound to the chest. According to reports, early Tuesday, July 4, 1961—the day of his demise—he was engaged in an altercation with patrons of Suggins' Suds 'n' Grub beer garden and Alma's Patisserie next door who were rioting in the street, which resulted in his being shot.

At the time of the investigation, it was unclear whether the wound was suicidal, homicidal, or accidental. Autopsy examination revealed a penetrating gunshot wound to the chest, which damaged the heart and resulted in internal bleeding. The bullet was recovered in two pieces from the spine and from the posterior thorax. While the ballistics findings allow some room for interpretation, the characteristics of the entrance defect are consistent with an intermediate- to distant-range fire wound which rules out suicide. In conclusion, the manner of death is determined to be:

ACCIDENTAL BULLET WOUND TO THE CHEST

SHB/MD – 4 July 1961 – 1:37 p.m.

Chapter 1

<u>Indian Lake, Ohio – Tuesday, July 4, 1961</u>

Technically speaking, my assignment was complete when the immortal soul of Billy Barnes departed his lifeless body this morning at 3:09 a.m. Eastern.

True, I'm free to move on to my next assignment. But my *Big Boss*—God the Son—lets us take a five-day breather between postings. And so, out of respect, I've chosen to stay back to pay homage to Billy, whom I've been responsible for since his birth in 1937.

What's more, I'm confused. This man's violent death so blatantly contradicts his life of civility, love, and respect for others. I would characterize Billy as a silent heart, taught to sing—like a tune out of his band's dance book, "Love Is a Many Splendored Thing." Billy's life was a song. It was poetry. The report from the (not-highly-esteemed) county coroner, Dr. Samuel H. Brown, is a cream pie in the face:

ACCIDENTAL BULLET WOUND TO THE CHEST.

I'm impugning the integrity of an elected official, I know, but his arrest record for DUI and public intoxication does cast a suspect light on his opinion. That's why those six words—*accidental bullet wound to the chest*—just don't hold water. Admittedly, I do tend to overreach my milieu, but think about it: based on the information in the autopsy report, there is no way that coroner character could know if Billy's death was accidental or intentional—as in *murder*, not suicide. I agree with this single pea-brained finding of the doctor—this was no suicide—but with no known eyewitnesses and without Dr. Brown having been there himself, there's something fishy about this "accident" business.

In truth, my instincts tell me that the coroner took the easy way out: a ruling of "accidental death" does not require him to appear in court to defend his conclusion. For a suspected homicide, though, the doc would have to don his Sunday best, address a jury from the witness chair, and receive a thorough grilling from some clever defense attorney. Accordingly, the coroner's political stock could be severely diminished. Better to say "accident" and go about the rest of his day.

Beyond the politics of it all, there's the question of *Why?* Why is my ward, Billy Barnes, the sole victim of last night's mayhem? Considering my own doubts about what really happened, I want to stand by until the memorial service on Saturday, to hear what the bereaved—especially Annabelle Lea—have to say about Billy's passing. Maybe one of them knows something or sees something that I can't.

Though I've known Billy for the past twenty-four years, I had no say in the matter of his demise. But I'm getting ahead of myself. Likely, you are curious about who I am. Well, I'm *not* the Creator, but I represent Him. You could say I work for Him by way of His son, and have for eons.

Let me explain.

In the celestial hierarchy, there exists a *pre*-antediluvian power structure and functional organization of nine choirs of angels. The top two you probably already know—Seraphim and Cherubim. But further down the pecking order, there's a group of us known as *Guardian Angels.* Many humans are aware of us, but have only spotty knowledge of what we actually do. Completely understandable, since there have been very few sightings of us in human history—but we *do* exist, and have for all eternity.

Our job description is published in 1877's *L'Osservatore Romano,* in a bit entitled "Angelica Commendatia" written by Pope

Pius IX in preparation for the First Vatican Council. Here, Guardian Angels are described as heavenly spirits assigned by God the Son, Second Person of the Holy Trinity—whom I refer to as the *Big Boss*— to watch over human beings during their lifetimes. Due to an editorial mix-up, what was inadvertently omitted from the article—and later restored in the *Sensus Fidelium*—is that we are messengers, protectors of nature channeling between the spiritual and physical worlds. And, yes, we do have names given to us by God the Son. Mine is *Anäel*, meaning one who oversees all matters of the heart— romantic love, passion, mutual love—and, if asked, guides those who call on him to see beauty in all of life, especially in artful and creative expressions.

You may know of certain public reports in which an angel appeared to someone for some purpose, and you may have found yourself skeptical of these stories' veracity. A good instinct, if also a cynical one: guardian angels *are* real, but our appearances are far more infrequent than the stories might have you believe. I'll focus for now on the angelic appearances recounted in the Bible. While there are some differences of opinion among the nine choirs of angels, there is a general accord that twenty-some of these appearances are valid.

I won't go through all twenty; chances are, even a layperson is familiar with the most famous biblical examples. To wit: an angel appeared to Zacharias the priest declaring he would have a son to be named John the Baptist; the angel Gabriel told a virgin named Mary that she would give birth to the savior of mankind, Jesus; and Mary's husband, Joseph, received at least three separate visits from angels—one regarding marrying Mary and two concerning the protection of the infant, Jesus.

And my personal favorite, from Acts 12:1-10: Christ's disciple, Peter, is asleep in his prison cell, and is awoken when someone—guess who—causes the chains to fall from his wrists and then accompanies him on a safe journey out of the city. The next day, of course, none of the prison guards know siccum about what's happened to their prisoner: they offer a chorus of "We didn't see nothin'!"

Funnier still is when Peter arrives at the home of Mary, mother of John, and has the servant inform the others of his presence. Those in the home do not believe the servant, exclaiming that "It must be his Angel" rather than Peter himself. This was the common belief of the Jews at the time, that every Israelite had a guardian angel assigned to him, and that the angel often appeared as the person he protected.

The point is that, in all cases, the angel acts as a messenger, a purveyor of vital information. And it is true that angels have the ability to assume a form recognizable to humans, but only in the most extreme circumstances. In truth, the day-to-day duties of a guardian angel are far less dramatic than the Bible might have you believe. We guide our charges to good thoughts, words, and deeds, and preserve them from evil. We will not interfere unless asked— and, typically, that comes in the form of a humble supplication from our ward, usually *sotto voce*, as in: *Dear God, please...*

We GAs also speak among ourselves, though not in the same way humans speak. If I were to use a word all humans know to describe the nature of GA communication, it would be *gossip*. But, since human gossip deals mostly with shadings of truth, that word would imply that lies are part of the angelic discourse, too—and *that* is simply not the case! Angels do not lie, have no reason or motive to lie. Ergo, *truth* is the currency of celestial dialogue: it is all we angels know how to speak.

We can appear with any other triad (the nine angelic choirs are grouped in threes). As supernatural beings, we are able to access any human's thoughts, not just our ward's, when granted the professional courtesy of their GA's approval—which is typically a given, *quid pro quo*. We also offer guidance on self-transformation—that is, turning from within—as well as death, birth, protection, and defense.

The most unique of our God-given talents is our ability to be present anywhere and anytime we deem it important to our ward's well-being. We travel to and from anywhere instantly. All GAs have their own calling card, a subtle and tangible clue of our presence in any given place at any given time, though most humans would never suspect it. In my case, my physical presence is a shaft of light shaped in myriad ways—a circle, a square, a rectangle, or some other obscure polygon. I could, for my reader's convenience, ascribe narrative meaning to the shapes themselves, and the color of the light contained within them. A circle could be *normal discourse*, a square could be *exposition*, a triangle could be *argument*; we may even add a color to the shape—a *green* square for all-clear, a *yellow* triangle for caution, a *red* circle for danger—to further communicate meaning. It could be a color-coded guide to the story I'm about to tell you of Billy Barnes. For now, suffice it to say that, when appropriate to do so, I will signal my presence to you, the reader.

In addition to the enormous power that comes from our

unencumbered movement through space, there is another means by which we GAs enhance our cognition. It's part of the GA's special armamentarium called *Penso Appositus,* or "Thread of Relevance." This is the ability to access and integrate recent past or present information outside our ward's awareness but related to our ward's well-being. However, it does not grant the ability to foresee our ward's future or identify a lurking peril in advance by any means other than our keen intuition.

By no means are we omniscient or infallible. In fact, we are vulnerable to *Conscientia Defectum*—a failure of awareness—whereby we miss something that happens to our ward. Such was the case early this morning, during the riot where Billy met his (not accidental!) demise.

In any event, our powers and endowments are neutralized upon the death of our ward, meaning it will take some genuine detective work on my part to suss out Billy's killer. While I have my suspicions about who killed Billy, I've learned from my GA colleagues that the best way to flush out the truth surrounding a mystery of this nature—an untimely death—is by recounting the full story for consideration and scrutiny. Accordingly, I will exercise my privilege as Billy's guardian angel to recount his life story in a way that portrays my profound affection for his *mostly* gentle spirit and washes away my disconsolate grief—while also, hopefully, teaching you something about your own humanity, too.

I'm telling you all this because the case history I'm about to share with you—told in my own words, largely from my own perceptions, but occasionally requiring me to draw on the perspective of an alternate witness for clarity—bears your understanding of my role in Billy Barnes's transformation, defense, and death. After all, your life will eventually be touched by these forces, too.

Fair warning: My narrative will include references to some of the ugly traits your imperfect human society tolerates—anger, hatred, greed, and what I would describe as blatant social injustice. I think you'll see what I mean.

I'll keep my own backstory short. After having been the guardian angel for some real doozies, I was fortunate enough to work with a few very well-known celebrity types, such as Joseph of Arimathea, Catherine of Aragon, Florence Nightingale, and on down the line, with several more contemporary souls, such as Gregori J. Zinovjev, the Russian revolutionary. After Gregori's death in 1936, I was assigned to the infant Rupiah Banda, born February 13, 1937, in the town of Miko, Gwanda. I was prepared to move on to Southern Rhodesia when, at the last minute, a colleague of mine, who had just come off a very tough stint with Rudyard Kipling, petitioned the Big Boss to let him swap his new ward, Willis Barnes, for mine. And that's how I came to be Billy Barnes's guardian angel.

Making the switch wasn't a big deal, but I did take a few minutes to catch up with the *Who*, *What*, and *Where* of Billy's arrival on God's planet Earth. (The *Why* part, you'll have to be patient for.) In doing so, I noticed some uncommon details. Willis was born of a gypsy mother whose ancestors—Romanichals from England—migrated to Ohio's Miami Valley in the mid-1800s. The Romani name for Willis's mother was Willa Mae Stanley, born May 4, 1905—a direct descendant of Matilda Stanley, Queen of the Gypsies. Willis's father, Thomas Patrick Barnes, was nicknamed "Jupie," as the planet Jupiter was visible as the brightest star in the evening sky on the day of his birth—St. Patrick's Day, 1903.

Jupie and Willa Mae met in June 1934 at a VFW statewide celebration held in Dayton, Ohio, honoring the wounded and deceased veterans of World War I with a memorial monument dedicated to the local heroes of The Great War. Their meeting took place in the food service tent, with Willa Mae entertaining on violin while her father, Yoska, accompanied her on concertina. Soon after the war ended, Jupie's father—Lance Corporal Daniel Joseph "DJ" Barnes—was awarded the Distinguished Service Cross, posthumously, for bravery. DJ served in the American 32nd Division as part of the French 10th Army, which spearheaded penetration of the enemy's main line on August 22, 1918.

As part of the celebration, Jupie had agreed to read a poem written by his father's army buddy, Danny Rapp, and sent to Jupie's mother, Dora Barnes. As a prelude to his reading, Jupie asked Willa Mae to play an Irish song in memory of his father. The crowd fell silent as she offered a poignant rendition of "Danny Boy."

Following Willa Mae's performance, a respectful silence greeted Jupie as he stepped to the microphone and read Danny's letter. It was an elegiac summary of DJ and Danny's service together, accompanied by a poem Danny had written to commemorate his friend's death. Jupie read the poem in a steady, strong voice; Willa Mae would never have suspected him of crying had she not been close enough to him at the microphone to see the tears welling in his lower eyelids, never actually falling.

One year later, Willa Mae and Jupie married at St. Mary's of the Woods Catholic Church in Russells Point, Ohio. On paper, it looked like a typical union between an average man and an average woman. But the description of their personality attributes and physical characteristics—extensively noted by their individual GAs—caught my attention. Jupie's GA, a kindred soul of *Balthial*, Angel of Forgiveness—grantor of unconditional forgiveness and help in overcoming jealousy and resentment—noted Jupie's Nordic stature and fiery red hair. Jupie was physically powerful, short-tempered but quickly mollified, kind and tolerant unless insulted.

Willa Mae's GA, *Soqed Hozi*—known for energizing intimate relationships by overseeing the balance between feeling and truth in one's life through one's partners (i.e., enriching intimate relationships)—described Willa Mae as nothing less than Madonna-like in natural beauty, assertive in demeanor, well-endowed in figure, and devoted to gypsy traditions, especially learning and teaching music performed on instruments such as the violin, accordion, concertina, and guitar.

And thus were the facts at my command as I began my tenure as guardian angel to Willis "Billy" Barnes.

Chapter 2

<u>Sunday, February 21, 1937 – 5:00 a.m.</u>

On that miserably cold Sunday morning, I was right there to witness the events surrounding the first few days of life for Willis "Billy" Barnes, son of Thomas Patrick "Jupie" Barnes and Willa Mae Stanley Barnes. Willa Mae struggled to comfort Billy, who squirmed and wailed as though he were in a torture chamber until relieved by suckling his mother's generous breast. He began his life in a peaceful place he came to find out later was a homemade tin-roof shanty attached to a roller coaster structure called the Silver Streak, built by a man named Pappy Wilgus, who opened Sandy Beach Amusement Park on Indian Lake in 1924. And that's where Billy's dad, Jupie, worked as the maintenance man on-call for every emergency, from broken lightbulbs to defective pinball machines to jammed gears on the merry-go-round.

At this point, I think it's prudent to mention that it was by God's unfathomable plan that my ward, Billy, was born and raised in the Midwest next to a body of water named Indian Lake. If asked today which historical time-period I've found most interesting, I could name more than a dozen possibilities of life-changing, soul-scorching, inimitable eras. For starters, there's the Holocene epoch, which began at the end of the last glacial period of the current ice age, circa 10,000 BC. Then, there would be the Roman Empire, the Birth of Christ, the Early Middle Ages, the Roaring Twenties, the Great Depression, the convulsionary Nazi scourge of World War II, and the Space Age. Oddly enough, I would choose the decade of the 1950s in America—dubbed "The Nifty Fifties"—as the era I've been most fond of, and during which my young ward grew from infancy through childhood, to adolescence and...well, we'll get to that adulthood part in a bit.

But the 1950s was the berries for me—and for a lot of reasons. There was a magic quality to it. World War II was a springboard to a new sense of freedom, legitimizing behavior that theretofore would have been considered "unacceptable." I remember James Dean dying in 1955, exemplifying the mantra "live fast, die young, leave a good-looking corpse." A feeling of permissiveness urged youth to experiment with everything: sex, drugs, fast cars, fast food, loud music, and revealing hemlines. Despite the negatives associated with the cultural changes, the positives outweighed them, and the dynamics of that rapid growth forced inevitable changes that have profoundly shaped our present day. Some call that evolution—and, for the most part, I would agree.

God does not ask His guardian angels to agree with His choice of locale for their assignments, but I honestly could not have been happier with the beauty, simplicity, charm, and allure of this bucolic venue. Even the breezes wafting off Indian Lake had a unique and soothing effect—exhilarant in summers, invigorating in winters. Beyond that, the icons of that time were so rich, vivid, colorful. Think about it...Indian Lake: Electric. Russells Point: Neon. Sandy Beach Amusement Park: Rip-roaring—sexy! There was a saying about Indian Lake: "If you ain't seen it, you ain't been nowhere!"

The amusement park alone had so much to offer: Roller coasters; Ferris wheels; twirling, spinning car rides. Speed and height, ice cream and cotton candy. Fun houses. Billowing skirts ("Man, look at those beauties: hubba-hubba!"). The merry-go-round and Sweeney's Dodgem. The penny arcade, buzzing and bopping. Shooting galleries pinging and popping. Lovers and lechers, darlings and dreamers, suitors and swains clambering over Dreamland Bridge to Paradise Island—home of Danceland's Stardust Ballroom and Moonlight Terrace Gardens—in search of a dance partner to share a longed-for intimate moment, a soulful kiss, a lingering sigh.

So, to me, the time, place, and people of that decade are like the very musical innovation flourishing during my guardianship of Billy Barnes: *Jazz!* Jazz and its sensory, energetic, youthful, creative power, its improvisational genius and intellectual potency. Billy and I both shared an enthusiasm for that wonderful music, though neither of us knew it yet.

April 1941

No surprise, my early experience with Billy was routine: Help him learn to walk, drink through a straw, and go to the bathroom on his own. A GA's help with these daily trials comes down to the question of *grace*. The guardian angel cannot force his ward to cooperate with grace—otherwise the will would not be free—but he acts as a channel of actual grace, working within God's providential design, to bring the person he is guarding in contact with outside occasions of grace: a good teacher, good words, and good examples. The more one cooperates with grace, the more graces one will receive. In Billy's case, Willa Mae was the channel of my help. At my request, Willa Mae's guardian angel, *Soqed Hozi*, imparted the grace of patience to her as she worked through her daily trials of raising Billy.

Soon enough, it was the spring after his fourth birthday. Willa Mae took Billy and his friends—Albert Martin, Helen Gordon, and Annabelle Lea—for a ride on the Silver Streak. It would have been hard to distinguish my presence as a warm ray of sunlight gracing the children's shining faces, but I was there amid the laughing, yelling, and screams of delight. From the coaster's highest peak, the children could see the whole amusement park: the Ferris wheel, the penny arcade, the carousel, the millrace ride, the funhouse, the dodgem cars. They saw the boardwalk to Sandy Beach for swimming and boat excursions, and the attractions across Dreamland Bridge on Paradise Island.

But it was the music, the unforgettable, mesmerizing music, which so quietly, inexorably affixed its indelible imprint onto Billy's entire being, as if it were a permanent code that would shape his life for the entire time God allotted him on terra-firma. And it did!

Afterwards, they had cake and ice cream at Willa Mae's favorite bakery, Alma's Patisserie—across from the park entrance and adjacent to local businessman Red Suggins's eponymous Suds 'n' Grub. Billy's eyes stayed wide as saucers while he ate and talked about the music they'd all heard coming from the amusement park, as if it were heaven-sent. From my vantage point, it was *that* outing that opened up Billy's imagination to the world around him, and without question—no prodding on my part—Albert, Helen, and Willa Mae felt that Billy was destined for a lifetime in music. Curiously, Annabelle's remark was contrarian: "I didn't like the music, it hurt my ears."

I don't like to interrupt the flow of my story, but Annabelle's remark caught my attention. Remembering that my resource— *Penso Appositus*—does not grant me the ability to foresee Billy's future or identify a lurking peril in advance, I and all GAs rely on our keen powers of intuition. And that's what kicked in when Annabelle complained of the music hurting her ears.

On its surface, her remark seemed trivial enough, but I've learned that seemingly trivial remarks often become the proof of one's very own pudding: a thought spoken in jest often bears out a truth which influences one's behavior or relationship with another. Yes, this was all speculation, but due to their close living proximity— a few miles separated the homes of Billy and Annabelle—I saw the distinct possibility of their growing closer over time...particularly since they would eventually both attend Lake Ridge High School— home of the Blue Jackets—as hormonal teenagers.

Accordingly, my intuition told me that, eventually, there would be a disconnect between Billy and Annabelle over music—not a far-fetched prediction, albeit of nominal consequence at that moment. However, since to be forewarned is to be forearmed, I vowed to do my best to steer Billy away from an alliance in which his aspirations of a career in music would be jeopardized.

Of course, I had to allow for the possibility that any number of complicating circumstances—not only a beguiling young woman—might enter the picture, and Billy's dream might be compromised in a completely unexpected manner. Moreover, the extent of his talent was yet to be weighed.

I didn't realize it at the time, but I was my own prophet.

Three weeks after that momentous ride on the Silver Streak, Willa Mae told Jupie and Billy that she'd heard from her bachelor brother, Willis Stanley, a professional carpenter. He had invited them to live in his cottage across from St. Mary's of the Woods Catholic Parish and "mind things" until he got home from his tour of duty with the United States Navy. Willis Stanley being his only uncle, and his namesake, Billy was disheartened by this departure—and for reasons Billy couldn't understand. What was a war? Why did his

Uncle Willis have to go? When would he be back? Billy worried that his own father might be next—but, fortunately, as a married man with a young son (and, it should be mentioned, profoundly flat feet), Jupie was able to avoid the draft.

Jupie jammed all the family's belongings into a clunky green Hudson Terraplane, on loan from Willis, and drove out to the cottage on September 5, 1941. It didn't take long for them to settle in, but something happened on their first Saturday at the cabin which I tried to prevent but couldn't. Jupie was working in the yard and Billy was playing on the porch when a car drove slowly by. In it were three men, each yelling separate epithets out the window—the loudest one screaming, "You better remember me—I'm Red Suggins! Me and my friends don't want you no-account gypsy white trash livin' in this here neighborhood or you'll damn well be sorry!"

By the time Willa Mae came out to see what was happening, the car had turned around and headed back their way. This time it stopped, and two of the men got out of the car brandishing clubs. When they saw Willa Mae, Red Suggins pointed to Billy and yelled at her, "If that kid's yours, you better not let him get near any of our kids."

Suggins was so busy having fun, he didn't see Jupie rush him from the side with a metal garden rake, planting it in his shoulder up to the hilt. Seeing blood gush down Suggins's neck and shirt as he pulled out the rake, Jupie turned to the second man and buried the rake in his rear-end as far as it would go. By that time, Father Stenz—pastor at St. Mary's across the street—was in their yard defending them, but when a police car finally pulled up to stop the fracas, the carload of bigots screeched away, free as birds. The policeman—rookie detective Joe Kuldau—advised Jupie to ignore the likes of troublemakers like Red Suggins and not to retaliate against them, lest Jupie be fined for disturbing the peace.

Fr. Stenz invited them to the parish house across the street to calm down, but Jupie—still shaking with rage over the blatant insults—disappeared into their house. Willa Mae and Billy thanked Fr. Stenz for his help, and he told Willa Mae he would look forward to enrolling Billy in the first grade at St. Mary's Parish School two years hence.

Later, at home, Billy asked his mother, "Why didn't those men in that car want us living here, or me getting close to their kids?" She explained that the men were cowards and hateful rabble-rousers who were jealous of them.

I was pleased that I helped Billy get over that jarring,

confusing incident. It took less work than you might think. I just had to place a comforting image in his mind: an image of his mother holding him on her lap.

Billy and his parents passed a gloomy Christmas season with the shocking news that Willa Mae's brother, Willis, was killed in action on December 7, during the Japanese sneak attack on Pearl Harbor. The letter Willa Mae received from the War Department extolled Willis Stanley's heroism, stating: "When on the morning of December 7, 1941, under intense enemy fire, Seaman Apprentice Willis Stanley saved the lives of five fellow seamen who had been washed overboard and left clinging for their lives to the sinking battleship, the USS *Arizona*."

The letter went on to say that Willis's selfless sacrifice of his own life would be memorialized forever by awarding him, posthumously, the Navy Cross—the United States military's second-highest decoration awarded for valor in combat—along with a commendation for the Purple Heart. That Christmas, Willa Mae placed the letter and the medals next to their tree, on an elegantly burnished driftwood table Willis had crafted. For Billy, it was the first time he had felt a sense of desolation from the death of a loved one, and he asked Willa Mae about it.

"Why do I feel so...so funny inside? How do I feel better?"

Willa Mae put a gentle hand on Billy's shoulder as they sat side-by-side on his bed. "Our gypsy heritage teaches that our deceased loved ones are travelling Romanis who leave signs called *patrins*—an old word for *leaf*—for those of us left behind, to remind us to follow their love to heaven."

"What...where is heaven?"

"It's a special place where your Uncle Willis is waiting for us."

"But how?"

"Just pray that God will take care of your Uncle Willis until we get there."

"When will that be?" said Billy, still puzzled.

Smiling, Willa Mae embraced Billy. "Not for a hundred years."

Uncle Willis had made most of the furniture in the house, including in Billy's bedroom. The room was tiny, with barely enough space for his skinny bunk bed, the small dresser with its cracked mirror affixed to the wall, a chair for studying at a drop-down table, and storage shelves Willis had built-in with two drawers for clothes.

Between Billy's room and his parents' room was a smallish bathroom, with a length of clothesline threaded through a plastic bath curtain secured to the opposite wall with a rusty bolt, a hose rigged overhead for showering, and a commode across from a sink with a shaving mirror. Their kitchen had a metal sink with one faucet that ran only a thin stream, but also a hand pump to bring water from a well dug near the southwest corner of the house. Willa Mae boiled water and fixed their meals on a four-burner Garland gas stove with an oven for baking her delicious bread, sweet rolls, cakes, and pies. Four wormy chestnut chairs and a matching table Willis had crafted sat centered in the kitchen. An icebox was tucked in the corner beside the back door, outside on the porch, next to a Maytag washing machine with a hand-cranked wringer.

In addition to the cottage, Willis's estate consisted of a gold Illinois railroad pocket watch, four buffalo-head nickels, a broken rosary, his carpenter tools and tote-box, a newsboy cap, a few clothes (including one blue suit that fit Jupie), a picture of Willis and Willa Mae's mother, Mary Klienman Stanley—and Willis's prized twenty-five-key Jaymar miniature piano.

The best thing about Willis's piano was that Willa Mae had learned enough from her brother to teach Billy some. She showed him how to use the color tags above each key to identify the fifteen white and ten black key names, and explained that the eight white keys between any two of the red-card tone labels equaled an octave. She taught Billy to play simple ditties such as "Happy Birthday" and "Silent Night." It took what seemed like a million tries for Billy to understand octaves, scales, sharps, and flats. But Willa Mae never gave up—and, as I would have predicted, neither did Billy.

Fall 1943

Billy's first-grade enrollment at St. Mary's wasn't the traditional patty-cake affair. Not that it was so different from the other kids'—it was just that Billy reacted as though he had been abandoned to a creepy, black-robed monster with tiny round glasses perched on its pinched face, peering out from a spooky, hooded headdress. I'm sure his fright was thanks to Jupie, who the night before had told Billy about a wicked witch named Sister Theresa who lived in the school basement and whose green smoldering cauldron was filled with wayward children—boys particularly.

After the first day of school, Sr. Theresa asked Billy to stay for a few minutes extra before going home. It was the ambiguity of her invitation that worried Billy: Was she going to make him go down to the basement and push him into the smoldering cauldron? Though anxious about not going straight home as expected, Billy nodded along. The last of the kids left, and Sr. Theresa took Billy by the hand. But it was fear that really gripped him. Was this it? Were they heading for the dreaded basement?

His heart in his throat, Billy followed Sr. Theresa into the activities room, where she showed him something he'd never seen before: a miraculous full-size piano. She opened the piano's dust cover, and there before him was a row of jewel-like ivory and black keys he counted to make eighty-eight gems. "Your mother told me you're very talented and wants me to give you lessons," Sr. Theresa said. "We'll practice on this piano once a week."

His fear permanently assuaged and music books tucked under his arm, from then on Billy trudged up Patterson Hill almost every Saturday morning at ten o'clock for an hour of Sr. Theresa's piano lessons.

Chapter 3

<u>Wednesday, July 5, 1961</u>

How I wish Billy's troubles had stayed within the realm of cartoonish ghouls quickly proved gentle souls, or even carloads of bigots easily deterred by a strategically-placed garden rake. This morning's report in the *Bellefontaine Examiner*, the local newspaper, contains the first written account of the riots that led to Billy's death:

RIOT KILLS LOCAL RESIDENT

Popular local entertainer dies of gunshot wound

Patrick McBride, Associate Editor

July 5, 1961 – Russells Point, OH – As common as flag-waving, fireworks, and ice cream were the riots that broke out on the evening of Monday, July 3, and carried on into the early morning of July 4 in the village of Russells Point.

Growing in size, a crowd of ten, fifteen, even thirty

thousand young people converged on the scene to wreak havoc. According to this writer's investigation, Joseph Kuldau—Chief of Police, Russells Point Police Department—asked one beer-swilling teenager, "Why?" The woozy youngster giggled: "Just to raise hell." And they did.

"At its peak, in what was coined a 'night of irresponsible and senseless acts of lawlessness,' some three hundred persons were arrested or jailed," said Kuldau.

The chaos started early in the evening of July 3 when a young girl, angry that the Carnival Room was closed due to the recent death of the owner, tore a black mourning wreath from the establishment's front door and crowned herself with it. She led the procession down the main street, chanting, smashing windows, and uprooting anything not fastened down. Bricks, rocks, bottles, fireworks, and anything the mob could get its hands on were used as instruments of destruction. The wreath was later used to start one of numerous fires.

After two hours of watching in street clothes as the mob terrorized villagers, Sheriff Clifford Williams mobilized his units, as well as the Russells Point Police deputies and lawmen from surrounding counties. Still unable to quell the full-scale riot, Williams called in National Guard troops, who arrived with bayonets fixed at about 3 a.m. on July 4.

By that time, the rioting had centered in the street in front of Red Suggins' Suds 'n' Grub and the adjacent bakery, Alma's Patisserie. As the authorities struggled to restore order, a shot rang out in front of the patisserie, resulting in a fatal wound to Mr. Willis "Billy" Barnes, age twenty-four.

The emergency squad transported the victim to Mary Rutan Hospital in Bellefontaine, Ohio, where it was later learned that he was declared DOA at 3:09 a.m. Eastern by Coroner Samuel H. Brown, M.D. At that point, though most of the rioting had ceased, the Guard patrolled the streets breaking up a few smaller gatherings.

Sheriff Williams said of the night, "It's part of a worldwide trend. I don't know why, or how to solve it. It's been happening everywhere."

Mayor Bunny-Sue Macrath blamed parents "for not helping their youngsters."

###

Unfortunately, this article is more a fact recitation and opinion poll than an investigative report. In the absence of any compelling evidence as to the killer's identity, I cannot directly intercede in the police investigation: after all, an angel cannot play messenger without a concrete message to impart. The Big Boss would never approve a corporeal appearance if all I had to say was, "Hey, check your report—that bullet wound was no accident!"

Instead, I must simply watch in silence as the investigation unfolds. Thankfully, I have far greater faith in Joseph Kuldau than I do in Coroner Samuel Brown. Kuldau is a man of integrity. He was the rookie called to the scene all those years ago in the altercation between Jupie and Red Suggins: I still remember the hint of anger in the officer's tone when he suggested Jupie must just grin and bear the harassment, lest he be in hot water for "disturbing the peace." Kuldau is a man who recognizes the occasional absurdities of the criminal justice system and remains committed as always to the pursuit of truth, regardless of any political consequences.

Suffice it to say that I will keep as closely attuned to Kuldau's investigation as I can in the coming days—my instincts tell me that he is key to my mission of rooting out Billy's killer.

Chapter 4

<u>Saturday, April 20, 1946</u>

For Fr. Stenz and St. Mary's Parish, the official end of Lent
and the joyous celebration of Easter Sunday—Christ's resurrection—
began with a parish dinner following the Saturday evening vigil
mass. As usual, the Ladies' Altar Guild provided the traditional meal
of roasted lamb, vegetables, oven-roasted potatoes, green onions,
and hot cross buns, while Willa Mae contributed her *devastating*
apricot coconut cake.

A special musical presentation followed, with local pianist
and St. Mary's maintenance man Dukie Kincaid playing several of
his gospel song arrangements in the jazz idiom: "Were You There,"
"There Is No Greater Love," "Battle Hymn of the Republic," "This
Little Light of Mine," and "Amazing Grace."

Later, Fr. Stenz introduced Dukie to Jupie, Willa Mae, and
Billy. "Jupie is one of the hardest workers I know," Fr. Stenz told
Dukie. "He could be the perfect partner for that business venture you
mentioned to me." I was very interested to hear them discuss Dukie's
idea of opening a de facto jazz club on the Sandy Beach boardwalk,

to serve nominally as a barbecue restaurant managed by Jupie.

"We're going to be replacing that old upright piano Dukie played on tonight," said Fr. Stenz. "So that'll at least get you started." He lit a cigarette. "You'll have to get the approval of the Businessmen's Association, but our parishioner Bernard Sweeney is the head man. I'll talk with him and get things set up for Jupie to meet with them.

Before anyone could say more, the group was surprised when Billy spoke directly to Dukie. "Where'd you learn to play the piano?"

Worried that Billy's question was rude, Willa Mae held up her hand as if to silence him.

Nodding his approval to Willa Mae, Dukie sat forward, grinned at Billy, and said, "Georgia. Juke joint half a mile down the road from our shanty town. Old boy there named Jimmy 'Fats' Crawford took a liking to me and taught me how to play boogie-woogie, stride, some blues chords. I hung out with him every night until the wee hours watching him bang away on a broken-down upright. It was a rough scene, but I learned a lot just listening to him. That's the trick, my man—you have to *listen* if you want to be good."

"You lived in Georgia? How'd you get all the way up here?"

Arching his eyebrows in embarrassment, Jupie put his hand

on Billy's arm and said, "That's enough for now. Mr. Kincaid is—"

"I'm cool," said Dukie. "Fun to talk about it." After pausing for approval, Dukie continued: "Baptist Church sent me up here to sell bibles door-to-door. Didn't pan out, so Sr. Theresa hired me here at St. Mary's to do the maintenance and janitor work. If you're interested in learning jazz piano, maybe we can get together some time after school if your folks say it's okay. Dig?"

As excited as Billy was about meeting Dukie Kincaid, I was equally excited by Jupie's remarks to Willa Mae later that evening: "I don't know much about music, but I've been hoping to find something I can share with Billy as he grows up. I think the music tent—well, the food, too—will be a good fix."

With the summer season on Indian Lake about to kick in, Jupie had the opportunity to take advantage of Dukie's jazz club/barbecue tent idea, thanks to the help of Bernard "Bud" Sweeney, chairman of the Sandy Beach Businessmen's Association. As promised, Sweeney had given Jupie permission to present his plan for opening a tent on a vacant space near Dreamland Bridge in the middle of the boardwalk.

Ceremonially chairing the Association's first meeting of the season, Mayor Bunny-Sue Macrath slammed the gavel down on the murmuring assemblage: barber Stump Brewster, restaurateur Red Suggins, bakery shop owner Alma Dinova, Danceland manager Mutt Pickering, horse trainer and gardener Marge Costin, bookstore owner Babbs Donley, insurance agent James Dressel, dentist Dr. Tommy Ryan, talent booking agent Johnny Mocha, and wholesale food distributer JoJo Gardini—plus Jupie Barnes, grounds manager for the amusement park and would-be barbecue magnate.

It was easy enough to convince the committee that Jupie's special-recipe barbecue would be a huge hit, and the natural accompaniment to ice-cold beer, tangy lemonade, and sweet tea—all served indoors, where customers could sit down out of the hot sun, feeling satisfied and refreshed. The real point of contention, though, was Jupie's plan to have live music on weekend nights— unbeknownst to the rest of the group, the *raison d'être* for the whole endeavor in the first place.

Willa Mae and Billy waited outside the open-windowed meeting hall to listen to the committee question Jupie about his petition. "What kinda music you talkin' about?" one man asked harshly. From where Willa Mae and Billy stood, the voice sounded familiar.

"Toe-tappin' music," Jupie said. "Blues, gospel, and jazz."

"Jazz? Blues?" The man sounded flustered. "Sounds like nigger bait if you ask me. We don't need no more colored attractions around this here resort."

"Hold on a minute, Red," Sweeney said. "Mr. Barnes has been a loyal and valuable employee of the park. He deserves a fair hearing."

Ignoring Sweeney, Suggins said to Jupie: "Ain't you that white trash hit me with a rake a while back?"

Before Jupie could answer, Mayor Macrath interrupted. "Red. Let's keep to the subject. Do you have anything else to say about the music Mr. Barnes is proposing?"

"You're damn right. I'm telling everyone that colored music ain't good for business."

Jupie refrained from mentioning the caravan of all-American white men who had threatened his son and wife on their first weekend in town. He held his tongue and waited to hear what the rest of the committee had to say.

Stump Brewster, owner of Stump's Clip Joint—Lakeview's most popular barber shop—pushed his chair back from the table and stood up. "I know all those big bands coming into Danceland and Stardust Ballroom have several negro musicians. They come into my place three, four, sometimes half-a-dozen at a time for a haircut. I cut their hair and listen to them talk about the music. Some call it jazz, others call it swing music. It's a hell of a lot more popular than that hillbilly or rock 'n' roll stuff. And by the way, Red—if I'm not mistaken, I saw you and your missus dancin' up a storm to one of them big swing bands last summer at Moonlight Terrace. The place was jam-packed. For my money, that music is good for business."

"They come into my bakery, too," said Alma Dinova. "They're very polite and buy a lot of my special pastries, especially my biscotti. Sometimes they'll eat half a dozen biscotti and drink two or three cups of espresso."

Red was barely chastened. "If you're telling me that swinging a dead cat around by the tail and hitting more coloreds than whites is good business then my name ain't Red Suggins."

"Hold on, Red," said Mayor Macrath, "there's no need for—"

"Okay, I'll hold on—for now. But don't say I didn't warn ya." Turning to Alma Dinova, Red stabbed his finger on the table, bobbed his head, and said, "You ever decide to sell that bakery of yours, sweetheart, I'll top any offer anyone makes—and that's a promise. Once that spot's bulldozed, I can expand my beer garden, probably double my profits."

Alma's face betrayed no particular emotion, but I sensed she wasn't at all threatened by Red's bluster. Suggins ended his tirade with one last pathetic appeal: "We're talking trouble from that colored jive music, and that's why I vote *no!*"

(I probably shouldn't interrupt, but witnessing this idiotic outburst goes back to my "fair-warning" of certain social elements tolerating the ugly human inclinations toward anger, hatred, jealousy, and greed. Thinking about that now, I would submit a fifth element: *stupidity!*)

Despite all the riffraff, when Jupie came out of the meeting hall, he was grinning. He hugged Billy, winked at Willa Mae, and said, "We got all but one vote—so I hope to hell you know how to make a good barbecue sauce!"

"Where do you plan on getting all the supplies and food?"

Jupie was quick with his answer, having obviously given it a fair deal of thought. "Most of the supplies and dry goods from JoJo's Wholesale in Lima, the meat from Tony Fisher's butcher shop. Then there's ice, soft drinks, and tea from Gillespie Distributors—and, of course, bread, buns, and pastries from Alma's."

Willa Mae cocked her head. "What about the help?"

"What about it?" said Jupie.

"Who and where?" replied Willa Mae.

Jupie shot Willa Mae a puzzled stare. "I was counting on you for that, my dear—this is a *family* business, after all!"

Chapter 5

Friday, May 24, 1946

I admit that when Billy brought home a note from Sr. Theresa at the end of his third year at St. Mary's, I looked forward to seeing what it said:

Dear Mr. and Mrs. Barnes:

My staff and I are eager to discuss Willis's accomplishments with both of you, and perhaps share some ideas about Willis's future. If convenient for you, we'll meet in the Rectory Office at 4:00 p.m. next Friday, May 31. Please let me know if this is convenient for you and Mr. Barnes.

Cordially,

Sr. Maria Theresa Parks, O.P.

It would be misleading for me to say that guardian angels know the future. Yet in our special way we know so much more than our wards do about what awaits them, as we understand the causes of things both more universally and more perfectly than humans. (That's why I hate the word *fate*—more on that later.) That said, for as many resources as a guardian angel has or may call upon if necessary, a crystal ball is not one of them.

Still, given Billy's own ideas about his future as a famous jazz pianist, I knew I would enjoy hearing his parents' and Sr. Theresa's takes on his grade school performance and musical aspirations, which might possibly be at odds with each other.

Luckily for everyone, it was a beautiful, tranquil day for the meeting. Things began on a very cordial note, with Willa Mae expressing regret that Jupie was in the middle of a huge dodgem repair job at the amusement park following a raucous Memorial Day.

"I'm so sorry to miss your husband, Mrs. Barnes. Perhaps we'll meet some time over the summer vacation months. In the meantime—"

"Please, Sr. Theresa, call me Willa Mae."

"Yes, by all means, Willa Mae. As I was about to say, I never would have thought that your son, Willis—"

"Excuse me. We named Billy 'Willis' after my brother, Willis

Stanley, who died at Pearl Harbor. But my husband didn't like calling him Willis, so we call him Billy. Has Billy gotten into trouble of any kind?"

"No, not at all. In fact, he is the model child a teacher hopes for. He's smart, polite, considerate, and outgoing. He pays attention in class and, well, frankly, I'm hopeful he will one day consider—you and Mr. Barnes in agreement, of course—becoming a priest in the Dominican Order. I wanted you and your husband's permission to speak with Fr. Stenz about Billy joining the priesthood, though the training itself wouldn't be for quite a while—fifth or sixth grade."

"Do priests play jazz piano?"

"I...well...I'm not sure. I don't really know. Why do you ask?"

"Billy wants to be a jazz pianist. That would be the only way any of us would consider him becoming a priest."

"I'll inquire about it when I see Fr. Stenz this weekend."

"Do you know Dukie Kincaid?"

"Yes. Wonderful man."

"Mr. Kincaid has offered to give Billy lessons on the school's piano. Has he mentioned that to you?"

"Indeed he has."

"When can it start?"

"Start?" I almost felt sorry for Sr. Theresa, whose face took on a look of such excitement at the prospect of one day serving at the Mass of one Father Billy Barnes. "You mean...?"

"Billy taking lessons from Mr. Kincaid."

"Oh." Sr. Theresa, ever diplomatic, allowed her face to fall only slightly. "Well, nothing has been formalized yet."

Willa Mae stood to leave. "My husband and I would appreciate it if you would arrange for Billy to take music lessons from Mr. Kincaid beginning this fall when he enters fourth grade. If that's not possible, we'll have to enroll Billy in the public school and ask Mr. Kincaid to give him piano lessons on the weekends—which we'll pay for with the St. Mary's tuition money we'll save."

From the look on her face, I could tell Sr. Theresa knew she was beat. "Well," she conceded, "there's no denying Billy has excelled through his first three years here at St. Mary's. I'm sure things will work out with Mr. Kincaid. Thank you, Mrs. Barnes, for your candor."

"Thank you, Sr. Theresa, for your understanding. And please," she added, before closing the door behind her, "call me Willa Mae."

###

Friday, September 6, 1946

I had to hand it to Willa Mae. Most people would have been intimated by a nun's clerical habit, but not her. And *it*—piano lessons with Dukie Kincaid—finally happened that September of Billy's fourth-grade year, several months shy of his tenth birthday.

What's so special about that, you ask?

It would never be my intention to bore you with the details of Billy's learning curve with Dukie, but any jazz pianist worth his salt would appreciate Dukie's meaning, at that very first after-school lesson, when he said to Billy, "Lemme show ya a couple of things..."

However, if it's your first time really thinking about jazz, you should know at least a bit about the vernacular, jargon, and theory. So, here's my abbreviated account of that September afternoon, beginning with Billy ambling into the parish hall to meet Dukie for his first lesson.

Dukie chuckled, sat down at the piano, and beckoned Billy to join him on the bench. He spoke those magic words—"Lemme show ya a couple of things"—and spread his hands over the keyboard. Billy watched Dukie's fingers slide from one piano key to another, using all five fingers on both hands—up and down together, then in opposite directions. Dukie played a funky tune and hummed along as he said, "C-seven, D-seven, G-seven, C-seven."

Hypnotized by the sounds coming out of Sr. Theresa's piano, sounds he never knew were there, Billy listened as Dukie played four notes at the same time. To Billy's ear, they sounded odd, as if there were something missing. Not waiting for Dukie to explain, Billy said, "How do you make that sound?"

"It's all in the chord structure, man. You gotta listen."

"I am. I just—"

"Ya know your scales?"

"From my mom," Billy said.

Dukie's hand fingered a four-note formation. "This here's a B-flat seventh chord. That top note I'm playin' is the flatted seventh tone on the B-flat scale."

"What's making that sound?" Billy asked. "Like it's sort of hanging?"

"It is hangin'. That's a dominant seventh chord."

"But...it's—"

"Here's the B-flat scale," Dukie interrupted.

Billy watched as Dukie started on middle-C, moved down one white key, and put his finger on the adjacent black key to the left. He counted off the notes going up the scale and, when he got to the seventh tone, moved his finger down to the next black key and tapped on the note. As he sounded four notes together, he said, "If you want to play a dominant seventh chord, it's the same in any key. You play the first, third, fifth, and flatted-seventh tones of the major scale together."

Dukie played the chord again, pulled his hands off the keyboard, and stretched his fingers. He looked at Billy. "Ya hear the color in that chord?"

"I think so."

"Ain't no thinkin' to it, man, it's your ears!"

Emphasizing the black key, Dukie hit the chord three times, then turned to Billy. "Ya hear that? The dominant seventh makes it sound like somethin' else has to happen—like it has to go home. Dig?"

"Home?" Billy said.

"Yeah, man, home! E-flat—the fourth tone of the B-flat scale—it's called resolution. Dig?"

And, like a ravenous wolf, Billy spent nearly three hours each day practicing what Dukie showed him or told him to do. It was a marvel to me—watching a hopeful master learn from a true-to-life one—and, for Billy, it was even more incredible.

###

Saturday, December 21, 1946

Having agreed to let Dukie's new pupil perform at St. Mary's Christmas Party, Sr. Theresa politely *informed* him that she expected Billy to play "White Christmas" while several Knights of Columbus members led the parish children one-by-one through a holiday themed *elfin* workshop, ending at the lap of Santa Claus, to whom they would reveal a daunting list of coveted gifts.

At nine that morning—with Willa Mae helping Jupie don the Knights' aging Santa costume—Billy took his place at the piano on the parish hall stage, ready to play. Anxious to please Dukie and Sr. Theresa, Billy waited for Fr. Stenz to signal the beginning of the event.

The allotted half-hour was about to end when Billy noticed Sr. Theresa and Fr. Stenz talking in the stage wings as if sharing a deep secret. Curious to Billy was their periodic nod in his direction.

As the children bid Santa a boisterous farewell and the Knights set up the movie projector to show the children *The Bells of St. Mary's*, Fr. Stenz beckoned Billy to join him at one of the tables near the parish office. To Billy's surprise, Sr. Theresa brought a tray of cookies and a pitcher of punch and sat down with them at the table. Feeling sweat drip from his armpits, Billy sat anxiously as though waiting for some kind of bad news: Didn't they like his piano rendition of "White Christmas?" Was Fr. Stenz leaving St. Mary's? Was Sr. Theresa being transferred to another parish? Was she...having a baby?

Before he could wonder any further, Sr. Theresa beamed broadly and solved the mystery of their impromptu meeting.

"Billy," she began, "all of us here at St. Mary's know you are very talented." She turned to Fr. Stenz. "Isn't that right, Father?"

"Absolutely! By all means," he said. "Everyone admires you and everyone—especially Sr. Theresa and I—hope you'll join us one day as our parish priest." He paused, chuckled, then added, "After I'm gone, of course."

Gulping for air, Billy's mind went blank as he groped for something to say. "I...I hope...maybe I should talk with—"

Before he could finish the thought, Sr. Theresa took over. "You know, Billy, God has made each of us in his image and likeness. He has created us with a specific purpose in order to share his love with the world. Haven't you ever wondered if God is calling you to be a priest?"

"No," he said, "I haven't. I've been...I want to be a musician."

"That's even better," said Fr. Stenz. "Our diocese is in desperate need of a professional music director. It's a big job, planning all the holy days and special events. I think you'd be perfect. And, if you like, I'll speak with the bishop to get you early enrollment in the seminary. Let's see, you're how old now?"

As if seized by some tormenting demon, Billy stammered: "No. I mean, yes, ten in a couple months, but—do you know where my mom and dad are?"

"Follow me," said Sr. Theresa as she stood up. "I know right where to find them."

Patting Billy on the back as he passed by, Fr. Stenz said, "Give it some thought, son, and we'll talk about it after the New Year."

Yes, there is a practical benefit to God's omniscience. Though it is not our prerogative to challenge the Big Boss's plan, there are moments when every GA feels the need for change—refreshment, or a restoration of vigor. Luckily, a key element of God's omniscience—my favorite almighty power—is His gift of mercy granted to us GAs in the form of *Intuitive Adjuration.*

Here's how it works: Just by meditating on it, GAs derive the Almighty's gift of rejuvenation, particularly as it relates to the four essential attributes we strive to perfect in our ward's soulful growth: inspiration, inclusion, jubilation, and compassion.

These four essential attributes ultimately play a role in how and which way we choose to nudge our wards. It comes down to the basic question of the purpose of one's life—or, better said, in one's *ward's* life. For example, I consider my strongest asset to lie in the area of *acceptance*, a sub-component of *inclusion*. In short, I have a particular knack for reconciling seemingly incompatible truths—a conflict embodied most strikingly in the question of whether Billy should become a priest or a jazz musician.

It was an interesting paradox, that Billy's God-given musical talents were a potential obstacle to a higher calling by that same God. While this paradox appeared to trouble Sr. Theresa and Fr. Stenz immensely, I was still on the fence, myself: while I believed vehemently in the primacy of Billy's musical growth to his overall development as a human being, it had also occurred to me that he might not have the combination of talent, timing, and good fortune required to actually make a successful career of his musical craft.

To that end, it seemed prudent to have a back-up plan—in this case, the priesthood—in mind. And yet I could tell that Billy's heart was not with the Church as much as it was with his piano, and my ultimate purpose as a guardian angel was to provide for Billy's happiness and spiritual fulfillment—so, as I say, it was quite the dilemma.

Billy was similarly conflicted. His mood at dinner that night betrayed his angst, and did not escape the notice of Willa Mae.

"What's gotten into you?" she asked as she served Billy and Jupie a mountain of freshly-churned vanilla ice cream.

"Oh, nothing." Billy absentmindedly picked at his dessert. "I was just wondering if priests and nuns hang out together or, um, get married?"

Willa Mae reared her head back just slightly—first, to let out a quick, good-natured laugh, and then to catch her husband's eye.

"That's your father's bailiwick," she told Billy. Then, to Jupie: "I think it's time you and Billy *talked*."

After a bit of grumbling over having this "birds-and-bees" subject sprung on him so suddenly, Jupie instructed Billy to finish his ice cream while he fetched some wood. "This is the sort of talk we should have over a roaring fire," he explained.

I was especially interested in the outcome of this conversation, understanding that it could tip the scales one way or the other in terms of Billy's future vocation. Still, despite my extensive knowledge of "the facts of life," I felt awkward listening to father and son's exchange of deeply personal disclosures.

"Your mother is a wonderful woman," Jupie said as he leaned against the mantle and sipped a cup of fresh coffee Willa Mae had brewed for him.

"I know," said Billy. "Is that what we're going to talk about?"

Jupie stood straight, meandered to the front window, and looked out on a surprise evening snowfall. "No," he said. "We're going to discuss how you got here."

"How I got here?"

"What do they teach you in school?" said Jupie. "About where you boys and girls come from?"

Billy bobbed his head indifferently. "Sr. Theresa and Fr. Stenz talk about God creating us in His image and likeness."

"What do you think that means?"

"I don't know." Billy squirmed a bit in his seat. "I guess it means God made us...for some reason he liked."

"And why do you suppose God created us?"

Billy shrugged his shoulders. "Sr. Theresa says it's to know Him, love Him, and serve Him in this world, and...and to be happy with Him in the next."

"What do you think about that?"

"It's cool by me," Billy said. "Why?"

"Did they teach you about how someone is born?"

Billy arched his brow. "Just about Jesus in the manger. I think it was in Jerusalem somewhere. I don't remember."

Jupie paced the room, then sat next to Billy on the sofa.

"For now, what you need to know is that when men and women marry, part of their living together is to have intercourse. Do you know what that is?"

Billy nodded. "Albert Martin told me all about it. I didn't pay that much attention until he showed me this rubber thing he called a raincoat. He said he was going to put it on his pecker when he screwed some girl so she wouldn't get pregnant." This information having been delivered in the most matter-of-fact tone I had ever heard from my ward, Billy concluded with, "That's all I know."

Suppressing a grin, Jupie drew in a deep breath and said, "So, you know what a man does with his...*pecker*...when he has intercourse with a woman?"

"Albert said his dad told him the one thing men like about a woman's privates is her—uh, he calls it her *love pouch*, I think."

"That's a new one." Jupie shook his head and put a hand on

Billy's shoulder. "It seems like your friend Albert is full of information. You shouldn't believe everything he says, but he's right about one thing: If you put your penis inside a woman and release your sperm in her, you may become an unwanted parent—or wanted, depending. Do you understand?"

"Fr. Stenz said it's a sin to do that unless you're married."

"Be that as it may, I don't think he knows a hell of a lot about it—you know, being celibate and all."

"What's celibate?"

"Priests take a vow of celibacy. It means they promise to abstain from sexual activity. Intercourse."

"What about the nuns?" asked Billy.

"I'm pretty sure it's the same for them, too."

"Why do they decide to do that?"

"I was taught it's a special calling from God." Jupie paused. "So think about your conversation with Fr. Stenz and Sr. Theresa. Understand that becoming a priest means you won't have children. What your mother and I did to make you? Priests and nuns don't do that. If you'd rather have a family than be celibate, then say so."

Billy thought on this for a long moment. Though I am always privy to my ward's thoughts, in this case I was just as on-edge as

Jupie, unsure of what Billy would say next.

Finally, he said, "I want to be a jazz pianist. Is that a problem for having a family?"

Jupie chuckled. "Not if you're married to the right woman."

"Someone like Mom?"

"You should be so lucky," said Jupie. "And I pray that you are."

The matter apparently settled, Billy thanked his father and went to his room to listen to a new jazz record Dukie had lent him. Jupie, meanwhile, returned to the kitchen to help Willa Mae clean up the remainder of the supper dishes. At her eager grilling on the outcome of the conversation between father and son, Jupie offered Willa Mae a simple summary: "I doubt it Billy's gonna be a priest, if that's what you're askin'!"

Chapter 6

<u>Friday, October 21, 1949</u>

I'm always privy to my ward's thoughts, but sometimes it's extra fun to hear how he expresses them out loud. Unbeknownst to Billy, after a lesson with Dukie on an unseasonably cold Friday night, he was especially entertaining.

"I've told myself a dozen times," he said shaking his head: "'Billy, you don't know how lucky you are!'" He looked over his right shoulder, then his left, marching up the street from St. Mary's to his house. No audience—or so he thought—which meant he could let it all out. "Yup," he laughed, "I'm bragging now! I didn't expect to learn so fast, to get as much done as I have in barely three years of lessons with Dukie.

"I know all my scales" —and here he waved his fingers in midair, playing an invisible piano—"major, minor, chromatic, harmonic, whole tone, pentatonic, and blues. I can play 'Billie's Bounce'"—and now he *did* bounce, sailed from one square of sidewalk to the next—"'My Heart Stood Still,' 'Jelly Roll Blues,' 'Stormy Monday Blues,' and 'Long Tall Mama.'" All of these melodies went along with the blues chord format Dukie had been teaching him.

"And now," he said, "I'm getting to put some *soul* into it, half-singing, half-talking through those crazy lyrics. Those *stories*, man. Whiskey and Cadillac cars, all that trouble between men and women, or someone getting shot in Memphis."

While Billy had made great strides in playing, I knew he had a lot more work to do to get on par with the best of his role-model jazz pros—Oscar Peterson, Red Garland, Art Tatum, Hank Jones, and Willie "The Lion" Smith.

At the same time, I had to hand it to Billy: no one in my eons of experience had exuded more enthusiasm for achieving their goals than he did. His dedication rivaled that of my nineteenth-century ward, Dr. Ludvig von Fancher, who sought in a most enigmatic fashion to prove his hypothesis that organisms in the presence of stress can adapt and thrive. The crux of his theory? If one were to pour warm coffee into a subject's ear long enough, that ear would eventually become a mouth. As Ludvig's GA, I can personally vouch—zany as he was—for his try-and-try-again, single-minded devotion to overcoming setbacks and proving the naysayers wrong. Though Ludvig never could prove his ears-to-lips theory, I had always admired his persistence.

Suffice it to say that I saw that same grit and determination in Billy—and, what's more, I had far higher hopes that his dreams might actually come to fruition.

Later, at Percy's Diner, Billy's excitement seeped from every pore as he regaled Albert Martin—his best friend, clarinetist, fellow jazz buff, and apparent expert on the goings-on between the sexes—with his *grand plan:* "I've been thinking it would be cool if we could start a little combo—you know, a quartet or something like that. I bet we could even get Sr. Theresa to let us practice in the parish hall at St. Mary's. What do you think?"

"Man, that's a cool idea, but I don't think I can swing it."

"What's the problem?"

Albert sighed. "Since my mom and dad split up, I live with her all the way over in Cranberry Cove. There's no way I can get anywhere except on the school bus."

The circumstances surrounding the dissolution of the union between Margo and Eugène François Martin are worth mentioning here. After a "misunderstanding" over finding Eugène François in the kitchen of his first restaurant—Café La Poulette—with a seminude young waitress who strongly resembled Eartha Kitt, Margo packed up her and Albert's things and served the elder Martin with divorce papers. The ensuing debacle brought a premature end to Café La Poulette, not to mention the budding romance of Eugène François and Eartha.

Eugène François scrambled to refinance and rebuild, and—with the help of Vincenzo "Whitey" Bianco and Whitey's younger brother, Little Angelo-B, owner and proprietor of the Alpine Grotto in Lima, Ohio—the Café des Amis was born. The new restaurant featured a cozy piano bar, a mini wine bodega, and a limited French menu including *pommes frites*, *crêpes suzette*, and a variety of *croque monsieurs*—boiled or fried ham and different cheeses. Eugène listed them on the menu as *Messieurs Crunch Wells*. Café des Amis opened in Flourish after Little Angelo-B and his crew came to *ancillary* terms with Eugène François——which I'll explain later.

The seedy details of the Martins' divorce notwithstanding, Billy had a hard time understanding how their separation made it impossible for their son to play in Billy's proposed new band. "Your mom can't drive you?" he asked.

"She's too busy at the flower shop—she works there for extra dough now that my dad's gone."

"What about your dad? Can't he drive you to rehearsal instead?"

"Nah, man, he says he's too busy picking up food and stuff for his new restaurant."

I sensed Billy's desperation as he continued to needle Albert on the subject of Saturday band practices. "Couldn't you tag along and he could just drop you off when he's finished?"

"It's a bar, Billy. He doesn't want a kid there." Albert grinned. "But I bet, if we somehow manage to start up a band, he'd give us some gigs at the Café—if he thought we were any good."

As Billy finally resigned himself to the present impossibility of forming a band, he was surprised by two squealing voices entering Percy's Diner and heading toward their booth in the back.

Albert slapped a hand against his forehead, feigning contrite surprise. "I forgot to tell you, man: I invited Helen to have a Coke with us. Anna, too. Cool?"

Before Billy could respond, Helen slid into the booth next to Albert, squeezed his arm, and said to Billy, "Long time no see, Barnes. I think this might be the first time all four of us have been together since that crazy rollercoaster ride on your birthday—what, eight years ago?"

In the years since that fateful first ride on the Silver Streak, Billy had kept in touch with the three witnesses to his artistic awakening—though his lessons with Dukie and subsequent hours of solo practice occupied most of his free time. Still, he considered Albert, Helen, and Annabelle his closest friends. He was happy to be with all of them at once.

Billy grinned at Helen's remark. "Something like that." Turning to Annabelle, he said, "C'mon and sit down."

As she scrunched into the booth next to Billy, the sweet scent of her perfume enfolded them. Billy bumped Anna's shoulder playfully and said to her, "What I remember most about that rollercoaster ride was you covering your ears because the music was too loud. Do you remember that?"

"I didn't *cover* my ears, I just said it was so loud it *hurt* my ears."

Completely enamored with Annabelle's cool demeanor, Billy was eager to find some way to endear himself to her. He quickly lit upon the perfect opportunity: St. Mary's annual All Saints' Day Invitational Mixer. In addition to his or her own date, each student was also permitted to bring another couple. And so, Billy extended an invitation to the trio in his most cordial manner:

"If you guys aren't busy—and if the music won't be too loud for Anna here—will you all be my guests at my school dance on the fourth?"

As if accepting for everyone, Helen slapped her hand on the table and yelled, "You bet!"

"Dig the enthusiasm, Helen." Billy turned to Anna. "That sound okay to you, Lea?"

Anna gave Billy a look that was not quite a frown, not quite a smile. She said it sounded fine to her: not an emphatic acceptance, but still music to Billy's ears.

Friday, November 4, 1949

Though I had promised myself I would do my best to steer Billy away from any undue influences seeking to undermine his musical aspirations, the fact is, premonitions, passions, and promises aren't compatible forces. In other words, my trying to steer Billy at the height of his amorous interests was as pointless as my efforts to steer my first ward —a thirty-third-century BCE merchant named Kushim—away from his best client's wife, who offered Kushim her "personal" services in exchange for settling her husband's debt of 27,850 measures of barley. I won't go into the consequences of Kushim's consummating the bargain, but soon his son, Kozmayed I, took over the management of the family's grain business.

All of this is to say that I could see Billy falling in love that Friday night, at the annual All Saints' Day Invitational Mixer.

The two boys arrived together, and while Albert secured a table and grabbed four glasses of punch, Billy waited just inside St. Mary's parish hall for the girls to arrive. He examined the red carnation in his hand. Boys could give the girls a small floral memento, to be pinned to their sweater, and they could dance together for a whole hour to the music of a DJ hired by Sr. Theresa.

As Billy imagined what it might be like to dance with Annabelle, she and Helen arrived. Billy stood riveted in place and allowed his eyes to scan them from head to foot. Helen stood in silhouette with her elbows jutting out like coat hangers, her tight-fitting white sweater clinging to her curvy bust. She was in the same grade as Billy and their other friends, but a year older than him, and though she was pudgy and bucktoothed, she oozed a sensuality that set her apart from the other girls, whose catty remarks belied their jealousy. Anna, meanwhile, was lanky, taller than Helen and less developed. Her curly black hair framed her oval face; short bangs at the top of her deep-set dark eyes tickled her rounded eyebrows. In beige slacks, flat heeled shoes, and a knitted cardigan sweater over a dark brown long-sleeved blouse, Anna was the most dressed-up of the girls attending the mixer.

Billy held her carnation to his nose, gave it a sniff, and began to shuffle forward. As he approached, Annabelle stepped to the side to make room for him between her and Helen.

Uncertain about what to say, Billy raked his fingers through his unruly hair and felt his hands moisten. Anna's enticing scent teased him, reminding him of the gardenias his mother cultivated in her sunny kitchen window box. He thought of saying this, but didn't, and instead extended the carnation to Anna without a word.

She accepted the flower and pinned it to her sweater. Then she said, "Let's go in and sit together."

For most of the mixer, Albert huddled with Helen and tried to kiss her. When they danced together, Helen would let him hold her close. But as far as Billy knew—and despite Albert's incessant claims to the contrary later—Helen never actually let him kiss her.

Billy sat next to Anna and leaned close to her as the DJ played the right song to set the mood: "Imagination" by Ella Fitzgerald.

"That's a good song for dancing," Billy said.

"It's too mushy," Anna said. "I'm not very good at dancing, anyway."

"What do you like to do?"

"I like reading, especially poetry. Our class is reading poems out loud. We take turns with different verses."

"Like what?" Billy asked.

"Right now, we're reading Poe's 'Annabel Lee.'"

Between songs blaring over the parish hall's speaker system, Billy groped for something else to say. He might have asked Anna if she was named for Poe's poem, which he'd never heard of before, but he suspected he would not be the first person to ask that question, and he didn't want to risk annoying her. Anna was smart, he thought, and it made him feel less so. She had a quiet mystique about her, as if she harbored some secret power.

As Billy fumbled for his next remark, Anna gave him an unexpected opening.

"I took my first piano lesson from Mr. Chapman last week," she said.

"Wow, hey, I have a piano at home," Billy said. "I practice all the time. How did you like your lesson?"

Anna shrugged. "He said I had a pretty voice."

As the DJ started playing another tune—"I'll Be Seeing You" by Bing Crosby—Billy turned to Anna. "The mixer's about over," he said. "Let's dance...just this one time."

Moving slowly toward the dance floor, Anna said, "Remember, I'm not very good."

Embracing Anna gently, Billy put his right arm around her back and took her right hand in his left. Making only the slightest moves, Billy guided Anna's tentative steps in unison with his. As the song went on, Billy gradually pulled Anna closer to him, hoping she would feel the romantic mood. When they returned to their table, Anna smiled as Billy held out her chair for her to sit down.

"Maybe next time I'll know how to dance a little better," she said.

Billy wanted to ask her about that "next time," but he was stopped short as Sr. Theresa appeared at their table. All business, she said to Billy, "You are scheduled to play in fifteen minutes—unless you're too busy."

Billy glanced at Anna, swallowed, then looked back to Sr. Theresa. She had promised him fifteen minutes at the end of the night to practice his piano for a captive audience.

"No," he said, "I'm ready."

Sr. Theresa gave a sharp nod, then walked away. Anna leaned toward Billy. "When you said you practice piano, I didn't realize that meant you performed in public."

This felt like a compliment to Billy, though Anna had worded it almost like a question.

"What kind of music do you play?" she added.

He dared to take her hand. "I play jazz. Will you come up by the stage and watch me play?"

Anna tilted her wrist to look at her thin silver wristwatch, and Billy's hand gently slid away from hers.

"Maybe for a few minutes," she said. "My dad is picking me up pretty soon."

"Oh," Billy said, clearly dejected.

Seemingly oblivious to Billy's disappointment, Anna added, "My father actually thinks jazz—and jazz musicians—are, well, *weird*."

"Well, what do *you* think?" Billy asked, trying to keep his tone light.

And now Anna smiled, just slightly. "I'm reserving judgement."

Billy returned the smile, newly emboldened. "Do you have a favorite song I could play for you?" he asked.

"Not really."

But he thought he had just the song for her. "I'll play 'Star Dust' by Hoagy Carmichael," he said.

Anna cocked her head and said, "Is he from around here?"

"No," Billy laughed. "He's from Indiana. But I've heard him on the radio from the Steele Pier in New Jersey. If you like, we can go down to DeLong's Record Store sometime and listen to his new album."

Billy fancied this a rather sly way to ask Anna on a date—but she ignored it entirely. "Hurry up and play," she said, "before my dad gets here."

As you'll recall, I had made myself a promise to keep an eye on Annabelle Lea, in case she sought to undermine Billy's musical aspirations. I do not mean to vilify Annabelle, but even if she had no conscious intention to steer Billy off course, she still might accidentally do so in word or deed.

That said, she was mesmerized by Billy's performance at the All Saints' Day Mixer. Her face glowed a rosy, bashful pink, and her eyes closed as though hiding her most secret thoughts. And Billy—himself mesmerized by Anna's mystique, smile, scent, and charm—played "Star Dust" as if he were Hoagy Carmichael incarnate.

As I've learned over the centuries, things happen that elbow their way into one's best intentions, changing them—sometimes for the good, other times for the not-so-good—but definitely *changing* them. Looking ahead, I didn't need a crystal ball to tell me that Billy and Annabelle were harmonically in tune. All that didn't change the fact that I was still Billy's GA, but now I saw myself more as a watchdog over Billy's personal life. God help us both!

Chapter 7

<u>Saturday, June 10, 1950</u>

Billy's turning point? I'll tell you what: here's one that impressed even *me*. I would call it a true kick-start to Billy's adulthood—one even more profound than the All Saints' Day Mixer with Annabelle Lea.

One Saturday night, Dukie, Jupic, and Willa Mae took Billy to a place not many of Billy's age group had ever been: The Ritz Club, a jazz joint on the north side of Indian Lake at Atkinson's Landing, run by Fern Atkinson—owner, bartender, and bouncer.

The Ritz Club was crowded, the air foggy with cigarette smoke. Amped-up jazz blared over the club's speaker system. Men and women flirted and drank and danced close. It was a world of roiling, swirling motion bristling with pent-up energy about to explode. A slender man, hair parted in the middle and face sporting a thin black mustache, wore a black t-shirt and baggy pants. Billy watched as he put his hand on a woman's shapely backside and whispered into her ear as they danced. The woman wore a skin-tight skirt and halter-top. Her hoop earrings dangled loosely, and a silver chain with a small pendant teased the top of her large bosom. The woman smiled, pulling the man close as they gyrated together to the blaring music. This was nothing like the moves Billy had seen at St. Mary's parish hall last November, nothing he'd ever dreamed himself capable of doing with Annabelle Lea.

Turning back to the bar, Billy saw more than a dozen men dressed in sporty clothes and women wearing close-fitting slacks, tight sweaters, or loose blouses with plunging necklines and fancy jewelry. The mirror-back bar took up about a fourth of the club's floor space and ran down the left wall's expanse to the restroom area in the back. At right angles against the south wall, six booths stood opposite five tables, centered between them and the bar. A tiny service aisle ran between the booths and the tables. Every seat was filled—mostly with couples, but a table or two of only women sat together.

Toward the back of the seating area, an elevated bandstand overlooked the dance area. The black-and-white diamond-block linoleum dance floor was pocked with tar marks and peeling up at the corners. On the right side of the bandstand, a rickety upright piano sat nestled tightly against the wall; a large, richly-burnished wooden stand-up bass leaned against it. A set of drums sat cramped against the back wall, and a floor-stand microphone teetered at the front edge of the bandstand.

Jupie and Willa Mae grabbed a table. Meanwhile, Dukie led Billy into a small room behind the bandstand where a man stood smoking with his friends. The smoke in the room had a sweet, pungent aroma. Their little fat homemade cigarettes weren't like anything Billy had ever seen.

"Moss." Dukie gestured to Billy. "This is Billy Barnes—blows fine piano. You remember I told you about him?"

Moss took a long drag on the cigarette, sucked in the smoke, and held his breath. Stubbing out the butt in a coffee can, he nodded and introduced the other men, starting with a lanky fellow standing beside him.

"This is my brother, Otis. Plays bass." Turning to his left, Moss continued. "This here's J.J. on sax, and that's James Jackson, our drummer."

As all the men shook hands with Billy, Moss turned to Dukie and said, "You ready to wail?"

"I'll play the first tune, but I want Billy to play with the group after me. He's only ever done solo, and I want him to see what it's like when you're backed by the best bluesmen in town."

Moss agreed, and led the other musicians out of the back room and onto the bandstand. As Moss introduced the first tune—"C Jam Blues"—Billy took a seat with Jupie and Willa Mae. His gut clenched at the prospect of playing with Moss's group in place of Dukie after the first set. How could he follow that—how could a nobody like Billy Barnes play as masterfully as a jazzman like Dukie Kincaid?

Billy's mind blanked, until Jupie punched him on the shoulder and pointed to Dukie, who stood beckoning Billy to the stage.

Moss addressed the microphone. The crowd buzzed in readiness. As Billy sat down, sweat dripped from his brow onto the piano keyboard. A sudden chill seized him as Moss spoke to the noisy crowd.

"Wanna introduce my new piano player, Billy Barnes. Stand up, Billy, and take a bow."

To a smattering of applause, Billy stood and nodded bashfully. He felt his cheeks flush. A heightened sense of exhilaration surged through him, just as it had the first time he'd heard the jazz music playing at Sandy Beach all those years ago.

"Won't be long before he'll be playing all over town," Moss

said to the crowd, then quietly spoke to Billy and the other musicians: "I'll play an eight-count solo intro. Billy, you come in when James hits his first drum lick. Relax and be cool, man."

That was the turning point: Billy's first time playing for a real audience. His hormones got an equally significant kick-start about thirty minutes later, during the bows, when he noticed a full-bosomed, seductive woman in a loose halter-top reaching for his hand. It was the same woman Billy had seen earlier, gyrating on the dance floor while the man she danced with rubbed his hand on her behind. When their own hands touched, she tickled Billy's palm with her finger.

"You're cute," she said. "Can I buy you a drink?"

"He's with me," Willa Mae rasped as she stepped in front of the woman.

Still at the microphone, Moss interrupted their exchange.

"Got another blues number, so get down," Moss announced. "Here's 'Long Tall Mama.'"

Lost in the reverie of the woman's touch, the hot lights, the smoky air, and the thrill of having lived up to Moss's expectations, Billy sat down automatically on the piano bench.

James reached over and tapped Billy on the arm with a

drumstick. "Cool, man."

J.J. leaned over and patted Billy on the back. "Like Moss said, man, you got the *mo-jo!*"

As the band started playing again, Dukie turned to Willa Mae and Jupie.

"That was Billy's baptism with Moss," he said. "He would never let anyone sit in like that if they didn't have good chops."

"We owe you, Dukie," said Willa Mae. "Any other place around where Billy can get some more experience sitting in?"

Turning point? Yeah! Billy's first night at the Ritz Club—and two months later, the Colored Elks Club for Moss's birthday.

Sunday, August 13, 1950

Dukie brought Billy to the Colored Elks Club on West Williams Street for Moss's birthday bash and jam session. The club was crowded, smoky, dank, dimly-lit, and packed with men and women from age eighteen to eighty. Most of the men wore jackets and thin-ribbon ties or big blousy shirts with bold designs and gold necklaces. The women wore low-cut party dresses and high heels— arms loaded with bangles, fingers adorned with large, jeweled rings. Billy had never seen so many people with big hair. As groovy, laid-back, and cool as the Ritz Club was, Moss's Elks Club was hot, noisy, and frenetic.

It bewitched Billy, the sight of everyone drinking, smoking, and jiving all over the dance floor to the music blaring over the club's maxed-out sound system. Moss led Dukie and Billy to a table near the stage. "This is my reserved table, so you can see all of the action. I'll get you both a drink. Dukie, man, what'll it be?"

"I'll have a glass of sweet wine and whiskey," he said.

"You want something, Billy?"

"A Dr. Pepper, please."

As they sat down, Moss hailed a waitress, said something over the noise to her, and gestured to the table where Billy and Dukie sat. Then he jumped onto the stage and took the microphone. Everyone whistled and clapped for Moss, then quickly quieted down.

"Now hear me, everyone." Moss grinned. "It's my birthday."

The crowd started singing "Happy Birthday," drawing it out with "*And many mo-o-o-re...*"

Moss clapped his hands back at the crowd and continued. "I want to introduce you to a couple of special friends sitting over there who came out today to help me celebrate."

Moss gestured toward their table as a small spotlight beamed on Billy and Dukie. The applause kicked back up, and they both stood and waved timidly.

"That young man is Billy Barnes, my new piano player," Moss said, pointing to Billy. "That guy next to him is the jazz legend Dukie Kincaid, four-time *DownBeat Magazine*-awarded blues composer. Now put your hands together and let's get that little old white boy up here on the stage. He'll be black before the night's over, I guarantee it!"

Billy was so rattled by the loud applause that he tripped on the stage step and fell flat onto the bandstand. The crowd howled and jeered at his embarrassing, clumsy debut. Laughing, Moss helped Billy up off the floor and walked him over to the piano. Billy looked over and could see Dukie mouthing the words *Are you OK?* He nodded and smiled back at him.

Moss grabbed the microphone.

"See that? He can't walk, but he can sure wail on the piano!" Moss bellowed.

Though he'd gotten used to the hot lights, smoke, and crowd noise, Billy felt his whole body tense up in the unfamiliar setting. Sweat gushed from every pore of his body. Moss turned to him and said, "You cool, Billy?"

Billy croaked a weak response, "I'm good," then his voice quit working.

The crowd buzzed as Billy fidgeted to get comfortable on the piano stool. It was lower than the one at the Ritz Club—even lower than Willis's piano. Moss saw Billy's dilemma and came over to him.

"Twirl that piano stool around, man—couple of twists makes it higher," he instructed.

After adjusting the stool height, Billy, Otis, J.J., and James took their positions as Moss picked up his trumpet and got ready to play.

"We're gonna start off this set with a blues tune called 'Drinkin' Wine Spodie-odie.'"

Billy knew that "Wine" was the same twelve-bar blues as most of the other songs Moss loved playing (and making up his own version of the lyrics for). Just before they started, Moss walked back over to the piano and put his hand on Billy's shoulder.

"It's the same as the Ritz Club, man—only better. Just be yourself and relax."

Moss turned and dipped his head toward Billy and the others to make sure they were ready to play. Listening to Moss count off the tune, Billy thought the tempo was hot enough to singe the hair off everyone in the room. On the first beat, Billy hesitated briefly, but Moss ignored him and began singing. More nervous than ever, Billy started feeling Moss's groove and the group's swinging rhythm. After the first few bars, Billy settled down.

Dukie sat, rapt, and nodded every time Billy looked his way. When it came time for his solo, though, Billy was hesitant and uneasy. The fluid moves required to glide over the keys were lost in the fast tempo. Tentatively, Billy struggled to make sense out of his improvisational phrases. It wasn't his best effort.

As Otis and James traded four-bar solos, Billy wiped his brow on his shirtsleeve. Moss leaned toward him and chuckled. "Calm down, man, and play like you know you can!"

Billy nodded, focused on the keyboard, and got ready to play again. Moss and J.J. alternated soloing through three passes of the blues classic, and Billy was glad to be getting near the end—and a welcome break in his first performance at Moss's club. Just before the last four bars ending the tune, Billy started to relax—until Moss surprised him.

"Take another solo, man!"

With Moss and J.J. grinning, James and Otis held the swinging tempo behind Billy as he played his best ever. Without realizing it, Billy had soloed through the blues form twice and kept playing though the third. When he looked up, the crowd was clapping and shouting. Even Moss applauded before finishing the tune.

When he was through playing, Billy went back to the table to be greeted by Dukie. "Proud of you, man," he said. "Got a few new ideas for you when we get back together."

Later, on their last break, Billy went outside to get some air. When he returned, neither Dukie nor Moss were anywhere in sight. Billy saw Otis and James standing by the bandstand and moseyed up to them.

"Looking for Dukie," said Billy. "You seen him?"

James turned toward the bar and pointed over the crowd.

"He's right over there, next to Moss."

Billy spotted Dukie and Moss standing in a small space at the far end of the bar. He could see them huddled together, grinning as he approached.

Dukie's eyes were red and watery, his speech slurred. "One more set, man," he said, raising a near-empty tumbler of whiskey. "Then we'll split."

Billy watched his teacher and idol stagger and wobble through the crowd back to the bandstand. There was little doubt in his mind: Dukie was in trouble. On an impulse, Billy turned to Moss and said, "Dukie is sick. We need to get him out of here."

Moss reared back, shot Billy a long face. "Nothin' wrong with the Dukester he ain't had before. I'll get him a nightcap and he can sleep it off in the back."

I was very proud of Billy's response after Moss walked away: he went to the payphone and called his parents. Willa Mae arrived to take him home. On the way home, Billy's solemn mood struck Willa Mae odd. "Are you okay?" she asked. "What happened tonight?"

"Where's Dad?" asked Billy.

"Home. He said hello but he has to get up early tomorrow."

"I'm sorry he couldn't come," said Billy. "He doesn't care much for me playing piano, does he?"

"It's not that he doesn't like it. He just...he worries about the environment at these jazz clubs."

"What do you mean, the environment?"

"Billy..." Willa Mae paused, measuring her words. "Your father and I admire you and your ambitions to be a professional musician. God has given you a wonderful talent, and we are all thankful for His gift. As young as you are, you've been fortunate to have the benefit of a good teacher to prepare you for the future, so that part of what I have to say is positive."

Billy said nothing. He was waiting for the other shoe to drop.

"On the negative side..." Willa Mae sighed. "Your dad and I are worried about the life of a jazz musician. From what we can see, these jazz joints—to be honest—your father has a word for it."

Willa Mae slowed the car and spoke in a somber tone. "Many of the places we've seen aren't very respectable. They seem to be...the word he uses is *sleazy*. When we were at the Ritz Club watching you play, while you were onstage, a man who called himself Mouse-Something kept walking by the table offering us—what did he call it?—*hash*. Dukie finally had to tell him to go away."

Billy didn't wait to respond. "Mom, I don't pay attention to any of that. And Dukie—well, tonight was the first time I've seen him go too far with the drink."

Willa Mae pulled over, stopped the car, and turned to Billy. "Your father and I have always trusted you. And we care very much for Dukie Kincaid—I pray he gets the help he clearly needs. Just don't let yourself be dragged down by drugs and alcohol, okay?"

"Mom...I promise. I know better than to let that stuff ruin my life."

Willa Mae put her hand on Billy's arm. Her tone was unequivocally assertive: "Stand up and be accountable. Don't depend on anyone but yourself to stay out of trouble."

It was a strange word to Billy, "trouble." *Trouble* was the feeling of being onstage, worrying he couldn't keep up with Moss and his band; *trouble* was feeling like he'd bitten off more than he could chew. But the reefer, and the liquor—hell, even the women— that all felt like something he could avoid. A temptation he could easily overcome, since it wasn't all that tempting in the first place.

All that mattered to Billy was the music. And he knew Dukie felt the same way: he was in it for the love of jazz, even if he sometimes overindulged at the bar.

That night at home, I knew what Billy was thinking. Dukie was a friend—and Billy would stand by him, no matter what. At the same time, he made the promise to his parents: he wouldn't let them down or disappoint them by behaving the fool with drugs and alcohol.

###

Tuesday, September 5, 1950

When Billy went to his next piano lesson, he found that Dukie had mysteriously disappeared. Nothing more was said about him until school took up after Labor Day. Following the opening prayer on the first day of school, Sr. Theresa said, "Everyone close your eyes, say a prayer for Mr. Kincaid, and sign his Get Well card. He's in the hospital."

After class, Billy approached Sr. Theresa. "What happened to Dukie?" he asked.

She gave him a kind look. "Some people are afflicted with heart trouble, sugar diabetes, or diseases like arthritis. Dukie is one of the unfortunate ones who—I'll just say—is allergic to alcohol. It's called an addiction. I pray for Dukie every day that God will help him."

"Where is he now?" asked Billy.

Sr. Theresa turned to her desk, retrieved a pamphlet, and handed it to Billy. "This will explain things for you," she said.

Billy read the brochure:

St. Rita's Medical Center is a drug and alcohol rehabilitation center with a primary focus on substance abuse treatment based at 730 W. Market St. in Lima, OH. The provider specializes in a program called Addiction Services. The facility provides detoxification services to the public. The treatment center provides outpatient, partial hospitalization, and hospital inpatient care. Clerical referrals are encouraged.

His eyes moist, Billy looked up at Sr. Theresa and thanked her for helping Dukie.

Sr. Theresa was able to help Dukie Kincaid in a way I wasn't able to help Billy. I know I shouldn't think this way, but it's hard not to wonder how one emissary of the Big Boss could have such luck saving a wayward soul from danger, while another could fail at it so miserably. I might be feeling some professional jealousy, it's true.

The trail of my continuing inquiry into who shot Billy is going cold: Police Chief Kuldau seems to be sitting on his hands while he waits for the state of Ohio's ballistics report to return from Columbus. With no real witnesses to Billy's shooting (not even me), I suppose it's understandable for things to stall out: Kuldau hasn't got any leads or anyone to talk to, and if he has any suspects in mind he's so far kept that information to himself.

This all reminds me of the so-called *official inquiry* by Premier Josef Stalin into the crimes of one of my wards I mentioned earlier, the Bolshevik revolutionary Grigory Yevseyevich Zinoviev. As Grigory's star began to rise in the Soviet Communist party, Josef Stalin sought to eliminate the competition. By 1926, Grigory was ousted from the party's leadership, and the day after his conviction at 1936's Trial of Sixteen—a sham of a legal proceeding and the forbearer to the Great Terror in Russia—he was promptly executed. Other than a preliminary investigation led by Grigory's paramour, Carla Sokolovski, there was never an official inquiry, hearing, inquest, or even the most cursory probe into his disappearance; Carla was subsequently ostracized and banished to the far reaches of Siberia, never to be heard from again.

I mention this example to remind myself that searching for Billy's killer is not a risk-free endeavor—if not for me, then for his loved ones on Earth. Still, I'm committed to discrediting Dr. Brown's specious *accidental death* verdict, with or without the help of the Russells Point Police Department.

Chapter 8

I won't go so far as to say Billy was drifting without Dukie's influence, but I feared the possibility. With that in mind, I was tuned in on all levels when Anna, Helen, Albert, and their little colony of eighth-grade graduates clustered at the auditorium entrance for their first day at Lake Ridge High School. A hulking kid—the biggest kid Billy had ever seen, actually—stood with three other boys inside the auditorium by a bank of seats. The boy looked like a redheaded tree stump with stovepipe arms. He held up a hand-lettered sign with an arrow pointing to an empty section of nearby seats:

MACKRIL SNAPPERS SECTION —

WELCOME CATLICKERS.

"I guess they don't teach spelling here," said Annabelle. "Or how to use apostrophes. But since you're the only *catlicker*, Billy, you lead the way."

As they took their seats, two teachers escorted the big

kid and the three other offenders out of the auditorium, not to be seen again that morning.

Principal Josh Freeman addressed the student body: "On behalf of our faculty and staff, we welcome our returning upperclassmen as well as our entering freshmen. Lake Ridge High has always been an egalitarian community..."

Albert leaned over Helen and Anna to whisper a question at Billy: "What's that *eagle* word?" he said.

"Ask Anna," said Billy. "She's the genius."

"Shut up." Annabelle sighed. "It means everyone's *equal*."

LRHS boasted a student body of more than four hundred. There were nearly a hundred and twenty-five students in Billy's freshman class alone—more than the entire student body, kindergarten through eighth grade, at St. Mary's. When Billy looked around the packed auditorium, he recognized a few other transplants from St. Mary's, but no one else. He felt as if he were a nameless drone in the middle of a beehive.

Following the assembly, Billy huddled around the hallway lockers and reviewed his class schedule with Albert, Annabelle, and Helen. Annabelle had changed since their dance at the All Saints' Day Mixer nearly two years ago. Her dark curly hair was fixed in a French braid, and her black eyes were now shaded with a faint tint of lavender; her eyebrows were thinner, her lashes longer and more pronounced. She wore a bright red cardigan sweater over a sleeved blouse with a white linen collar, Spalding saddle shoes, and white bobby socks. Her lipstick was dark pink, and her fingernails were painted in a matching tone. Billy had thought about her all summer: he hoped he would have another chance to impress her with his piano playing.

Helen, too, had changed. Her fingernails—once cracked and nubby—were neatly filed into smooth oval shapes, and her legs were now cleanly shaven. Her bulky eyeglasses had been replaced with contact lenses, which made her amber eyes seem deeper and better aligned. Her eyelashes were longer, her smile broader, her complexion richer and creamier. Her flowing blond hair was pulled back into a ponytail and fixed with a ribbon. Though still pudgy, she wore a tight brown sweater that emphasized her legendary bosom. When she smiled at the boys who stopped to stare at her figure, Billy saw that she wore braces.

Looking over his class schedule, Billy discovered the four of them shared several classes: Latin, English, Algebra, and Business Accounting, as well as a weekly health class. Separately, Helen and

Anna elected to attend home economics classes, and Billy and Albert had their own choice of extracurriculars—an additional gym class, or an optional music class. As I had expected, and to my delight, Billy and Albert decided to join the school orchestra.

That first day, the group ate lunch together in the school cafeteria. Except for Helen, who had purchased an apple and a square of cherry Jell-O, everyone's tray was loaded with Sloppy Joes, potato chips, fruit salad, and milk. As they sat down, Billy whispered to Helen, "You're not eating much. Aren't you hungry?"

"I'm trying to lose some weight," Helen said, quietly. Then, more animated, she addressed the group. "You'll never guess who I met: Leon Muncy. The call him 'Beef.'"

"Who?" Annabelle asked.

"We saw him at the first assembly," Helen said.

"Holding up that *sign*," Albert said.

"Looked like the Hunchback of Notre Dame," Billy quipped.

"Beef's our freshman football star," Helen said. "He's so *big*!"

Nodding cynically, Billy turned to Anna. "You meet any *big guys* yet?" Annabelle just shook her head and sipped on her carton of milk.

###

At 3:15, Billy poked his head into the music room for the orchestra class he'd chosen. Mr. Hamilton, the music teacher, introduced Billy to the other musicians. "I heard from your old teacher, Dukie Kincaid, that you play quite well. Why don't you try out the piano?"

A six-foot, ebony Baldwin Grand stood centered in the room. Billy sat down at the piano and played "Cottontail," using many of the chords Dukie had taught him. The whole time he played, a girl seated in a chair near the piano watched him closely. At the end of the tune, Billy moved away from the piano as the entire group of student musicians sat motionless. Finally, Mr. Hamilton applauded, and the student musicians sprang to their feet and did the same. Mr. Hamilton shook Billy's hand and gestured to the girl who had been watching him.

"This is Sarah Flowers," he said. "Sarah is a senior. The two of you will be sharing piano assignments for our orchestra."

Though she appeared to be well proportioned, Sarah was stout, larger than Anna and not as curvy as Helen. Her skin was a rich porcelain texture, her face round but well balanced with soft rosy cheeks and bud lips. When she smiled at Billy, eyebrows arched over her hazel eyes, the corners of her mouth turned up to reveal perfectly symmetrical, straight white teeth. Her chestnut hair was cut in pageboy style, shoulder length, with the ends of her hair curled smoothly in a loose roll. Raising her eyebrows in greeting, Sarah extended her hand. Billy took it, and felt the strength in her fingers from what he assumed to be years of playing piano.

"You play super!" she said.

"Uh...thanks," said Billy.

Sarah turned back to the piano and winked over her shoulder at him. "Sit next to me," she said. "We can talk."

When Billy sat on the piano bench next to Sarah, it felt as though her large frame required more of the bench than Billy's slighter one. She put her hand on his shoulder and whispered into his ear, "I think it's super we'll be playing together." Her warm breath sent a tingle down his spine, and he could smell her lingering floral scent. After listening for a half-hour to the orchestra tune up and play simple ensemble exercises under the tutelage of Mr. Hamilton, Sarah handed Billy a sheaf of music.

"These are copies of the piano parts for our repertoire," she said. "You can look them over before our next rehearsal. Mr. Hamilton said that we'll start with 'Finlandia.' Do you practice every day?"

"Almost," Billy said—though less than usual, now that Dukie was gone. "Do you?"

"Every day." Sarah smiled. "I know you like jazz. So do I."

"What do you practice?" said Billy.

"I don't know many jazz songs, but I practice the jazz scales and how they work with chords. I think it's just super fun."

"Jazz scales? Are they different from the regular scales?"

"Doesn't your teacher talk about jazz scales?"

"Some. I'll ask him the next time I see him. Who's your teacher?"

Sarah stood and packed up her music. "My dad. He plays guitar. He studied with a famous guitarist in New York named Johnny Smith. He taught my dad how to use the jazz scales to improvise over a lot of the classics. That's what my dad is teaching me—to learn how some classical compositions can be improvised with jazz scales and chords. Isn't that just super?"

Billy was intrigued—and I was pleased. For the first time since Dukie had left for St. Rita's, Billy's eyes showed the spark of curiosity: he wanted to learn something new, to innovate, instead of dutifully repeating the scales and chords Dukie had already taught him by rote.

"Did your dad ever show you an example?" Billy asked Sarah.

She nodded. "He played 'Bourrée in E-minor' by Bach. And he showed me how the opening melodic line, except for tempo, was the same as this song called 'You'd Be So Nice to Come Home To.' Cole Porter wrote it for a movie, *Something to Shout About.* Do you know it?"

Billy shook his head. He was beginning to wonder if he knew much of anything.

"It's really super," Sarah said. "Doesn't your teacher make you learn the jazz scales?"

"Dukie?" Billy stumbled over the name—it had been so long since he'd actually said it out loud. "Dukie teaches me jazz tunes and their chord patterns. I have good pitch, so he makes me cover my eyes so I can't see his hands, and we practice tone association so I can identify the chord he's playing by name."

Sarah gave him a look he couldn't quite describe. Not pity, or doubt—I would have called it a soft, polite incredulity. "Billy," she said, "do you want me to ask my dad about the jazz scales?"

"Yes," Billy said, a little too emphatically. Then, cooler: "I mean...well, sure."

At home, Billy leafed through the orchestra repertoire for the year:

Gershwin's Overture from *Porgy and Bess*, "The Russian Overture" by Rimsky-Korsakov, and "Finlandia, Op. 26" by Sibelius. Looking forward to playing with the orchestra and getting to know Sarah, Billy practiced the piano part for "Finlandia." The following week, at the first full Wednesday orchestra rehearsal, Sarah made room for Billy to sit next to her on the piano bench. As he sat down, he once again felt the spread of her rump taking up more than her half of the piano bench. He noticed her skirt, pleated black plaid, and almost felt its fabric pressed against his own slacks.

Sarah opened her music portfolio and turned to Billy. "Did you practice?" she asked.

"A little," he said.

"Isn't Jean Sibelius just super? He's one of my favorite composers," she said, as Mr. Hamilton raised his baton. "Do you mind if I play the first time or two?"

"I'll listen," Billy said.

Billy studied the score as Sarah played. To his astonishment, Sarah played through the first three rehearsal segments without a mistake. At the break, while Mr. Hamilton worked with the brass section, Sarah stood and turned to Billy.

"Your turn," she said.

"No, that's OK," Billy said.

"Are you sure?" Sarah leancd closer to Billy and added, "Do you want to go to Percy's after rehearsal? I can tell you what my dad said about the jazz scales."

"I have to meet someone," Billy said. Still, he did want to hear what she had to tell him. "Maybe next week?"

I was disappointed with Billy for putting off Sarah in favor of spending more time with Annabelle Lea—and, what's more, with the lie he had told to manage it. Perhaps you would find the word "fib" more appropriate, but for GAs there are no gradations when it comes to untruths: there is only fact or fiction, and Billy's so-called "meeting" with Anna was the latter. It was not a formal or mutual appointment, but a romantic impulse Billy needed to satisfy.

The two of them stood at their hallway lockers at the end of the school day. Anna was loading schoolbooks into her backpack as Billy pulled a neatly wrapped gift from his own bag and held it out to Anna.

"I thought you might like this," he said.

At first, Billy thought Anna hadn't heard him, but suddenly she looked at the proffered gift and stepped back. She glanced at Billy, then back to the package. Her curiosity piqued, she said, "What's this?"

"Just a little gift," Billy said, and pushed the package toward Anna's hand.

She took the package and held it to her ear. "It isn't ticking or anything," she said, grinning

"Open it," Billy said.

Anna unwrapped her gift: a palm-sized book of poems by Edgar Allan Poe. Opening the cover to see the first poem, "Annabel Lee," she smiled as she scanned the first verse:

> *It was many and many a year ago,*
>
> *In a kingdom by the sea,*
>
> *That a maiden there lived whom you may know*
>
> *By the name of Annabel Lee;*
>
> *And this maiden she lived with no other thought*
>
> *Than to love and be loved by me.*

Anna beamed and hugged Billy.

"I'm glad you like it," Billy said. "I picked it because you said you liked poetry. But mostly because your name is Annabelle, just like Annabel in the poem...but spelled—"

"It's really wonderful, Billy. Thank you." As she tucked the book into her bag with the others, Anna smiled at Billy. "By the way," she said, "I hear Sarah Flowers thinks you're really cool."

This surprised Billy. "We...just...play together," he stammered.

"Sounds like she wants to play more than piano with you," Anna said

"That's not—"

"Everyone says that Sarah's real...well, *I* think she's real nice," Anna said. "We're in the same gym class."

"Will you go to the football game with me Friday night?" Billy blurted. He'd never attended a football game in his life, but it was the first excuse he could think of to spend some time with Anna outside of school.

Anna nodded, ambiguously. "I...I don't know anything about football."

"Me neither, really. But Albert does. And Helen..."

"I'll talk to her about going with us," she said. "But Albert plays in the marching band, so we'll be on our own when it comes to figuring out the game."

Chapter 9

Over my years as a guardian angel, I've never had an assignment with a sports figure—no gladiators, Olympians, or anything in between—which is to say that I was just as clueless as Billy at that first LRHS game. It was a cool fall evening, the air light but damp and filled with the smell of smoke from the previous night's pre-game bonfire. Since Albert was playing in the marching band, Billy and Anna were alone in their search for Helen in the mobbed grandstand. Wiggling their way into a first-row seat meant for one person, they squeezed so close together that Billy could inhale the sweet scent of Anna's heady perfume. From over his shoulder five rows back, he heard Helen call, and looked up to see her waving to him and Anna.

"Come up and sit with me!" Helen yelled.

I'm fine right here, Billy thought to say, reluctant to give up his forced proximity to Anna. Still, he stood when Anna did and followed her up the bleachers, stumbling over the other fans until they finally reached Helen. Thankfully, seat space was still limited, so Billy and Anna wound up pressed nearly as close together as they had been five rows down.

"Do you like my corsage?" Helen asked, as Billy and Anna settled. A yellow mum sat perched just above her right breast, striking against the bright red of her sweater.

Billy glanced at her floral adornment. "Nice."

"Don't tell Albert, but Beefy gave it to me for good luck." She turned to Anna and said, "Isn't that cool?"

Within minutes of the game beginning, Beef Muncy scored his first high school touchdown. With the crowd going berserk, Helen pounded on Billy's back. "Billy! Did you see that? Beefy just bulled over everyone. He's so big!"

"Amazing."

At halftime—the Lake Ridge Blue Jackets leading 24 to 3 over their archrivals, the Urbana Hill Climbers—Billy, Anna, and Helen made their way to the fan-swamped concession area. As they waited to move up, Anna and Helen studied the menu offerings, which hung from the awning of the snack stand on brightly-lit placards.

Suddenly, Billy felt a tap on his shoulder, and turned to a familiar voice greeting him. "Hi," Sarah said. "Enjoying the game?"

Billy shrugged. "What I can understand of it, I guess."

Sarah laughed. In the same confident tone she'd used at orchestra practice to ask him out to Percy's, she said, "I was wondering if you're going to the victory dance tomorrow night at the Cottonwood Inn. We could go together."

"Oh, I have a gig tomorrow night at the 151 Club," said Billy. Another lie: Billy hadn't performed at a club in months. "But maybe some other time," he added. "You still owe me your dad's jazz scales."

She grazed Billy's wrist with her trailing fingertips. "You know, we can have a lot of fun together besides playing the piano," she said—and, with that, she was gone.

Apparently less absorbed in the menu than Billy had thought, Annabelle and Helen turned to him and smirked. "If you want to go spend some time with Sarah," said Anna, "I can get a ride home with Helen."

Billy sighed. "Let's just go watch the rest of the game," he said.

Back in the stands for the second half, Billy felt miserable. Even the closeness of Anna's body to his own offered little comfort, after the hint she'd dropped about Sarah—the ease and disinterest with which she'd suggested Billy might go out with her. He just watched as Beef Muncy scored touchdown after touchdown, and listened to Helen's screams of encouragement—"Go, Beefy!"—every time.

After the game, Helen rushed the field in search of either Beef or Albert—Billy wasn't sure which. He and Anna ambled out of the stadium alone. They had planned for Billy to walk her home, but now—inspired, perhaps, by Sarah's own brazenness—he decided to press his luck.

"Do you want to grab a milkshake at Percy's?" he asked. "If you had the Poe book with you, I thought maybe we could read 'Annabel Lee' together. I've never read it."

"Color me surprised," Anna said, but the mockery was gentle. She adjusted the strap of her purse on her shoulder. "I do have the book, but I think you should just walk me home. I promised my father I'd be back right after the game."

"Oh," said Billy. "Some other time, maybe?"

Anna smiled. "Sure, Billy."

"What about the dance at the Cottonwood Inn?"

"I thought you were playing at the 151 Club tomorrow night. That's what you told Sarah, isn't it?"

I don't mean to gloat, but this is one of the reasons why GAs are so constitutionally opposed to lying: one lie invariably leads to another. Billy hoped that Anna might be flattered by the lie he'd told Sarah—*See*, he might say, *I was really hoping to go with you instead*—but he knew her well enough to know she would instead be disappointed in him, possibly even offended.

"Shoot," he said, "that's right. Maybe next time?"

"Sure," Anna said. "Maybe next time."

The next Friday, Billy was still sulking over his missed opportunity with Anna. A few minutes before rehearsal with the orchestra, he sat apart in the music room and reviewed the piano scores for the Thanksgiving concert. As he studied the piano part for each, Albert Martin blustered through the door, plopped his clarinet on the piano bench, and turned to Billy.

"Where's the tubbette?" said Albert, gesturing with his arms in a big circle. "She's got the woodwind charts."

There was something about Albert that irritated me, and I got the sense that Billy humored him unnecessarily, as though doing so would boost Billy's stock with him. True, Albert was smart, talented, and reasonably attractive with his tall, wiry physique and deep-set dark eyes. But, for some reason which I didn't care to investigate—*Penso Appositus* notwithstanding—I thought he relished belittling people so that he could nurture his own superiority complex. That's why I took every opportunity to steer Billy away from Albert's boorish behavior—and, to my mind, this was one of those opportunities.

Billy looked up from the Gershwin score and said, "Who?"

"Flowers," Albert said. "Tubby Flowers."

I tried to put in Billy's mind the thought of Helen sitting at the cafeteria table on the first day of class, lamenting her weight; I tried to make him see that there was little difference between a girl like Helen—whom Albert had been actively, unsuccessfully courting for years now—and one like Sarah. I wanted Billy to understand that, just because Helen and Sarah's bodies were not perfectly thin, that did not make them any less worthy of affection—and, more importantly, respect. Unfortunately, I failed in my attempt: all Billy could see was Sarah's rump on the piano bench beside him, requiring more than her fair share.

Billy laughed out loud at the thought—but the revelry was short-lived. Almost immediately, Billy heard the sound of Sarah's voice. He turned to see her standing in the doorway of the music room—early for rehearsal, of course. Her face was red as she sneered at Albert. "I heard what you called me," she said. "I'd rather be fat than stupid like you."

Embarrassed, Billy stood and said, "Hi, Sarah, I—"

Sarah strutted over to Billy and slammed a music folder on the piano stand. "I thought we were friends, Billy."

"We...we are."

"I heard you laughing at what Albert said."

Billy groped for words. "Sarah, I didn't mean...I'm sorry."

Sarah dabbed at her eyes with a tissue and thrust an envelope into Billy's hands. "You don't deserve it, but my father and I went to a lot of trouble hand copying those jazz scales for you last night. Now, if you could just break away from your moron friend Albert and practice them..."

Tears flowing, Sarah turned away from him and stalked into Mr. Hamilton's empty office. She slammed the door behind her.

As the other orchestra members arrived, Billy felt smothered by regret for letting Sarah be insulted. And now, belatedly, he thought about all the nasty things he'd heard other girls say about Helen, which only augmented his shame. There was no difference between mocking a girl for her large chest and mocking a girl for her large behind. It was all stupid—Billy saw that now. And I was proud of him, too, even though the revelation had not come sooner.

When Mr. Hamilton finally strolled into the room, he glanced around and asked Billy if he'd seen Sarah. "She was supposed to come in early and organize the scores for rehearsal."

Albert disappeared into the reed section as Billy nodded toward Mr. Hamilton's office and said, "She's in there."

As the players tuned their instruments and waited for Mr. Hamilton to begin rehearsal, anxiety tightened Billy's back. Fifteen minutes later, Mr. Hamilton stepped out of his office and beckoned Billy to approach. He was livid.

"I can't tell you how disappointed I am with you, Willis Barnes. I just listened to the most anguished account from a lovely young woman about how you and Albert Martin insulted her beyond words."

"Mr. Hamilton, I..."

"Don't say anything. As of now, you and Mr. Martin are suspended from further orchestra participation until you can show some respect for your classmates and fellow musicians."

Shaking his head, Billy stepped back. "May I please see Sarah?" he said, sheepishly. "To apologize?"

"It will take more than an apology to get you back on that piano bench, Billy," said Mr. Hamilton. "If I were you, I'd go home and think about how to resist the urge to make careless remarks that hurt people—especially someone as kind and hardworking as Sarah Flowers."

You might expect me to have taken issue with Mr. Hamilton's punishment for Billy—determined as I was to keep my ward free of those who would prevent him from growing as a musician—but in this case, I agreed that Billy needed some time to adjust his thinking. It would mean nothing for him to be the most talented jazz musician of his generation if he managed to alienate the friends who had helped him develop his talent in the first place.

My own mind made up on the matter, I was curious to see how Billy's parents would react to the news of his suspension. He managed to avoid the topic until the next morning, as Willa Mae filled a bowl with cereal, topped it with plump red fruit, and sat it in front of Billy.

"What are you thinking about so early on a Saturday morning?" she said.

Billy hesitated as he stirred the berries into his cereal.

"I got in trouble at school yesterday—at orchestra practice. I hurt Sarah Flowers's feelings by laughing at Albert's stupid joke about her...being fat."

Willa Mae wiped her red-stained fingers against her apron. "Did you apologize?"

"It wasn't me that said it, it was Albert. I just laughed."

"That's no better than saying it yourself, Billy."

"Yeah, I know." He held his spoon over the bowl of cereal, too preoccupied with anguish to actually take a bite. "Anyway, Mr. Hamilton suspended me from the orchestra."

"For how long?"

Billy pushed his cereal aside. "I don't know for sure."

Willa Mae put her hands on her hips. "Well, no matter how long you're suspended from the orchestra, you need to call Sarah and apologize to her immediately."

Billy nodded. "Would you call her mother for me and..."

"I will *not* call her mother." Willa Mae shook her head. "*You* call her this morning and be man enough to admit to being rude and thoughtless."

Billy stewed over what he would say to Sarah. Should he apologize for Albert...for himself...what? Finally, at 8:45, he called the Flowers home. A woman answered: "Flowers residence."

Mustering his courage, Billy said, "Mrs. Flowers?"

"Speaking."

"This is Billy Barnes. May I speak with Sarah?"

After a long delay, Mrs. Flowers said, "I don't think Sarah is interested in speaking with you, Mr. Barnes."

Billy forged ahead.

"Mrs. Flowers, I know Sarah's feelings were hurt yesterday at school. But I—"

"You and your little friend did more than just *hurt her*

feelings—you devastated her!"

Billy could feel the tension seize his throat.

"I...could you please...*please* ask Sarah to come to the phone?"

After more thumping heartbeats than Billy could count, Sarah's voice sounded on the other end of the line: "I don't want to talk to you, Billy, but my mother—"

"Sarah!" Billy interrupted. "I know I did a very awful thing laughing at Albert's dumb insult. Will you give me a chance to apologize?"

Sarah was quiet for a long while. "I'm going shopping with my mother," she finally said. "I'll stop by Percy's around eleven. If you're not too busy thinking up stupid jokes, maybe you can stop in."

Realizing he had never thanked Sarah for the scales she and her father wrote out for him, Billy grabbed the envelope before he left for Percy's. He arrived at the restaurant fifteen minutes early and staked out a booth in the back. Waiting anxiously for Sarah to arrive, he practiced what he would say. But as soon as he saw Sarah enter with a woman dressed to the nines who must have been her mother, he forgot the words. As he stood and rushed toward them, the woman whispered into Sarah's ear and left the restaurant.

Taking Sarah's coat, Billy tried his best smile, but Sarah seemed oblivious.

"I have a booth in the back," Billy said.

"I can't stay. My mother is waiting."

"Couldn't we just have a Coke?" Billy asked.

"Fat people shouldn't drink Cokes," Sarah said.

Billy's shoulders slumped.

"Sarah, I was very...thoughtless...and rude...and..."

Sarah shrugged—but, sensing that she was the tiniest bit receptive, Billy continued.

"I'm sorry for laughing at what Albert said. I apologize."

Sarah sighed. The hint of a smile crossed her face as she said, "At least you were man enough to admit it. I accept your apology."

Heartened, Billy put his hand on Sarah's arm and said, "I never thanked you for the scales you and your father showed me. Do you have a minute to talk about them?"

Sarah nodded and watched as Billy removed the manuscript paper from the envelope she'd given him in the music room the day before. He read the note attached to it:

Dear Billy: Here are five scales my father recommends you learn for jazz improvisation. My father said that you still have to study the chords to know what notes of the scale are also in each chord and how to use these scales in your improvisation. Have fun. Sarah.

Shaking his head at what he knew still hurt Sarah, he scanned the page quickly and pushed it across the table to her. Sarah turned the page around for Billy to read as she pointed to each of the first four scales—major, minor, dominant, and diminished—and described them and their usage.

Billy studied the notation as he followed along with Sarah's instruction. "Do you know all of these scales?" he asked.

"My dad's still teaching me. He wants me to learn some of the alternate names for the scales or modes, like *Dorian* and *Phrygian* and *Ionian*. Their names go all the way back to the Middle Ages."

Billy's head was spinning at these terms—and Sarah could see that. To reassure him, she added, "My dad said you shouldn't worry too much about those names—just memorize their uses."

Now, she placed her finger on the final scale: the blues scale. "Dad says this is one of the first scales jazz musicians need to know."

"Yeah." Billy nodded. "Dukie taught me a lot of blues tunes, so I'm pretty much hip to that one."

Sarah smiled, just faintly. "It sounds like Mr. Kincaid is a super teacher. You must really enjoy being his student."

"I do," said Billy. "But it's been great learning from you, too. I love playing piano with you in orchestra."

"Thanks for saying that, Billy." As Sarah stood to leave, Billy grabbed her coat and held it for her. "I appreciate it."

"I'm playing a solo in the assembly room at Thanksgiving," Billy said. "Will you come and sit with me while I play?"

"I can't," Sarah said.

"You're still upset with me?" he said.

She shook her head. "I was going to tell you this yesterday, but then—well, you know."

"Tell me what?"

"My dad just got a new job teaching calculus at Xavier University in Cincinnati."

"Cincinnati?" said Billy.

Sarah nodded. "We're moving in two weeks."

###

Billy and I were both disappointed by Sarah's abrupt departure from his life—and, more importantly, his musical education. So we were both heartened when, in the early months of 1952, Willa Mae handed Billy a sealed envelope postmarked CINCINNATI, OHIO. Extracting the enclosed handwritten note, Billy learned that good things actually do happen to deserving people. Sarah's closing words:

> *...and guess what??? I just got accepted to The Juilliard School of Music in New York. Isn't that just super?*
>
> *Your Friend,*
>
> *Sarah*

And here's my own post-script: Any GA worth his salt will exert his influence with his colleagues to teach his own ward a valuable lesson. In this case, I persuaded Sarah's GA to nudge her toward writing Billy this note. I simply wanted to stimulate Billy's awareness that one musician's hard work and diligent practice could pay off—and to encourage him to stay the course with his playing, even in Dukie Kincaid's long absence.

Chapter 10

March 1952

The freezing winter weather kept everyone trapped in the cafeteria for lunch. With Albert rehearsing with the marching band, Billy was left to his own devices. Anna stood next to him in line, but she was too busy reading over an algebra textbook in preparation for an upcoming test to pay him much mind.

I had a preferred vantage point for staying close to Billy and his lunchtime entourage: a small stage set in the corner of the cafeteria for noon-time announcements by Principal Freeman and other faculty members. And, though it wasn't within my purview to oversee anyone else's conduct, I could tell by Beef Muncy's swagger and brazen petting of Helen's shapely behind as they entered the cafeteria that he was the self-appointed reigning Adonis of Lake Ridge High School.

On this particular day, Beef chose to exert his dominance by first elbowing his way in line between Billy and Anna, then brashly exhibiting to the cafeteria crowd that Helen was a timely target for furthering his reputation as a bully. As Helen served herself two sloppy joe sandwiches and reached for a cupcake, Beef took the items on her food tray and hastily trashed them in a nearby waste receptacle.

"Beef, stop," Helen protested, weakly.

Beef turned to the others in line. "Listen everyone! My friend Helen here"—Beef gestured to Helen and smirked—"wants to eat all this fat food so she can try out for the circus. All she'll have to do is grow a beard!"

Instantly recalling his cruel insult to Sarah Flowers, Billy pushed Beef out of the line. Forcing his way back in, Beef exploded: "Barnes, get your candy ass out of my way, I'm ahead of you!"

Billy was astonished when Anna suddenly looked up from her book, pushed past him, and confronted Beef. "You should be ashamed of yourself, Leon—you are nothing but a bully."

Beef tapped his finger on Anna's shoulder. "I don't take no crap from a snob-puss like you, Lea," he growled. "This is about Gordon's fat ass, so mind your own fucking business."

Shocking everyone, Helen took dead aim and launched her chocolate-frosted cupcake at Beef's head. "Mind your own frigging business yourself, you moron," she yelled.

Helen's cupcake missile in hand, Beef charged her.

Intercepting Beef, Billy grabbed him and, exerting more strength than he thought himself capable of, forced Beef out of the lunch line again.

That did it: Beef grabbed Billy by the shirt and they both fell into a cafeteria table. Chairs flew and food scattered over the floor. "I been waitin' to get a piece of you, Barnes!" Beef roared. Billy swung wildly at his head. His left fist connected with Beef's right ear and a cracking noise like firewood being split with an axe resounded through the cafeteria.

Before Billy could duck, Beef's roundhouse punch smashed him on the bridge of the nose. Blood spurted everywhere, and Billy sank to the floor. Sprawled there, tears gushing from his eyes, he tried to rebound from the sharp pain. Soon enough, he staggered to his feet. Beef began a new charge forward and Billy was prepared to lunge, but just then, Mr. Freeman yanked them apart.

"You two go straight to my office," he ordered.

Inside the principal's office, Billy and Beef sat next to each other, opposite Mr. Freeman over his desk. Billy regarded his throbbing, swollen hand. Wincing with pain, he sulked over how fighting—especially with someone as stupid as Beef Muncy—would affect his playing piano at the spring concert. Beef sat leering at Billy as Mr. Freeman pulled out a file from his desk drawer and scanned it.

"With your dismal record, Mr. Muncy, I have no choice but to suspend you from school for a month," he said.

Beef stood—towering over Mr. Freeman. "Who gives a rat's ass," he bellowed, and stomped out of the office.

Mr. Freeman watched Beef's retreat, unmoved, then looked at Billy. He was holding a bloody handkerchief over his nose.

"You better see the nurse and get some ice on that nose," said Mr. Freeman. "Meanwhile, I'm putting you on probation."

Billy glanced at the sign outside the nurse's office—MARY K. TALBOTT, R.N.—and rubbed his hand gently as he pocketed his bloody handkerchief. With Billy seated on a chrome clinic stool, Nurse Talbott examined his injuries. Coddling his left hand, she pressed on the center of the swollen red mass. Stabbing pain shot through his hand up to his elbow. Jerking back, eyes watering, Billy thought about playing piano and moaned, "It isn't that bad...is it?"

"Bad enough that you should get X-rays," Nurse Talbott said. With little ceremony, she pinched Billy on the bridge of his nose and shook her head. Seeing his eyes water as he recoiled, she said, "Your nose is definitely broken, too. I'll wrap your hand in an ice pack. Go home and have your mother re-wrap it with fresh ice. Unwrap it every hour for fifteen minutes and re-wrap it again until you get to the doctor."

As Billy watched Nurse Talbott stretch an elastic bandage over the ice pack, he said, "What about playing piano?"

"Are you kidding?" she said.

Billy stepped out of the nurse's office, clunked down the stairway to the music room, and made his apologies to Mr. Hamilton.

"Nurse Talbott thinks I won't be able to play piano for a while."

"I heard about your little cafeteria incident," Mr. Hamilton said, leaning against his desk. "It's a shame my star piano player keeps finding himself in situations that *prevent* him from playing the piano."

"It's pretty dumb," Billy agreed, as he turned and exited the room.

Upstairs, Billy slammed his locker door closed, spun the combination lock, and donned his winter coat. Stalking out of the school's side exit to walk home for more first-aid, he stopped short when he heard voices behind him. Turning, he saw Anna and Helen following him. Arriving at Billy's side, Anna reached toward him, patting him on the shoulder, as Helen shook her head in dismay.

"I didn't mean to start a fight," Helen said.

When Billy turned to greet her, Anna saw his swollen face and bandaged hand. She covered her mouth and gasped. "My God, your nose is broken! And...your hand?"

Billy held up his injured hand and frowned.

"No piano for a while," he said, as he adjusted the ice pack the nurse had given him.

Anna touched his bandaged hand and whispered, "If I had any idea..."

"It'll heal," Billy said. "I'll be able to play in a few weeks."

Gently, Helen touched Billy on his cheek. "Beef Muncy is a real jerk, Billy. He and I are finished, and good riddance."

"I'll walk you home," said Anna. "Helen has to go back and get her things in the girls' locker room—we were getting changed for gym class when we saw you out here."

Fifteen minutes later, Anna escorted Billy into the Barnes living room, where Willa Mae frowned at his swollen nose and ice-packed hand.

"How in the world did this happen?" she said.

Billy gestured timidly to Anna and said, "Beef Muncy insulted Anna here and I...just... lost it."

Willa Mae examined Billy's left hand and shook her head.

"I admire your chivalry, but really..."

Billy looked at his swollen hand, redder than before, numb and throbbing.

"I'll be fine," he said. "It's just...not being able to play the piano."

"I'm taking you to see a doctor," said Willa Mae.

"I'm fine," said Billy. "Really..."

Before he could finish the thought, Anna interrupted. "My dad is a doctor. If I may use your phone, I'll call him. He'll be happy to treat you."

As Anna dialed the number, Billy reared back. "See your *father?* Isn't there someone else?"

"What's wrong with my dad? He'll take good care of you."

"I thought you said he doesn't like jazz musicians. Didn't you?"

"Calm down," said Willa Mae. "It's very nice of Anna to do this."

As she hung up the phone, Anna turned to Billy and Willa Mae. "My father is busy with the flu season, but he promised not to make you wait too long." Anna regarded Billy for a moment, some sweet sentiment warming her features. "Call me, Billy, and let me know when you feel like going to Percy's for a milkshake."

"And the poem," Billy reminded her.

As Willa Mae donned her winter coat, Anna gave Billy a smile. "Right," she said. "And the poem."

As Billy and Willa Mae entered Dr. Lea's office suite, the smell of winter sickness took their breath. The receptionist behind the sliding glass window greeted Billy's mother.

"Do you have an appointment?"

"Dr. Lea's daughter, Anna, called ahead for us."

"Take a seat," the receptionist said. "We'll work you in."

Plopping down beside his mother in the last two thinly-padded armchairs, Billy scanned the waiting room walls: framed, faded bucolic scenes from anonymous locales. Picking up a three-year-old copy of *Family* magazine, he turned to his mother.

"Are all doctor's offices like this?"

"We're lucky Dr. Lea will see you today," she said.

Three outdated magazines later, the door to the inner office opened and an X-ray technician led Billy and his mother back to the radiology lab. After having his hand X-rayed, Billy and Willa Mae were taken to Dr. Lea's exam room.

Dr. Lea was already examining Billy's broken nose when the technician moseyed back in to deliver Billy's scans. Dr. Lea removed a large, dark celluloid object from a brown envelope and stuck it onto the backlit translucent fixture mounted on the wall.

Billy saw the white areas illuminated by the backlight. As in a spooky Halloween image, Billy saw the outline of his skeletal hand. Dr. Lea studied the image and turned to Billy.

"So, you've been in a fight?"

"Not really," said Billy. "I..."

Billy's mother moved closer to the examination table.

"Is it bad?" she said.

Dr. Lea flicked off the panel light and wrote on a pad of paper. When he finished, he snatched down the X-ray film and stuffed it back into the envelope.

"You have what's called a Boxer's Fracture," Dr. Lea said. "Cracked your fourth metacarpal, but you're lucky it isn't worse. Take a couple of aspirin twice a day for the pain and keep your hand iced. Keep ice on your nose, too."

Dr. Lea handed the note he'd written along with the brown envelope to Billy's mother.

"Give these to my nurse," he said. "She'll tell you where to get a soft cast put on his hand."

As the doctor opened the door to leave the examination room, he turned to Billy.

"By the way, Anna has told me a lot about you. She said you play piano. Are you trained in the classics?"

Billy jumped off the examination table.

"I play jazz. How soon can I start playing again?"

"Jazz? I never cared much for jazz. I like classical. Can you read music?"

"Yes, I play in the school orchestra. How soon will I be able to play?"

"At your age?" Dr. Lea considered. "Maybe a month or so. You can take that soft cast off—but wait at least two weeks."

With this new bump in the road of Billy's progress toward becoming a jazz musician, I couldn't help but feel as if I wasn't having as much influence on him as he needed—as much influence as I was capable of providing. Jerk or no, it bothered me how quickly Billy resorted to physical violence with Beef Muncy. To me, it all spelled trouble.

Chapter 11

<u>Saturday, November 1, 1952</u>

The woman in the nurse's uniform seemed less than friendly. She barged into Sr. Theresa's office and plopped a folder of papers on her desk right in the shadow of a shaft of orange sunlight. In other words, I had a perfect view of the scene.

"My name is Kathy Lewis," she said. "From St. Rita's Rehab in Lima."

Sr. Theresa stood to greet Nurse Lewis, but she ignored the extended hand and pointed to the stack of papers she'd tossed on the desk.

"That's Kincaid's file," she snorted. "Tough bird, Kincaid. Eighteen months of detox and another nine months to get the reckless driving charges dismissed. It's all there—the bill, too— itemized and enclosed in accordance with the treatments we administered."

"Has he recovered?"

"Recovered? Ha! His kind don't recover. My years of working with alcoholics tell me they just need a rest now and then so they can build back enough strength to pop the cork off the next bottle of booze and hoist it to their lips."

"I don't think Mr. Kincaid—"

"I wouldn't worry much about him. He's like all the other musicians. Too much booze is never enough."

(This is a perfect example of where, as a guardian angel, I would like to correct an erroneous perception about addiction and send the message that jazz is not the only harbor for it. Nor is alcoholism the only vice otherwise goodhearted people might find themselves persuaded by. Let's not forget sex, gambling, gossip, drugs, and gluttony, for example.)

"And where is Mr. Kincaid now?" said Sr. Theresa.

"He asked to be dropped off across the street at the home of Jupie and Willa Mae Barnes. He's there now. I just stopped by here to drop off the paperwork and get the balance of his bill paid. Can you give me a check—now?"

"I promise I'll mail it tomorrow."

"That's what they all say. But you being a woman of the cloth, I'll trust you."

Following Nurse Lewis out of her office, Sr. Theresa gathered her skirt and ran across the road to the Barnes residence.

Inside, the house rang with music from Willa Mae's concertina. The aroma of fermented apples filled the air. In the kitchen, Jupie stood at the stove tossing vegetables into a large, black iron kettle—along with chunks of raw red meat, peeled from the bloody pelts of what appeared to be two plump rabbits laying atop a newspaper on the counter—the main ingredients for the Irish concoction of *hare and cider stew*. A fog of yellowish vapor wafted from the soup pot toward the ceiling fan.

Dukie led Billy in clapping hands and bouncing shimmy-shake in rhythm to Willa Mae's music. All things considered, it appeared to Sr. Theresa that the biblical account of the Prodigal Son was being re-enacted, with Dukie playing the central role.

Sr. Theresa stepped inside the house and knocked on the doorjamb as loudly as she could. In unison, Willa Mae let her squeeze box collapse in a breathy *sh-sh-shush*, and beamed at Sr. Theresa; likewise, Jupie stopped stirring the soup pot as Dukie and Billy cut short their merriment, stood ramrod straight, and blushed at the unexpected surprise of being caught in the act of being themselves.

As quickly as the scene turned from jubilant to somber, Sr. Theresa reversed it by rushing up to Billy and Dukie, gathering them to her, and singing the opening words to "The Battle Hymn of the Republic" in a surprisingly crisp alto voice.

Soon, Jupie offered the adults in attendance a bottle of Carling Black Label beer. Declining Jupie's offering, Dukie said, "Thanks, Jupe, but I don't touch it anymore. More trouble than it's worth. But you could help me out with a place to stay for a few days until I get back to work over at the school." Dukie turned to Sr. Theresa. "Can we talk tomorrow?"

"No need to talk tomorrow, Mr. Kincaid," said Sr. Theresa as she sat down. "Just come to work as usual—seven in the morning."

"And you plan to stay right here," Willa Mae said. "No hurry moving on until you get settled. Besides that, Billy's been moping around and not practicing, so I guess you two can get back to work."

"I didn't quit," said Billy. "I just...feel like I'm getting stale."

The broken hand hadn't helped matters, of course, but Jupie and Willa Mae were too polite to mention it. Jupie, in particular, held his tongue on the matter of inviting Dukie to stay in their home. He considered Dukie a good friend and a good business partner—but he had never quite gotten used to the way Billy idolized Dukie, looked up to him as a father figure superior to Jupie in one specific regard: his aptitude for music.

And yet Jupie had to admit it: seeing the bounce in his son's step as he sang and danced with Dukie in the living room, he knew Billy belonged in that world—not in the kitchen, with Jupie, fretting over skinned rabbits and a bubbling soup pot. Jupie knew he would have to learn to take joy in his son's joy, without imposing a life's path on Billy that he did not want. Anything else, and he'd be just as bad as Fr. Stenz pushing the priesthood on Billy.

In the midst of Jupie's reverie, Dukie rummaged through his travel bag and pulled out a small, cloth-wrapped package. As he uncovered it, Billy reared back: though clearly discernible as an electronic device, he was baffled by the unfamiliar object's purpose. From the looks of it, Jupie, Willa Mae, and Sr. Theresa were likewise perplexed.

"This is called a magnetic sound recorder," Dukie said. "I had a very good friend with me in rehab over at St. Rita's. His name is"—and now Jupie's eyes began to water—"or, I should say, his name *was* Johnny Hirst. I was with him when he passed away. We played in Sammy Kaye's big band together—me on piano, Johnny on trumpet."

Dukie handed Billy the tape player, which he studied as if it were a relic from some ancient cult. "How does it work?" he asked.

Enjoying the moment, Dukie said, "It's very complicated."

"Really?"

"Yes, very." A smile spread across his entire face as he said, "Just plug the player in the outlet and turn it on."

Shocked at the player's simplicity and clarity, for the next twenty minutes everyone riveted their attention to Dukie as he played the tape and narrated the litany of tunes and artists featured on his friend Johnny's recording. He had recorded a number of featured pianists over several months of barhopping in New York City: Hank Jones, Red Garland, Wynton Kelly—to name a few.

"It's like I told you at our very first lesson," Dukie said to Billy. "If you want to be good, you have to listen—but that's only half of it."

"What do you mean?" said Billy.

"It's not just about listening—you've gotta *feel* how these cats play." As the next song geared up, Dukie clapped his hands. "Now here's the guy for you: Willie Smith. They call him 'The Lion.' Listen to his stride piano style."

"What's stride?"

Dukie paused the tape and walked over to Billy's miniature Jaymar keyboard. "Watch what I'm doing with my left hand on the keys—and listen to that rhythm!"

After a flawless rendition of Smith's "Echoes of Spring," Dukie turned to Billy and grinned. "Tell ya what, man—you get back in the groove, get your chops in shape, and we can start thinking about forming a band."

And just like that, Dukie and Billy were back in business.

And *just-like-that,* too, Sr. Theresa's hopes of recruiting Billy to the priesthood dissolved. She had by now come to the same conclusion as me: Billy could demonstrate true loyalty to God by acknowledging his God-given talent for music and pursuing it as far as it would take him.

As she departed for the evening, Sr. Theresa said as much to Willa Mae: "All things being equal, I think God's will is pretty clear. Billy will be a better musician than he would be a priest."

As Sr. Theresa waved goodbye to Willa Mae, it was also *pretty clear* in their exchange of knowing smiles that the two women were in agreement on this point.

Chapter 12

January 1953

That winter—with six friends, plus the help of Dukie and his deceased trumpet player friend, Johnny Hirst, who had given him a box of ensemble lead sheets—Billy started his own group: Billy Barnes & the Swing Kings. Given Billy's popularity and growing reputation as a cool jazz pianist, it wasn't hard to find six fellow jazz buffs to fill the Swing Kings' chairs. In addition to Billy—the band's founder, leader, and pianist—you had the following:

Albert Martin on reeds, clarinet specifically, though he was also a gifted alto sax player. He had won a statewide competition for his playing—and, more importantly, he and Billy had managed to mend fences since their blow-up over the Sarah Flowers insult. In the year-plus since Albert's cruel joke, I hadn't seen him mature all that much—he was still cocky, fond of describing himself as the best clarinetist and sax player in the whole Midwest, the second coming of Charlie Parker or Paul Desmond—but he was Billy's best friend and first to join him in the band.

Ike Gough was on trumpet. Ike was the diminutive leader of

the trumpet section in the high school band and orchestra. He was also the youngest player in Satan's Angels Drum and Bugle Corps. Ike was a good player, but his argumentative personality—he was frequently wrong in his opinions, but never in doubt—often made him the butt of sarcastic critique. His trademark response when his "authority" was challenged was to hoist his middle finger and present it to the offending challenger with a corkscrew-like motion toward the sky. When it came to jazz, though, Ike was all business.

Ned Beam played trombone. He was a tall, lanky kid and captain of the high school marching band who wore ducktails and long, bushy sideburns. A talented musician, Ned had grown up under the narrow musical perspective of his father—an amateur brass band cornetist—who started his son on a baritone horn but switched him to trombone for easier access to Dixieland ensembles. Ned's speech impediment obscured his witty quips, sometimes making them more comical than intended.

At first, Jack Roush—electric guitar—seemed to be a perfect adjunct to the Swing Kings' rhythm section. Known for his solid time-keeping, he also excelled at improvisation, *à la* the lyrical style of Wes Montgomery. Jack was as handsome as he was talented, with dark curly hair and deep-set dark eyes. Sporting the sleek build of a long-distance runner, his long, slender fingers embraced the guitar frets seductively. From my vantage point, though, something wasn't right with Jack. He was always late for rehearsals, and I worried, in a different way than I worried about Albert Martin, that Jack might prove to be a bad influence on Billy. But, so far, Jack's transgressions had been slight enough that I, and Billy, could let them go.

Jay Walter, on bass, dressed as though he were a cover model for *Esquire* magazine: hair slicked back in ducktails, shirt freshly-pressed, slacks sharply creased, shoes of blue suede. Admittedly, Jay was handsome, athletic, and quick witted. To his credit, he practiced incessantly and taught himself to play standup bass. Jay tried to emulate the solid groove of Ray Brown, learned to keep good time and intonation—and told good stories about his love life.

Georgie Weaver, drummer, insisted on being called "Styx," in reference to his musical accoutrement—drumsticks. The alternate spelling was based on something he'd learned in Latin class. He relished explaining to all who inquired that it derived from the River Styx, located in the underworld, which served as a barrier separating the world of the living from the world of the dead. To his credit, Styx played drums as if he were the patron saint of groovy brush work, inventive solos, swinging groove, and water-proof timing.

With Dukie Kincaid guiding them, they rehearsed every Sunday afternoon in the St. Mary's parish hall. Here, they prepared for the high school gigs—and an occasional St. Mary's mixer—under the strict supervision of Sr. Maria Theresa Parks, O.P. After only a few months, though, the Swing Kings would find themselves playing bigger gigs in bigger and better venues.

Thursday, April 23, 1953

As I'd hoped he would, Dukie placed a call to Karl Ruhl, owner of the Golden Ruhl jazz bar in Lakeview. Though Karl hadn't expected Dukie's call, he was happy to hear from an old friend. He'd hired Dukie at his place dozens of times during the summer seasons. Dukie sometimes sat in with a big band when their pianist was ill or unavailable, and frequently served as the audition pianist for aspiring vocalists hoping to hit it big with one of the bands on a road tour. Usually Karl would let him go after a few weeks of too much booze, but he'd heard Dukie had dried out. Karl loved him—always helped him when he needed help—and Dukie hadn't let him down yet.

"What's happening, Dukie?" Karl asked.

"Need a favor."

"How much of a favor?"

"No money. Just listen to a friend I've been teaching piano the past few years. Solid young cat. If you like him and his group—give 'em a summer gig."

"Okay, I'll listen—five minutes. Have him meet me at my place next Monday morning about eleven o'clock. What's the name of his group?"

"Billy Barnes & the Swing Kings."

Good name, Karl thought. "Tell him I'm busy getting ready to close for the season," he said, "so if he isn't here on time, it's his problem, not mine."

Just as Karl unlocked the front door at 10:45 Monday morning, he saw an old green clunker pull into his parking lot and skid to a stop. When Billy jumped out of the car, he looked like a cross between an altar boy and a lost dog. But I give him credit, he walked straight up, no slouching, and reached for the door to go in. Karl beat him to the punch, though, yanked the door open, and held out his hand in greeting. "Barnes, right? Friend of Dukie Kincaid?"

Billy's anxious hand squeezed Karl's as he said, "Yes, Mr. Dukie...I mean, Mr. Ruhl."

"Skip the formalities and follow me."

I could see Karl's mind churning: Nothing about this kid so far convinced him that Dukie knew what he was talking about, but he reminded himself that he had promised Billy five minutes. He walked Billy onto the stage and rolled back the dust cover on his relic of an aging piano. I could hear Billy's heart thump as he studied the decrepit condition of the old upright, a Lester piano. "I've held onto this beaut since my grandmother passed away and left it to me," Karl said. "Let's hear whatcha got, Billy-boy."

Billy sat down, adjusted the bench, flexed his fingers, and ripped through George Shearing's swinging composition, "Lullaby of Birdland," then the Gershwin Brothers' "It Ain't Necessarily So." He finished with an up-tempo version of Jerome Kern's "All the Things You Are." It was clear from the expression on Karl's face that he was surprised to be twenty minutes into his agreed-upon five-minute audition, and that he could've listened another half-hour. He told Billy so, and offered his band a play-date.

"You're a good pianist, so if you're interested, I'll try out your band—what's the name again?"

"The Swing Kings."

"How many?"

"Seven, counting me."

"Okay" Karl said. "The Swing Kings will kick off the Ruhl's season. You'll open on Memorial Day weekend. Seventy-five bucks a three-hour night. That's ten bucks apiece and five extra for you.

"But don't expect tips," Karl added. "My customers don't come to listen to music, they come to drink and find someone to go home with."

I was proud of Billy's performance, and pleased to see him with his first official, paying gig as founder and leader of the Swing Kings. And not in some scumbag joint, either, but one of the top two clubs on Indian Lake, second only to the Ritz.

Then, as with some of my other experiences...wait, let me start over. I've mentioned that the word *fate* is one of my most despised words. Here's why. You'll recall I mentioned earlier that GAs can *nudge* a little here, *push* a little there? That's why I despise this belief that things just happen as they're "supposed to." There's more to it than meets the eye, and it has quite a bit to do with your GA's little *nudge* here or there.

It takes a lot of hard work on our part, is what I'm saying, which is why those handy little phrases—you call them aphorisms— really inflame me. They're just poor patches on the cloak of lame excuses when something untoward happens.

And—just like that—I sensed something coming to knock Billy off his lofty throne of prideful satisfaction. The blow that did the damage was a phone call in the first week of May 1953 from Karl to Billy:

"Kitchen fire destroyed the tavern," Karl said.

I'll pause here to note that I had my suspicions about this fire—which was ruled an *accident* (there's that word again!) and not an arson. For starters, the telephone company reported so-called "trouble on the line" the night of the fire, which delayed the emergency alarm call to the fire department. When the fire department finally did arrive—far too late to keep the Ruhl from near-total destruction—they found a single piece of evidence suggesting foul play: a charred matchbook remnant with the partial word *GROT* barely visible. It didn't register with me at the time, but later on that truncated title—*The Alpine Grotto*—would lead me to believe that the Ruhl fire was an arson perpetrated by a particular criminal element on Indian Lake.

But I'm getting ahead of myself. On the day he received the call from Karl, Billy saw his own future going up in smoke.

Karl tried to assuage these worries. "Keep your chin up, Billy-boy, but don't count on any play dates at the Ruhl until...probably next spring. Don't worry, I won't let you down."

I couldn't help but sympathize with Billy's tortured thought as he hung up the phone:

Don't worry? Next spring? Man...by then I'll probably be fucking dead.

Chapter 13

Thursday, May 13, 1954

Karl's call to Billy almost a year later fulfilled his promise: *Don't worry, I won't let you down.*

"I know it's short notice," Karl said, "but if you and your boys aren't booked over Memorial Day weekend, I'll give you three dates. Thursday, Friday, and Saturday, May twentieth, twenty-first, and twenty-second."

Of course Billy was thrilled, and immediately accepted. Assembling the Swing Kings to rehearse, however, was problematic. For the entire seven days between Karl's call and their first gig, there was only one date that everyone could be there: Sunday afternoon, two o'clock. There were no questions for Karl, but Billy's band had plenty for him, starting with Ike. "Billy—what's happening with the bread, man?" he demanded. "I ain't playing the gig at the Ruhl unless we get at least twenty bills."

"Ike, trust me. The ten dollars Karl's paying is just a start, man. We play good, he'll book us a dozen times over the summer."

Unmoved by Billy's assurances, Ike vigorously shook his

head. "You're good at making promises, Billy, but everyone's tapped out, man."

Ike did have a point: In the year since the canceled Ruhl gig, the Swing Kings had pieced together a resume of high school dances and victory parties, with the odd banquet or religious celebration at St. Mary's thrown in for good measure. The exposure was good, and so was the practice, but they'd been paid a pittance for all that hustling. While I disagreed with Ike's tone, I appreciated his frustration—I had begun to share it, myself.

Still, I was proud of Billy's response to the complaints. "Don't make a mutiny out of this, Ike," he said. "I'm working on it. Now let's rehearse!"

Thursday, May 20, 1954

Dukie Kincaid was the best publicity agent the Golden Ruhl ever had. He told Billy he wouldn't believe his eyes, and it was true—Billy thought the fire might have been the best thing to ever happen to the club, a gift from the gods of Timely Treasures.

The newly remodeled Golden Ruhl was a stunning mix of bright, shiny new woodwork and polished chrome accessories. Soft talk, seductive lighting, and the lush sounds of Coleman Hawkins's

"Body and Soul" buzzed around Billy as he made his way to the bandstand.

The lazily changing pastel colors of the overhead mood lights washed over the crowd, highlighting women dressed in skimpy shorts and scant tops mingling with men in tight jeans and t-shirts. Three bartenders in dress shirts and plastic bowties poured mixed drinks from chrome cocktail shakers. Waitresses sporting spiked heels, black fishnet tights, and revealing halter-tops circulated through the crowd, taking orders and serving drinks. Bounding up the steps to the bandstand behind the bar, Billy signaled each of the Swing Kings to gather around. As usual, Ike was the first one to complain.

"Billy? When do we get paid?" he whined.

"C'mon, Ike. When the gig's over, man. O-V-E-R!"

"Billy. Everyone digs this scene, man," Jack said. "But, man—it's like we're always behind getting the bread, and frankly it's a drag."

Now was one of the few times Billy revealed his latent irascibility.

"The Swing Kings was my idea," Billy growled at Jack. "I put it together. I do all the arrangements. I pay the expenses. I book the gigs. And, unless you haven't figured it out yet, I call the shots!"

"Billy, no one's arguing that," said Jay. "When we started, though, it was like you said we'd go on the road, make some records—dig?"

"So what are you saying?"

Albert—whom Billy considered to be very loyal—surprised him. "What we're all saying, Billy, is that it's time to shit or get off the pot. You know?"

"Here's what *I* know," Billy rasped. "*I* know you all don't have a clue what it takes to keep things afloat financially. *I* know that I've paid you everything I owed you to date and Karl will pay you for tonight when the gig's over. *I* know there isn't a band anywhere within fifty miles of here that's so busy they can't wait for you to sign up. *I* know that your collective asses would be scratching shit with the chickens if it weren't for me. So...that's what I know. And if you know better, then I'll wish you well on your way out the door."

The minute the words left his lips, it was clear from Billy's flushed face that he felt pangs of regret for losing his cool. Fortunately, Albert switched course and saved Billy from further embarrassment.

"Nobody's going anywhere," Albert said. "We all have the

same dream, man. We want to make it big like the pros—Ray Anthony, the Dorsey Brothers, cats like that. They all got a break somewhere along the way. That's what we're hoping for. So, man, it seems like the end of this year, or at least by next spring—that's a good goal to set for ourselves. We'll leave it up to you to work it out."

Just as Billy said, "Trust me, we'll make it," Karl signaled for him to start playing. Expecting to be hung with Karl's old Lester upright, Billy stopped in his tracks to check out the new Baldwin Studio upright. Easing onto the bench, he tapped the concert A tuning key three times. All tuned, he counted off a groovy tempo to "How Deep is the Ocean."

An hour later, Billy had to admit that the Swing Kings played better together than they had in a long time. Still, it didn't change the fact that unless he struck oil in his backyard, something special would have to happen to brighten the Swing Kings' financial picture. I wanted to help, but my influence in financial matters was minimal. At best, I could provide a measure of inspiration to never give up.

Finishing what he thought was a bang-up dry run for Karl's opening night in his very cool new tavern, Billy decided to ask Karl if he thought he could count on a few more play dates for the summer. He was so wound up when Karl said he would book the

Kings for one weekend every three weeks, Billy barely had the presence of mind to thank him as he raced out to the parking lot to give the band his very good news—at least for the moment.

On the way home, Billy thought about what he'd said to the band: "Trust me, we'll make it." But what his friends had said was true—he hadn't been successful at expanding the Kings' bookings after that first setback with the Ruhl.

More importantly, at the moment, he hadn't been successful in expanding his own repertoire or improvisational skills. Thinking back to one of his earliest conversations with Dukie about practicing like the pros practice—five to six hours a day—he knew the only way he could achieve that level of commitment was to drop out of school.

It wasn't the first time he'd had that thought, but now it seemed that his best chance of growing musically and improving his technique was to drop out of high school and knuckle down full time.

At home, rummaging through the refrigerator, Billy spied his favorite sweet: Willa Mae's candied apple tart. As he seated himself at the kitchen table to enjoy a generous slice, he was startled to hear Willa Mae call out, "Jupie, I hope you're not eating that apple tart— I'm saving it for my garden club luncheon tomorrow afternoon."

"It's me, Mom," Billy said, forking a huge bite of the tart into his mouth as Willa Mae appeared in the kitchen doorway. "Sorry, I didn't realize you were saving this."

Scrubbing the sleep from her eyes, Willa Mae shrugged at the scene before her. "Ah, well, the ladies and I will have to improvise tomorrow. Is the apple tart any good?"

Before Billy could reply, Jupie's booming voice resounded from the living room. "What's all the noise about? I'm trying to get some sleep!"

Rounding the corner and entering the kitchen, Jupie blinked at the bright light and plopped down on a kitchen chair. Glancing at the wall clock, he shook his head. "Hey, I thought you were saving this for tomorrow."

"The best laid plans," said Willa Mae. "Do you want a slice, too?"

"Don't mind if I do," said Jupie. "We're all up, now—no one's in a hurry."

As Willa Mae sat down beside him, Jupie turned to Billy. "How did you and your band do tonight?"

"Everyone played good, but the guys are getting sort of jumpy on the subject of money. They want more gigs—and I don't blame them, I want more gigs, too. It's just that, with school and all, I don't have time to scour for gigs, or even to practice all that much."

"So what are you going to do?" said Willa Mae.

Billy paused, got up, and put his dessert plate in the sink. Turning to his parents, he spoke haltingly. "I'm...I mean...I'm going to quit school."

Willa Mae shared a brief look with Jupie, opened her hands as though bewildered, and frowned at Billy. "But you only have one year left," she said.

"Mom, it's the only solution I see. I've talked with Dukie about it, and the fact is, I have to practice and get a lot better if I'm going to have any chance of really making it." Billy turned to Jupie, wondering if he might have better luck with his father. "Dad, you see what I'm talking about, don't you?"

I sympathized with Jupie: rarely had Billy sought his counsel. But with tension growing palpable between mother and son, Jupie was caught flatfooted. He decided to play it neutral, for now. "I want to hear more about why you think dropping out of school is a good idea," he said.

Billy turned a chair around and straddled it. "First," he said, "I don't have to spend a lot of time studying things I don't need.'

Willa Mae arched her eyebrows. "Don't need? You don't need to know how to read or write or do the arithmetic everyone uses in business?"

"I already know all that," countered Billy. "And speaking of business: it takes money to keep an operation like the Swing Kings above water. If I quit school, it'll be easier for me to get a part-time job, or a few solo gigs on my own."

Growing visibly uneasy by the back-and-forth between Billy and Willa Mae, Jupie finally saw an opening. "If that's the case," he said, "I'd be thrilled to take you on at the amusement park and train you—and the barbecue tent, too. I can talk to Mr. Sweeney about it first thing tomorrow."

Billy was surprised by the excitement in his father's tone. He'd never talked about the park or the barbecue tent before—not in this way, at least, not as a thing he expected Billy to take over for him some day.

"I appreciate that, Dad—really, I do. But I'm not a maintenance guy, or a cook. I think it'd be better to get a job that's more, you know, related to music."

I had to give it to Jupie: though Billy's words cut deeper than his son realized, Jupie remained calm and level-headed. He spread out his hands, rested them on the table, and tapped his fingers slowly. Looking down, then up, he addressed Billy. "Billy, I won't lie: I'd love for you to work with me at the park some day—hell, I guess I've always sort of hoped you might take over the barbecue tent when I'm too old for it. But I know that's not where your heart is."

There was a lilt at the end of that sentence, as if Jupie were posing a question and daring Billy to refute his read on the situation. Instead, Billy stayed quiet.

Jupie smiled in a small, sad way. "No matter what," he said, "your mother and I will always support you." He took Willa Mae's hand and lifted her from her chair as he rose from his. "Now, if you don't mind, it's off to bed for the two of us."

Laying close to each other in bed, Willa Mae whispered to Jupie, "Those were good things you said to Billy. I hope he'll be okay."

"He'll be fine." Jupie kissed Willa Mae on the forehead. "He's old enough now to make his own mistakes."

Chapter 14

Having resolved to drop out of school so he would have more time to practice and play the bars and clubs, Billy coaxed Albert to meet at St. Mary's parish hall every Saturday morning at 10 a.m. to rehearse, expand, and polish the Kings' repertoire. At their first rehearsal, Billy handed Albert an article Dukie had given him by the music and entertainment writer for the *Toledo Blade*.

"What's this?" said Albert.

"A great duet idea for you and me to try out with the band. Go ahead and read it out loud so I can hear it again."

Unfolding the article into the light, Albert began with the article's headline:

The Study of a Rare Musical Bird

"Ornithology" is the study of birds. In music, it's a "contrafact tune," which means it's based on a previously existing chord progression. This compositional device originated from the blues and was particularly important during the development of bop in the 1940s. Its title is a reference to Parker's nickname, "Bird." The Charlie Parker Septet made the first recording of the tune on March 28, 1946 on the Dial label. An example of a contrafact tune is a newly created melody written over the chord progression of another song, such as "How High the Moon." In Bird's case, "Ornithology" is the name of the contrafact.

Albert inhaled deeply. "So what?" he said.

"*So what* is, I'll play 'How High The Moon' on the piano and you'll blow 'Ornithology' on clarinet."

"I don't know 'Ornithology,'" said Albert.

"No problem, Dukie has it. He'll be here in five."

I will say that this was one of Billy's better ideas for a swinging jazz performance. And I will also say this: two hours of "Ornithology" combined with "How High the Moon" was enough to convince me—not to mention Albert and Dukie—that it would be an impressive tribute to Charlie Parker's saxophone genius, and a great addition to the Kings' set list.

At home, just as Billy stepped into the living room, still buzzing with the success of his session with Albert and Dukie, Willa Mae called to him from the kitchen.

"Phone call." As she held the phone toward Billy, she whispered, "It's a girl."

Anna and Billy had rarely seen each other since the formation of the Swing Kings, and his heart raced now at the sound of her voice.

"Hi, Billy. I'm having a cookout on Sunday night over the Fourth of July weekend," Anna said. "I hope you aren't busy playing piano somewhere."

"I'm not," Billy quickly responded. "Who all's coming?"

"You, Helen, Albert—the usual suspects," she said. "About four, OK?"

###

Sunday, July 4, 1954

Orchard Island's main road led to Chautauqua Boulevard, where Anna lived. Billy saw the brightly-painted mailbox glistening in the sunshine. A redbird mounted on a hand-carved boat oar held a wooden plaque in its mouth identifying the cottage: *LeaWard Rest*.

Helen and Billy in tow, Albert Martin drove into the driveway of the modest two-story house built with Nantucket brick and cinnamon-stained cypress. A canopy of leaves from four towering cottonwood trees shaded the house from the July sun. The well-manicured lawn was punctuated by a half-dozen evenly spaced tri-color beech trees. A copse of dogwood trees on the southwest side of the property protected it from the prevailing winds.

"Cool view of the lake," said Helen. "I hope we go swimming."

"What's Anna's old man do?" asked Albert.

Thinking back to Dr. Lea's help with his broken hand, Billy said, "He's a doctor."

Nervous at seeing Anna for the first time since school had adjourned in June, Billy took a deep breath and hoped for the best. As Albert parked his car in the driveway, Billy jumped out to see Anna emerge from the house. She wore white capri pants, a hot-pink sleeveless blouse with a matching wide-brimmed mesh sun-hat, and strappy pink sandals. She greeted Billy with a friendly but quick hug.

"Looks like the party's all here," Anna said. "Follow me—I just finished setting up the chips and drinks on the picnic table by the lake."

The lake sparkled in the afternoon sun. Two water skiers jumped the wake from their classic twenty-foot wooden Chris Craft, sending rooster-tails high in the air. As they descended, the beads of water created a rainbow over a metal fishing boat, its clunky outboard motor bobbing helplessly in the skiers' wake.

The fisherman yelled at the ski boat and gestured to a NO WAKE sign next to the channel marker. Billy couldn't decipher his swearing as the dissipating waves lapped at the stony beach. Besides, he was more interested in the music Anna had playing on the old portable record player, which she'd set on a tree stump several feet from the picnic table: a recording of "Don't Fence Me In" by Bing Crosby and the Andrews Sisters. Corny, sure, but at least it wasn't the classical music Anna's father decidedly favored.

The aroma of charbroiled burgers wafted over from the black steel kettle grill a few feet away, manned by Dr. Lea himself. He was surrounded by a couple of older guests: a pudgy man in a commodore's coat, a captain's hat, and aviator sunglasses, smoking a black cigar; and a woman dressed as if she were on a swanky ocean cruise—white blazer, blue and white striped blouse, sleek white pants, gold sandals, and a white wide-brimmed sunbonnet that left only her oversize sunglasses visible.

Approaching the couple, Billy extended his hand to greet the big man. "My name is Billy Barnes," he said. "I'm a friend of Dr. Lea's daughter, Annabelle."

"My pleasure," the man said. "I'm Carter Duffy. I own the First Lakeview Bank." Then, pointing to the woman next to him, he said, "And this is my little woman, Nadine."

Before Billy could say hello, Nadine shrugged, then—as if to inspect Billy closer—dropped her glasses to the end of her nose, blinked, and pushed them back up on her forehead. "Barnes," she said. "Billy Barnes. I know that name."

He felt suddenly uneasy, called out, as if he needed someone to come to his defense. But Anna had sidled up to her father to help plate the burgers and hotdogs, and Albert and Helen were piling chips into their mouths over at the picnic table.

"That so, ma'am?" he said.

To Billy's great relief, Nadine smiled. "I hear you play the piano."

"*Oh.*" Billy nodded, perhaps too vigorously. "Yes, ma'am, I do."

"Great. You can play some patriotic songs after the picnic," she said, and instantly shifted her attention to a passing sailboat a few yards offshore.

"I play *jazz*," he mumbled, to no one.

"What's that, Billy?" Dr. Lea's voice, and his hand on Billy's shoulder, was startling.

Billy turned to Anna's father. "Hi there, Dr. Lea," he said. "Great party."

"How's the hand, Billy?" said Dr. Lea, a small smile on his face.

"All good," Billy said. He twiddled his fingers a bit, to demonstrate. "Back in action."

"Good, good," said Dr. Lea. He led Billy by the arm, then motioned to Anna to join them. "Before I forget my manners," he said, "I want to introduce you to a friend of mine."

When Anna got there, her father embraced her and said, "I know you know my friend, Juliette Barlow. She's a nurse—and an excellent one, at that. Since she'll be joining me in my medical practice next month, I want her to meet more of my friends, as well as yours."

Stepping toward the refreshment table, Dr. Lea tapped a forty-something woman on the shoulder as she poured herself some lemonade. From what followed, it was clear to me that Dr. Lea and Juliette were well past boss-and-employee status. If anyone had any doubt about the two of them being romantically linked, they need look no further than the two's good old-fashioned amorous flirting—their eyes doing the job of what their hands would love to be doing in their place.

"Juliette," he began, nodding first to Anna, then Billy. "I want to introduce you to a friend of Anna's. His name is Billy Barnes. He's a musician—plays piano. Coincidently, he's also a patient of mine. Or was. He's healing up from a nasty hand fracture."

"Pleased to know you," said Juliette. "I'd love to hear you play sometime."

As if on cue, *sometime* came sooner than anyone might have guessed. Not a half-hour later, just as everyone had finished eating, it began to rain. Juliette, Annabelle, and her father herded everyone inside their modest kitchen.

"Please, everyone, make yourselves at home," Anna said. "Dessert will be ready soon." Anna turned to Billy. "Meanwhile—if you don't mind—Billy, will you please play something so we can all sing?"

The crowd clustered together in the small but elegant living room. At the sight of the Lea's white baby grand Steinway, Billy drew in his breath.

"It's beautiful," Anna said, her voice very quiet in Billy's ear. "Isn't it? It was my mother's—she loved to play for me when I was a baby."

Billy didn't know what to say. Anna's mother had died over ten years earlier—around the same time Billy's Uncle Willis was killed in action—and Anna rarely spoke of her.

"Wow," Billy said—at Anna's revelation, and at the piano itself. He pulled out the bench and sat down. He first ran his fingers over the keyboard, then played a trial note. The sound rang through the room like an angelus summoning worshipers to evening vespers. As Helen sat next to Billy on the piano bench, Anna frowned—Billy wanted to imagine this was jealousy—then motioned for Billy to play.

From my previous observations of Billy's preferred repertoire, I knew that group singing was his most despised form of music. But he knew all the corniest songs—"Take Me Out to the Ballgame," "I've Been Working on the Railroad," "Shine On Harvest Moon," "Home on the Range," "Camp Town Races"—and would dutifully play them, at Anna's request.

But it was Nadine, the cruise ship queen, who named the first tune. "Let's start with everyone's favorite, 'America the Beautiful,'" she said.

Helen wrinkled her nose at Billy and whispered: "Don't want to piss off the good humor lady." Remembering the song from grade school, Billy played with pride. The piano's silky soft action invited Billy's fingers to embrace the song and just feel the joy of playing the pristine instrument. After the final chorus, Billy looked over his shoulder to see if he could catch Anna's eye.

As if she'd read his mind, Helen whispered, "Spill it, Barnes—what's going on with you and Miss Anabelle?"

Billy turned to her and shrugged. "Don't know. What's with you and Albert?"

The crowd gestured for Billy to keep playing. This time, Carter Duffy suggested "Shine on Harvest Moon." Billy was surprised, and delighted, when Anna took the lead singing it. It was true: she had a lovely voice.

As everyone applauded at the end of the song, Helen leaned close to Billy and whispered, "Albert and I are going steady. He gave me his Hi-Y pin last weekend."

Before anyone could name a third song for Billy to play, Dr. Lea announced that dessert was ready. They returned to the kitchen and enjoyed slices of a fudgy dessert cake with ice cream and chocolate sauce. Billy stood in the doorway, near enough to still see that incredible Steinway piano in the living room. He watched Helen and Albert feed each other bits of cake from their forks, feeling both disgusted and forlorn.

"Thanks for entertaining the crowd," Anna said, sidling up to him. "I know those songs probably weren't your favorites."

"I sort of liked the second one," he said.

Anna looked down at her plate, but Billy caught the beginning of a smile on her face.

"You know, my father was a little worried when I told him I wanted to invite you tonight," she said.

"Worried?"

"Well, the last time he saw you, you'd busted your hand on Beef Muncy's face." Anna shrugged. "I think maybe he thought you're some sort of ruffian."

Her and those ten-cent words. "Ruffian?"

Anna smirked, apologetically. "A troublemaker."

"Oh." Billy let his fork fall to his plate. "Well, we can't have him thinking that."

Billy brushed his free hand lightly against Anna's forearm. She looked down at his fingers, then met his eyes. "No," she said. "I suppose we can't."

It was distracting, in the best possible way, for Anna to be looking at him like that. For her soft skin to be right there beneath his own fingers. It was a minor miracle that Billy was able to think of anything else in that moment—let alone the clever solution he'd devised to return to Dr. Lea's good graces.

"Hold my plate?" he asked Anna.

She obliged. "Where are you going?"

Billy returned to the Lea's piano and enacted his plan, playing Bach's "Bourrée in E-minor"—classical enough for Dr. Lea's tastes, and jazzy enough for Billy's. He hoped that might go some way toward smoothing tensions between the man who, Billy was now convinced, might one day be his father-in-law.

Chapter 15

Have I mentioned that I hate the word *fate*? Still, there are times when the word fits the situation—and, being an objective GA, I grudgingly accept that what happened at the Third Annual Holland Theater Talent Competition was, in fact, *fate*.

Despite Sr. Theresa's disappointment over Billy's rejection of the priesthood, she had become quite the Billy Barnes jazz fan, frequently requesting his services for school assemblies, dances, and other events at St. Mary's. In exchange for her generosity in letting him and Albert use the parish hall on Saturday mornings to rehearse, Billy had agreed to perform in the annual talent contest at the Holland Theater. "I'm one of the judges," she told him, "and even though I can't take my personal feelings about you into account, I'm sure my fellow judges would be simply taken away with your considerable musical talents."

Billy acquiesced, begrudgingly, even though he felt a small-time talent show was beneath the front-man of the Swing Kings. On the day of the show, he gave Sr. Theresa a quick hello at the judge's panel before gathering backstage with the other contestants.

There, Billy was surprised to see Anna. As always, she stood out in a special way that intrigued him. Pushing toward her, past a cluster of other contestants, his eyes were drawn to her jet-black hair brushing the tops of her shoulders, a bright red headband holding it in place. In profile, her features configured in a distinctive outline of soft curves. Arriving at her side, Billy suppressed a wave of anxiety— with all the time he'd been spending with the Swing Kings that summer, he hadn't seen her since her July Fourth picnic. He extended his hand to her.

"Hey, Anna, what are you doing here?"

"Same as you, Billy. I'm in the talent contest."

Before Billy could offer a rebuttal, Helen joined them. "Am I interrupting?" she said, her eyes shifting suspiciously from Annabelle to Billy.

"We're just talking about the contest," Anna said. "I think Billy was about to ask me, *bewilderedly*, what my talent is."

"I..." Billy cleared his throat. "It has to be singing, right?"

"Right." Anna nodded, briskly. "What about you, Helen?"

"Dance," she said. "After four years of lessons with Mrs. Sweeney, if I don't win this year, I'm finished."

Helen did not sound particularly bothered by this prospect. Without missing a beat, she dove into her knitting bag and produced a new Brownie camera. "My mom bought this for me for my birthday last week," she said. "Let me take a picture of you two."

Billy, Helen, and Anna scanned the backstage area for a suitable spot with good light and only a few people. When Helen found one, she motioned for the others to follow her. She stopped in front of a light blue backdrop and said, "This is perfect. Billy, you stand next to Anna on her left side and put your heads close together for the picture."

Helen snapped two pictures and returned the camera to her knitting bag, just as the voice of Marvin Dee—Master-of-Ceremonies for the competition—blared over the PA system: "Good evening, ladies and gentlemen, and welcome to our third annual Labor Day Youth Talent Contest. Now, here's the way the competition works: Each of our nine contestants' names have been drawn at random to determine the order of performance. You may applaud each performer as you wish, but after all nine are finished, they will be called back on stage to line up for your final applause. The loudest and longest applause will help guide our three judges in their determination of the winner."

As everyone scrambled to take their seats, Billy caught up with Anna. "Let's go to Percy's afterward, OK?" They had never made good on their plans to share milkshakes at the local confectionary. Anna nodded in favor of Billy's suggestion, and they sat together in the seats saved for the performers on the stage-left side of the theater auditorium.

As the competition proceeded, I could see Billy fidgeting in his seat. When Annabelle Lea took the microphone and sang "Too Young," something came over Billy that I can only describe as *distonishment*—my word—that is, a combination of *astonishment* and *dismay*.

Even though he had tried to be gruff and trivialize her participation in the talent competition, he didn't want to see her lose. But to compete with an amateur like her for a ten-dollar grand prize seemed unfair, what with Billy being a professional pianist and founder of the Swing Kings.

I could tell by the smirk on Billy's face after playing a flawless Duke Ellington arrangement of Billy Strayhorn's "Take the 'A' Train" that he clearly felt as though he had just stolen candy from the mouth of baby Annabelle and her love song.

And here's where that pesky *fate* comes into play. Though

what happened at the Third Annual Holland Theater Youth Talent Competition was a disaster for Billy Barncs, it was also an opportunity for him to finally make good on his intentions with Annabelle. So, OK, I'll admit it: *fate* had something to do with Annabelle coming in first and Billy coming in second in the talent contest.

As agreed, after leaving the Holland together, Billy and Anna stopped in for milkshakes at Percy's. Annabelle treated Billy to a double chocolate malt with her first-prize winnings.

"You sing great," said Billy.

"Oh, I'm not that good," Annabelle said.

Struggling to be a good sport but embarrassed about having lost to Annabelle, Billy nodded to her—and, in a way that he thought would flatter her, he said, "Good enough to win—you beat me."

"That's because nobody ever heard of Duke Ellington. What was the name of that song, 'Take a Train?'"

"It's called 'Take the '*A*' Train.'"

"What's the '*A*' train? Is it like trains are named for alphabet letters?"

Billy smiled at her. "Where did you learn 'Too Young?'"

"I listened to it one day down at DeLong's Record Store. Mr.

DeLong had the sheet music, so my dad bought it for me."

"I didn't see your father at the contest," said Billy.

"He had to make a house call to Mr. Duffy's," she said. "Mrs. Duffy is sick with the flu."

They were both quiet for a moment. Billy watched the delicate way Anna drank her own milkshake. For some reason, the thought of asking her to be his girlfriend seemed ill-timed. Finally, he said, "May I ask you a question?"

"As long as it's not about me winning the talent contest."

"No, nothing like that." Billy paused. "I'm, uh...I'm dropping out of school."

Anna furrowed her brow. "That's not a question," she said. "It's also a pretty dumb idea. We're starting our last year next week. We'll graduate in nine months."

Billy should not have been so shocked by her reaction—still, he tried to justify his choice. (For my part, I begrudgingly accepted that Billy's future success as a musician would have less to do with how many math and science classes he had taken at LRHS, and more to do with how many gigs he was able to book for the Swing Kings.) "You don't know anything about what it takes to be a professional jazz pianist," he said to Anna. "I need to concentrate on my playing.

It's the only way I can improve. I have to practice six or seven hours every day, and find jobs playing nights in different clubs."

"I was just trying to be honest," said Anna. "I think it's a mistake to drop out of school when we're so close to graduating. My dad says everyone now has to have a high school diploma to get a job. I didn't mean to hurt your feelings."

"*That* didn't hurt my feelings," he said. "But I'm really worried about what you'll say to my next question."

"That depends." Anna smiled. "Is it actually a question this time?"

Heartened by the softness of her voice, Billy found the courage to ask her the question he'd been chewing over since he'd heard her sing at the Leas' July Fourth picnic. He took Anna's hand and said, with all the confidence he could muster, "Would you be the vocalist for the Swing Kings?"

I'd seen disappointment on Billy's face before, but nothing matched his cheerless countenance at Annabelle's reply. "I don't think my dad will let me," she said.

"Is it because of the Beef Muncy thing?" Billy asked. "I thought he and I were square on that."

"No," she said. "It's just that—you know. He hates jazz and

popular music."

"Hates it so much that he'd keep you from singing in a jazz band?"

"I'm afraid so," Anna said, and dropped Billy's hand.

Not to be redundant, but, like I've said, I'm not a fan of the word *fate* because I don't believe in it; I'm a much stronger proponent of the word *coincidence*. There are hundreds of interesting examples of coincidence throughout history—here are three of my favorites:

1. The lives of Thomas Jefferson and John Adams, two of America's founders. Jefferson crafted the Declaration of Independence, showing drafts of it to Adams, who (with Benjamin Franklin) helped to edit and hone it. The document was approved by the Continental Congress on July 4, 1776. Surprisingly, both Jefferson and Adams died within minutes of each other on the same day, July 4, 1826—exactly 50 years from the signing of the Declaration of Independence.

2. The famous nineteenth-century horror writer (and scribe of "Annabel Lee"), Edgar Allan Poe, wrote a book called *The*

Narrative of Arthur G. Pym of Nantucket. It was about four survivors of a shipwreck who were in an open boat for many days before they decided to kill and eat the cabin boy, whose name was Richard Parker. Some years later, in 1884, the yawl *Mignonette* foundered, with only four survivors, who were in an open boat for many days. Eventually, the three senior members of the crew killed and ate the cabin boy. The name of the cabin boy was Richard Parker.

3. In 1893, Henry Ziegland broke off a relationship with his girlfriend, who, out of distress, committed suicide. The girl's enraged brother hunted down Ziegland and shot him. Believing he had killed Ziegland, the brother then took his own life. In fact, however, Ziegland had not been killed. The bullet had only grazed his face, lodging into a tree. It was a narrow escape. Twenty years later, Ziegland decided to cut down the same tree, which still had the bullet in it. The huge tree seemed so formidable that he decided to blow it up with dynamite. The explosion propelled the bullet into Ziegland's head, killing him.

There are hundreds more *coincidences* like that, but three are enough to make my point: There's no better word than *coincidence* to describe what happened out in Percy's parking lot as Billy and Annabelle left the restaurant. Just at the instant Billy tried to put his arms around her, Anna's father exited Insley's Pharmacy next door after picking up a prescription for Nadine Duffy. Looking to his left, Dr. Lea spotted Anna and Billy. Before either of them could say any more to each other, Dr. Lea ambled over, nodded to Billy, and patted Anna on the back. "How did the contest go?" he asked. "Did you take first place?"

Feeling awkward, Anna said the only thing she could think of that wouldn't embarrass Billy. She gestured to Billy and said, "We both won."

Dr. Lea extended his hand to Billy. "If you won, your hand must be pretty well healed."

"Yes, doctor—nice to see you again."

Turning back to Anna, her father said, "Congratulations to you both. I want to take this medicine back to Nadine—she's still sick in bed. If you want, invite Billy to come over to the house, and I'll catch up with you after I stop by the Duffy's. I want to hear all about this talent show."

Any excitement Billy felt at being invited back to Anna's house was neutralized by the presence of her father. However—*fortunately,* not *fatefully*—after only a few minutes of their conversation about the talent contest, Dr. Lea received a phone call. When he returned to the living room, he smiled apologetically and said, "That was the hospital. One of my patients won't stop badgering the floor nurse for more sleeping medication. A doctor's work is never done, I suppose." Turning to leave, he said over his shoulder, "There're some snacks in the fridge, if you'd like, and please help yourselves to the orange juice. My friend Juliette squeezed it fresh just yesterday."

After watching her father pull out of the driveway, Anna beckoned Billy to follow her to the kitchen. She opened the fridge door, stepped back, and said, "If you see something you like, just help yourself."

Billy shook his head, hoping to clear his mind. He worried that the pause might make Anna think he'd intended to say something inappropriate in response to her offer, but still he took a deep, nervous breath and said softly, "Anna...I like you. I liked being with you at the talent show, and Percy's after."

"Oh, that's just the double chocolate malt talking," she joked.

But Billy was undeterred, intent on making his point. "May I ask you a question about your song?"

"'Too Young?' It's a great song."

"I like the lyrics," said Billy.

Now Anna softened a bit. "Yes, they're very...romantic."

Billy reached for Anna's hand. "I want to see you," he said. "A lot. I want that song to be our special song."

Anna withdrew her hand, leaned back against the closed refrigerator, and took a deep breath.

"Honestly, Billy, I want to see you, too—but, with you dropping out of school, I don't know..."

"I'm not dropping out of life," Billy countered. "And I do want you to think about being my vocalist with the Swing Kings. Will you please think about it?"

Anna seemed to think it over for a moment, but then shook her head.

'You should go," she said. "I'll drive you home."

"I have my dad's car. It's parked behind the Holland Theater. And Anna—I want to see you again, soon."

At the door, Anna pulled Billy close and said, "I'll think about your question."

While GAs are known to spurn wishful thinking, they sometimes engage in it just for fun. Such was the promise I'd made to myself all those years ago to steer Billy away from anything that would undermine his musical aspirations—not only wishful thinking, but also a shade narcissistic. That night, I was forced to admit defeat: I was certain that Billy and Anna would be getting together on a regular basis.

I won't say more about that now, but there is no truer statement than *What you don't know won't hurt you.* Ironically, what Billy didn't know made him virtually invincible.

Chapter 16

In my time as a GA, I've learned many valuable lessons. For example, female wards tend to be more intuitive, more creative, more sensitive, and much less impulsive (i.e., more risk-averse) than male ones. Now—a few minutes past the 54-hour mark since Billy's death—I've decided to put this knowledge to good use. As the Russells Point PD spins its wheels on the matter of who shot Billy, it's clear to me that Annabelle Barnes (née Lea) might be my next best resource for digging up the truth.

While *Penso Appositus* denies me ongoing postmortem access to the thoughts of any of my deceased ward's surviving loved ones, in special circumstances (such as murder), the principle of *Immunitas Temporalis* provides me with modified access to this gift for up to five days—the same length as my furlough before the beginning of my next assignment, as you'll recall. With *Immunitas Temporalis*, I am able to follow people like Annabelle Lea, but am left to interpret their mental state only through the same visual cues and clues that any mortal might have access to. To that end, just after 10 a.m. today—going on 55 hours since Billy's demise—I arrive at Billy and Annabelle's home to find her at the kitchen table nursing a cup of freshly-brewed herbal tea. The pall of doom sapping her vitality, she sits staring into space. I notice a scrap of paper on the table, so close to the stagnant coffee mug that, at first, I mistake it for a napkin. But in fact, it is a torn bit of stationery, and in a bold but wobbly hand, Anna has written down a jumble of words: *Accident? Enemies. Mocha, Mutt, Suggins. The Beer Garden. Last council meeting...*

It's a seemingly incoherent stream of consciousness—unless, like me, you're suspicious of a particular coroner's findings on a particular fatal gunshot wound, and you're running down alternate theories.

It doesn't surprise me that Anna is speculating on the true cause of Billy's death. Thinking back to all those times when Billy's association with the unsavory personalities in the music business so alarmed Anna—and convinced her that something bad, or at least dangerous, might threaten Billy's existence—I must admit she was right. The point may be moot now, but it seems clear to me that Anna knows the coroner is inept and intends to prove it so.

At this very moment, as Anna and I both are lost in our

thoughts, the most unexpected thing happens: Jupie and Willa Mae drop in to visit. I haven't spent much time with them since Billy's death—trusting their respective GAs to offer the comfort they need—but I am grateful for their presence now (though the grief on their faces, deep and resigned, is almost too much to bear). Equally grateful to have them with her, Anna brews a fresh pot of coffee and sits with them.

Unwrapping her freshly-baked gypsy tart, Willa Mae serves Anna and Jupie as Jupie opens a sack, pulls three small crystal glasses from it, sits them on the kitchen table, and fills them with Pernod absinthe from a brand new bottle. Though Anna declines the beverage, Jupie hoists his glass and whispers to the heavens: "Let Billy be remembered forever." Willa Mae drops her eyes and utters a solemn prayer: "Yes...*vichnaya pamyat.*"

The ennui of their reflection leaves a solemn silence, until Anna turns to Willa Mae and says, "I have a good idea who shot Billy." She takes another sip of her tea, calmly, allowing her message to sink in. "And I won't give up until the bastard is arrested."

In the interest of fair play, here's what I know happened: Early in the morning of July fourth, I was with Billy at the barbecue tent, setting up for the holiday onslaught, when Anna called. There was a hint of fear in her voice when she told Billy to come pick up the tent's bun order for the Fourth as soon as possible, so she could lock up before the street rioters damaged the bakery. This was a slight adjustment to the original plan for Billy to stop by closer to 4 a.m., enjoying a sandwich on fresh Italian bread while he waited for the roll order to be filled, after which he would walk Anna home and the two of them would drift into a much-deserved sleep.

However, at Anna's request, Billy arrived at Alma's Patisserie at approximately 2:45 a.m. As he approached, the distinct scent of acrid smoke—more like gasoline than the smell of gun powder from fireworks—emanated from the direction of the bakery. Moving cautiously, Billy peered through the haze to make out the figure of a man wearing shorts and a billed cap who appeared to be torching the wooden sideboards of the bakery.

Despite the noise from the unruly crowd of drunken teenagers mingling in front of Suggins' Suds 'n' Grub next door, Billy's voice rang out: "Hey, you—stop! The police are coming! Stop—now!"

As the man turned in Billy's direction, he raised his arm. I didn't realize he was aiming a gun at Billy until I was stunned by the sharp report of a gunshot piercing the night air. Clearing my senses,

I saw Billy crumple to the ground, blood oozing from his chest as I heard his assailant yell, "I warned you, Barnes!"

Kneeling at Billy's side—choking on my bitter tears—my whole being trembled with fear that all of my twenty-four years spent protecting Billy Barnes—my most cherished ward ever—were meaningless. In the ensuing hysteria, I barely discerned hearing Anna exhort the emergency squad: "Please, for God's sake! Get him to the hospital now!" In accordance with God the Son's reminder that all GAs are imperfect, I was numbed by the harsh reality of *Conscientia Defectum*.

Still, in the far reaches of my memory, the voice of Billy's assailant haunts me.

Frankly, I cannot explain how I missed identifying the shooter who dispatched Billy to his eternal reward. All I can recall seeing is the aftermath: Billy, collapsed on the street, blood gushing from a wound in his chest, an emergency squad ministering to him and rushing him to Mary Rutan's emergency room, where he was declared DOA at 3:09 a.m. on July fourth.

I won't give up until the bastard is arrested.

There are times when a well-deserved epithet can have a

pacifying effect, but in this instance, it is clear that Anna's caustic tone has left a stinging impression on Jupie and Willa Mae. Not only is their consummate grief far from resolution—they must also contend with the profound trauma of realizing another person, this alleged "bastard," wantonly took their son's young life.

I am sympathetic to Jupie and Willa Mae's obvious grief—I share in it greatly myself, after all. But, more than that, I am pleased that Anna is so committed to finding Billy's killer. With *Penso Appositus* effectively lost to me, I make a resolution of my own: I will track Anna's activities for the remainder of my furlough and attempt to piece together the mystery of Billy's demise alongside her.

Chapter 17

<u>**Tuesday, September 7, 1954**</u>

I had my first real insight into Anna (*Penso Appositus*) many years back, when she discussed her thoughts about Billy with Helen. As usual, they met at Percy's for their *girl talk*—a version of which I had heard many times over my years as a GA.

"I don't understand what's bothering you about Billy," said Helen. "Why can't the two of you just hang out and have fun?"

"I'm not sure we're compatible. He's dedicated to his music; that's all he talks about. He dropped out of school to play piano full time. Since we only had one year left, I told him I thought that was a dumb idea."

"I'm sure he loved that."

"Don't you and Albert ever have a disagreement?"

"Only when I won't let him have his way with me."

Anna took a sip of her drink. "Helen, I'm serious. How can I be who he wants me to be without talking about it?"

"What does he want you to be?"

"His vocalist for the Swing Kings."

"What's to talk about? It sounds like fun."

Anna paused, filling her drinking straw with water and piping it into her mouth.

"My dad would flip. He thinks jazz musicians are second class."

Here's that word *fate* again. The minute Anna said *second class,* Billy appeared with Albert at their table and plopped down next to the girls. Billy forced a wry smile and said, "Who said musicians are second class? Was that you, Anna?"

"Excuse me," Anna said. "Helen and I were having a private conversation. Didn't anyone ever tell you that it's rude to butt in?"

Helen stood and gestured to Albert. As they turned to leave, Helen paused, winked at Billy, and said, "If you want my advice, you should share a banana split. See ya later, alligators."

From my vantage point—with Albert and Helen out of the picture—it seemed like a perfect time for Billy to revisit his earlier suggestion. I still wasn't entirely sold on Billy's choice of a romantic partner in Annabelle, but I couldn't dispute her talent for singing: if she got onboard with the Swing Kings, the band—and therefore Billy's musical prospects—could only improve. And so I nudged him that Indian summer afternoon at Percy's, the site where his attraction had first heated up, with Anna the unknowing catalyst when she said, "I apologize for saying it was a dumb idea for you to drop out of school. I only meant that, after thinking about being your vocalist for the Swing Kings, I would have to ask my dad, and he— he would..."

"He should hear you sing one of our tunes. We'll pick a song, practice it, and be ready to perform for him. You know, somewhere that he and some other people can hear you, and applaud."

Anna wasn't certain this plan would work, but the prospect of spending more solo time with Billy held an undeniable appeal, and so she nodded in agreement. "My dad is going to a medical seminar this weekend," she said. "We can practice all day Saturday. You can come over for lunch."

Saturday, September 11, 1954

In all my years as a guardian angel, I have been present for a number of my wards' intimate gatherings. My favorite of all time is the one held by Joseph of Arimathea—a member of the Sanhedrin— who took Jesus Christ's body down from the cross and buried it in his own tomb. It wasn't a celebration, but rather a respectful gathering in memory of Jesus and in honor of His beloved mother, Mary, along with Jesus's best friend, John (who became her guardian), Mary Magdalene, and Mary the mother of James the Younger. Even Simon of Cyrene stopped by for a cold one—wine stored in a goat skin kept deep in the water well.

Now, that wasn't exactly the scene at Anna's house on Orchard Island when she and Billy met to rehearse, but I was nonetheless looking forward to spending more time in her cozy home and listening to Billy play her mother's super-elegant Steinway baby grand. As in all of these situations, of course, it isn't about what's good for the GA, but about what's good for his ward. And for Billy, this was an occasion of great possibilities with Anna.

Just after eleven o'clock that Saturday morning, Billy appeared at Anna's front door, music satchel in hand, flashing a sparkling smile that said, *Don't make me wait too long!*

Scanning Anna's attire, Billy was taken by a feast of fall colors: floral printed trim-fit black slacks, an orange blouse under a green cardigan, and low-heeled flats. As he followed Anna into the living room, her sweet scent trailed behind her, teasing him. At the baby grand, a shaft of warm light washed over Anna as she turned and faced Billy. Her black tresses, combed into a tight bundle, lay close to her head, secured by a simple metal barrette. "Dad just had the piano tuned," she said. "The tuner said it needs playing."

Billy slipped out of his lightweight coat, tossed it aside, and opened the keyboard. Pulling out the bench, he motioned for Anna to sit down.

"You sit. You're the player," she said. "I'll just watch from here."

"No, I can teach you better if you're right here," Billy said, patting his hand on the right side of the upholstered bench.

Ignoring him, Anna remained standing next to the piano and inhaled deeply.

"Alright, Mr. Teacher," she said, exhaling an expectant breath. "What song are you teaching me to sing today?"

Billy shrugged his shoulders. "I think you should learn a good Hoagy Carmichael tune," he said. "Let's try 'Skylark.' It's my favorite love song."

"I remember you telling me he wrote 'Stardust'—you played it at the All Saints' Mixer, remember? Back in the eighth grade. Wasn't that fun?"

"Sure, until your dad showed up early and ruined things."

"He didn't ruin things. He just...he wants me to have fun, but he worries a lot."

"My dad lets my mom do the worrying in our house," Billy

said—and, as soon as the words left his mouth, he realized how insensitive they were. There was a very simple reason Anna's father was stuck with all the worrying: Anna's mother was dead.

Anna took the remark in stride, though. "I'd imagine you keep her pretty busy on that front," she teased.

"Yeah." Billy grimaced. "I can be a real jerk."

Anna gave a small laugh. "My father is very cool about you," she said. "He jokes that I should watch out so you don't lead me astray, being a jazz musician and all."

"*Me*?" Billy said. "Lead *you* astray? That's funny. When can I watch you polish your halo?"

"Right after I learn to sing 'Skylark.'"

Billy chuckled, patted the upholstered seat next to him again, and said, "You have to sit right here if you want me to teach you."

This time Anna acquiesced, sitting close to him on the piano bench. Billy fingered the keys and played a lazy introduction. "Okay, miss songbird, I'll play some chords and talk through the lyrics. The first thing for you to do is just listen and feel the mood of the song."

"What's the song about?" asked Anna.

"It's a love song...about longing...yearning. The melody was written by Carmichael but the lyrics were written by Johnny Mercer, who loved Judy Garland. At least that's what I read somewhere. Think about that as you listen."

Anxious to please, Anna said nothing—just closed her eyes and listened as Billy began:

> *Skylark...*
>
> *Have you anything to say to me?*
>
> *Won't you tell me where my love can be?*
>
> *Is there a meadow in the mist*
>
> *Where someone's waiting to be kissed?*

Billy cleared his throat and continued:

> *Skylark...*
>
> *Have you seen a valley green with spring*
>
> *Where my heart can go a-journeying*
>
> *Over the shadows and the rain*
>
> *To a blossom-covered lane?*

Billy vamped as he said, "This next part is called the *bridge*. It's the middle part of the song—"

"That brings something different into the song that helps explain the story." Anna nodded. "I know what a bridge is, Billy."

"Right. Anyway, I think a good bridge helps accent the mood, too. Especially in a love song. Listen..."

> *And in your lonely flight*
>
> *Haven't you heard the music of the night?*
>
> *Wonderful music, faint as a will o' the wisp*
>
> *Crazy as a loon*
>
> *Sad as a gypsy serenading the moon.*

"Now the song goes back to tell the end of the story," Billy said. "It's like making a promise. I think it's the hardest part of a love song to write. Listen and you'll see what I mean..."

> *Oh, Skylark*
>
> *I don't know if you can find these things*
>
> *But my heart is riding on your wings*
>
> *So if you see them anywhere*
>
> *Won't you lead me there?*

"That's it," Billy said. "Do you like it?"

In a rush of sentiment, the blush on Anna's cheek blossomed. On an impulse, Billy leaned close and kissed her.

Nuzzling close to him, Anna whispered, "Was that part of the song?"

"Absolutely," Billy said. "If we don't get that part right, we'll never impress your dad." Billy paused, looked to Anna. "Now it's your turn," he said. "Make me weep."

With Billy feeding Anna the lyrics, I was completely dazzled by her expressive, intimate rendition of the indelible ballad, as though she were impersonating Anita O'Day on her famous recording with the Gene Krupa Orchestra.

When she finished, Billy put his right arm around her shoulder. Gently pulling her to him, his left hand caressed her bosom.

Of course—if you have a scrupulous conscience—this would be an illicit moment of passion that you might consider sinful. But the lingering kiss that followed it nullified that notion—and, frankly, I appreciated the sincerity of it.

Finally coming up for air, Anna turned to Billy. "Where will we ever have a chance to sing for my dad?" she said, attempting to return to matters of business.

"Won't he be at his club's New Year's Eve party?"

Anna sat back. "He wouldn't miss it. He really likes this new girlfriend, Juliette—you met her on the Fourth of July, remember?— and they both love to dance. I'm sure he'll invite me, too, but you won't be there, so..."

Billy smiled from ear-to-ear. "I just booked the Swing Kings for that gig this week."

Anna smiled, too. "That should give us plenty of time to practice," she said.

Billy nodded. "Say, tonight is the last night for the Swing Kings to play at the Ruhl before Karl closes down for the season. Do you want to come with me?"

"I can't," Anna said. She brushed her thumb over Billy's cheek. "I promised Dad I'd be here when he calls."

It was the first time I'd seen Billy lack all enthusiasm for gigging with the Swing Kings. But given the demands of passion, and hoping he could return to Anna's for a reprise of their earlier—I'll call it *exchange*—his mood bounced between passive and anxious to finish playing so he could say goodbye to Karl and leave.

As in seasons past, the Ruhl's last night of business came to an early ending when—at 10:45—the last couple at the bar eased off their seats and waved goodnight.

What Billy didn't expect was Karl personally paying the Swing Kings a nice season-ending bonus, then beckoning Billy to follow him into his office. As the Kings packed up, it was obvious from Billy's fidgety haste that he was thinking more about a quick departure for Anna's than why Karl had asked him to his office. Seated across the desk from Karl, Billy watched him drum his fingers on the desk surface while he waited, as though enduring some kind of water torture experiment.

Finally, Karl sat forward and extended his hand across the desk to Billy. As though congratulating him for fathering a newborn baby, Karl pumped his hand.

"Billy," Karl said, "You're a real asset, as a jazz player—and you're a good kid. Listen, I need you to close things down this season, since my wife and I are leaving for Florida. Her arthritis is so bad, her doc says we should get out of here until next spring."

Stifling an urge to groan, Billy drew a deep breath and looked at Karl.

"What about—"

"I know what you're thinking," Karl interrupted. "The place

needs painting and cleaned from top to bottom. So why don't you do it? I figure since you're not going back to school you can use the extra dough, and I need someone reliable to be here and make sure there aren't any disasters brewing."

Speechless, Billy watched Karl take an envelope from his desk drawer and open it. He extracted three new ten-dollar bills and a handwritten note, handed them to Billy, and said, "Here's a start, kid—and my Florida address. I'll send you thirty dollars every week to do what needs to be done. Meanwhile, call me collect if you run into any problems."

"Thanks, Mr. Ruhl, I'll—"

"Hold on," Karl interrupted. "I got one more thing—sort of a favor, really."

Frustrated at being delayed, Billy inhaled a halting breath as Karl continued.

"After we get things locked down this week, I'd like for you to drive me and the missus to Florida. We'd want you to stay for a few weeks—help us get settled in, do some chauffeuring, that kind of stuff. You can head back here around the first of November and get the painting and cleaning done before Christmas. I come back for the holidays, but the missus stays put until spring when we come home."

Karl rocked back in his chair. He took a pack of Lucky Strikes out of his desk drawer, cracked it open, lit one, and exhaled the smoke across the desk. Studying the burning tip of the cigarette, Karl smacked his lips as though savoring a rich delicacy. "Have to give this up in Florida," he said, grinning. "The missus gets sideways with me when I smoke." Karl inhaled deeply and sniffed. "She thinks it's a dirty habit."

Billy stood, thanked Karl, and asked to use his office phone.

After three rings, Anna's sleepy voice answered.

"Anna," Billy said. "Can I come over?"

"Not now, Billy. Dad's on his way home. He didn't like the seminar and decided to leave."

"Can we talk tomorrow?"

"Sure. You can come over in the evening." She yawned. "The sunset is beautiful this time of year."

Monday, September 20, 1954

I couldn't help but empathize with Anna's frustrated disappointment over learning of Billy's obligations with Karl. Still, I was excited to ride shotgun in Karl's new, dark blue 1954 Oldsmobile 98. With Karl and his wife in the back and Billy at the wheel, I had the perfect seat to enjoy the jazz tunes emitting from the automobile's built-in cassette deck. Albert had copied them for Billy the day before we left for Florida. Keeping the volume low so as not to disturb Karl and his wife, Billy and I listened to *The Best of Albert* over and over. A track listing, for your consideration:

1. "Ornithology" by Charlie Parker

2. "Lullaby of Birdland" by George Shearing

3. "Walkin'" by Miles Davis

4. "Joy Spring" by Clifford Brown

5. "April in Paris" by Coleman Hawkins

6. "Well, You Needn't" by Thelonious Monk

7. "Billie's Bounce" by Red Garland

8. "Something Cool" by June Christy

9. "Poinciana" by The Four Freshmen

10. "Gone With The Wind" by Dick Jurgens

11. "Cheek-to-Cheek" by the Boswell Sisters

It was a days-long trip. Each night we would stop at a tourist home and, at Karl's request, Billy would go out for ice cream or snacks for his wife. On the drive, Billy would turn on the car radio and tune in to one of the famous radio stations featuring jazz—stations such as WJR in Detroit, WLW in Cincinnati, WWL in New Orleans, or Steele Pier in Atlantic City.

Other highlights of the long drive south included stops at Rock City, Stukey's Pralines & Pecans, Florida's Native Village & Gator Wrestling, Cypress Gardens for water skiing, and finally Ft. Lauderdale, Florida: 109 E. Valencia Street—one block from the Atlantic Ocean and its glistening sandy beach.

I won't detail Karl's daily list of errands for Billy except to say that by the end of our Florida sojourn I had a newfound appreciation for my ward's generous and compliant heart. After the four weeks Billy had pledged to Karl, he was put on a bus for Columbus, Ohio—and, five days later, on Monday, November 1st, 9:35 a.m., we pulled into the Greyhound terminal on North 4th Street. From there, Billy hitchhiked home, arriving that afternoon at 3:45.

For the four weeks Billy was in Florida, all Anna did was mope around and hope that his absence wouldn't change how he felt about her. But I had to give her credit for nurturing her affection for Billy, which she did by memorizing the lyrics to "Skylark," repeatedly humming the tune and thinking about Billy's explanation of how the song worked. He really did know—and love—jazz music. Anna began to share Billy's sentiments: the love stories of composers like Hoagy Carmichael were gifts from the muses, meant to warm the hearts of both performers and audiences.

Her burgeoning appreciation for jazz notwithstanding, I can honestly say that Annabelle's angst was getting to me. But, truthfully, I developed a new sense of respect for her as she tried not to be angry with Billy. Unfortunately, I didn't have the power to change the fact that Billy's circumstance was beyond his control, even though it afflicted her with a painful loneliness.

Her period of distress dissipated on the evening Billy returned. They met at Percy's and resumed planning her surprise performance for her dad at the Lakeview Country Club's New Year's Eve Gala.

Departing Percy's, slippery ice crunched under their feet as they walked in the winter darkness to Anna's car in the parking lot. Here, Billy's roaming hands found Anna's bosom. As his tongue pushed through Anna's inviting lips, she kissed him on his ear and whispered, "I'm sorry, Billy, but I have to go home and fix dinner for dad."

Chapter 18

<u>Friday, December 31, 1954</u>

Something important had happened during Anna's quote-unquote "separation" from Billy: she began to feel quite strongly that she wanted to be the vocalist for the Swing Kings. At the same time, she was aware of her father's view that jazz musicians were not in the same class as she was.

Despite her love for her father, appreciation for his difficult position as a single parent, and general respect for his opinions, Anna couldn't help but resent his view that jazz musicians were somehow second-class citizens. The whole thing was antithetical to her father's general good nature and belief in the value of all human life. Anna suspected his apparent disdain for jazz was actually just the manifestation of an overprotective streak: he feared for his daughter's safety, and would do anything in his power to keep her away from any unfamiliar characters or activities.

Even seeing the bigger picture this way, Anna wouldn't—no, *couldn't*—ignore her deep feelings for Billy. She vowed to do anything she could to make her father accept him.

Nevertheless, in my mind, Billy and Anna's plan to impress her father with a surprise performance of "Skylark" at the Lakeview Country Club's New Year's Eve Gala was a bit futile—tantamount to an evolutionist changing the mind of a creationist about where we are and how we got here. I realize we're only talking jazz—hardly a cataclysmic subject—but let's just say I had my doubts about the whole thing. Still, I sincerely hoped they would succeed, and that Anna would become Billy's vocalist for the Swing Kings.

The showdown—if you want to call it that—between Annabelle and her father came about as ongoing blizzards, piercing winds, and silver-dollar-sized sleet tormented, depressed, and angered the citizens of Logan County, who complained that the street potholes were big enough to swallow a large dog or a small child. The elements notwithstanding—puffs of breath freezing on their lips—Anna, Helen, her father, and his lady-friend Juliette arrived at the Lakeview Country Club on New Year's Eve, 1954. After stepping through the members' private entrance—a heavy, hand-carved wooden door from the Black Forest, emblazoned with the LCC crest of a golfer brandishing a club at a seagull flying by with a ball in its bill—they stomped the snow from their boots and checked their coats.

Entering the main dining room, Anna's palms moistened at the sound of a piano playing "White Christmas." Daring to look in the direction of the music, her heart skipped a beat as Billy beckoned her to approach. Though trying not to be obvious, when Anna's eyes met Billy's, she flushed red and began to fidget.

Trailing behind her father as the club manager led them to their table beside the dance floor, Anna sidled up to Billy and pecked him on the cheek.

"I went ahead and asked the head waiter to reserve this table for you," Billy said. "I thought it would be easier for you to get to the microphone when it's time."

"Do you know when that will be?"

"Probably after dinner when they start the Bananas Foster tableside dessert service."

Her brow furrowed, Anna asked, "What is *that*?"

"Apparently it's a big deal. They set bananas and liquor on fire and people love it."

"Give me a cue when you want to do 'Skylark,'" Anna said. "I've been practicing it all day in my room."

Winking goodbye to Billy, Anna took her seat next to Helen at the edge of the dance floor, a feather's toss to the stage, where my subtle ray of light washed over the Swing Kings as they played "Santa Claus Is Comin' to Town."

Though I shared Anna and Billy's resolve to impress her father, I assume you are familiar with the Scottish poet Robert Burns and his old bromide: *The best laid plans of mice and men often go awry*. Well, a tip of the hat to you, Mr. Burns—and hello, Bananas Foster!

On Billy's cue, Anna stepped to the microphone. As Billy played an introduction to "Skylark," Helen leapt to her feet, shouted *"Bravo!"* at Anna—and, in the process of saluting her best friend, bumped into the tableside Bananas Foster flambé server, just as he was pouring a spout of banana liquor from a bottle he held elevated over the simmering concoction. The ensuing chaos happened so fast, I couldn't see all of it (*Conscientia Defectum* rears its ugly head again), but it appeared that the server splashed the flaming liquor on Helen's hair, setting it ablaze. Rushing to Helen's side, the club manager doused Helen's rich head of hair with a pitcher of cold water from the sideboard. In the macabre scene that followed, Helen danced as though competing in an Irish jig contest, Billy stopped playing the introduction to "Skylark," Dr. Lea and Juliette stood in awe of the bizarre scene, and Anna rushed to Helen's side to console her over the loss of her newly coiffed, but now singed, Christmas holidays bouffant hairdo.

After all that, Juliette managed to save the day. "It's time to celebrate," she intoned. "I'll treat the table to a bottle of champagne if everyone will join Arthur and me in toasting our good health in 1955."

As all—including me—regained their composure, Juliette ordered Piper Heidsieck and did the honors: "Here's to 1955: a special year of health, happiness, hope, and love to our families, friends, suitors, and sweethearts."

In the end, I did have to grin at the fact that the only person convinced that night of anything was the club manager, who—after the tableside fiasco of the Bananas Foster dessert service—decided to remove it from the LCC menu.

As the night wound down and the crowd waned, the Swing Kings finished their final number, "I'll See You in My Dreams." Afterwards, Albert consoled Helen as he escorted her to his ice-covered '37 Flathead V8 Ford sedan, with Anna and Billy following, arm-in-arm. Anna's father caught up with them and said, "After I drop off Juliette, I'll see you at home, Anna."

###

Saturday, February 12, 1955

Following the Lakeview Country Club New Year's Eve fiasco, Anna didn't give up hope that somehow, she and Billy would have another shot at performing for her father—challenging his biases about jazz musicians and convincing him to give Anna his blessing to be the vocalist for Billy Barnes & the Swing Kings. Not two months later, on the Saturday before Valentine's Day, she got that chance: Billy invited her to accompany him to his gig at the Elks Club for its annual Sweethearts' Ball.

Though flattered by his invitation, Anna knew that Billy would be busy playing and so this wasn't a proper date; still, she resolved to be the band's best audience. And she would dress for the occasion: Billy had requested that she wear the same outfit she had worn on New Year's Eve, her Audrey Hepburn red swing cocktail dress and black silk high heels with embroidered pink hearts.

They entered the Elks Club through the musician's entrance in the back, and Anna sat at a small table to the side of the bandstand while the Swing Kings prepared to play. Scanning the crowd, it was very clear that she looked as snazzy as any of the other women in attendance, though most of them were much older.

A waitress came by. "My name is Bambi Jean," she said.

"What can I getcha?" After taking Anna's order for a Coke and some potato chips, she squinted at Anna and said, "Honey, I hope your boyfriend is watchin' out for you. That outfit you're wearin' is gonna stir up some hot blood with a few of the old geezers here who still think they can cut the mustard. Ha! Be right back."

As the waitress departed, Billy bounded off the stage and sat down in the empty chair next to Anna. She waited for him to say something, but he just sat there smirking like a cat savoring a canary.

"What time do you start playing?" she asked.

"Nine sharp," he said. "It's a big crowd and we play until one in the morning."

"What's the first song?" she asked.

"'Some Enchanted Evening.'" Billy grinned. "Sort of in honor of us."

"It's almost nine now," Anna said, glancing at her watch. "Shouldn't you get back up there?"

"In a minute—I have to ask you a question first." The grin on his face turned mischievous when he said, "Will you be my vocalist with the Swing Kings tonight?"

In honesty, Anna had been expecting this question—hoping for it, actually. Still, for Billy's benefit, she feigned panic. "Now?" she sputtered. "Tonight? Here? Are you serious? I don't think so. I mean..."

"It's a perfect time and place," Billy persisted. "At these parties, people drink a lot and don't pay much attention to the music, so—"

"So you want me to sing because nobody will hear me?"

"Anna! You know what I mean. Please, just a couple of songs starting the second set. 'Too Young' or 'Skylark,' and—and—what other songs do you know?"

"I know 'September Song,'" Anna said, playing things close to the vest. As the Swing Kings played their first set, Anna sat quietly, mentally rehearsing some other songs she had learned, unbeknownst to Billy: "As Time Goes By," "Peg o' My Heart," "Paper Doll," "When You Wish Upon a Star," and "You Belong to Me."

On the band's first, brief break, Billy ambled over to Anna, and—*sotto voce*—reminded her it was time for her to take the microphone. "I'll introduce you, then you'll start singing."

Anna rifled through her purse in search of lip rouge, and was surprised at a familiar voice from behind her. "You didn't tell me you would be here tonight," her father said. In the ambient glow of the stage lights, Anna turned to see him and Juliette, arm-in-arm, grinning as though they'd caught a disobedient child with her hand in the cookie jar.

As if protecting Anna, Billy stepped beside her and extended his hand to her father. This is where I have to hand it to Billy. No question, he intuited Anna's embarrassment and turned the sow's ear into a silk purse.

"It's so nice to see you again," said Billy. "You're just in time to hear Anna perform."

"Is that so?" said Dr. Lea, his voice neutral.

"Um, I mean..." Anna fumbled.

Billy nudged her in the side and whispered encouragement to her: "This is perfect," he said. "Just be cool and sing 'Skylark.'"

Dr. Lea arched his eyebrows and said, "When did you—"

"Arthur," Juliette interrupted. "Don't worry about the details. Let's just sit here and enjoy it." From my point of view, the coincidence (not *fate*) of Anna's father hearing her sing with the Swing Kings only ended so favorably because of Juliette's influence. I'm not saying that Anna's father reversed his opinion about jazz musicians—that would take a minor miracle from Our Lady of Perpetual Mirth—but his objections on the matter were largely quelled that night.

For Anna's part, she couldn't help but fall in love with Billy after observing his patience, persistence, and understanding in reconciling Anna joining the band with her father's views on jazz. In the seven hours between Anna's arrival at the Elks Club and her finally parting ways with Billy at 3 a.m., she experienced so many emotions. She swung from surprise to joy, courage to fear—and, finally, affection to love.

Starting with surprise-to-joy, Anna was *surprised* at the ease with which she got her nerve up to join Billy on the bandstand—and *overjoyed* to hear the audience applaud and to see the crowd, especially her father and Juliette, surround the bandstand insisting she sing yet another song. In order to overcome *fear* of revealing her secret to Billy that she knew a lot more songs than she'd ever told him, she mustered the *courage* to just turn to him and say, "Do you know that song by so-and-so, you know, Jo Stafford? 'You Belong to Me?' Can we do that?"

I have to admit it: Anna and Billy performing together on "You Belong to Me" couldn't have been a more poignant tribute to their burgeoning relationship.

With the crowd still exhorting Anna to sing more songs, Billy beckoned her to the piano. In a hushed voice, he said, "Okay, smarty, what other surprises do you have locked up in that song box of yours?"

They finished the night to raucous applause for Anna's renditions of "Peg 'o My Heart," Nat King Cole's "Mona Lisa," and two Doris Day tunes, "Secret Love" and "Sentimental Journey." After another short break, she finished the night singing a rendition of Tony Bennett's "Because of You," followed by "I'll Be Seeing You," popularized by the Four Freshmen in 1950.

By the time the Swing Kings packed up and Billy paid everyone, it was after 1:30 in the morning. Since Billy had driven and picked Anna up for the Elks gig—and, since Anna had seen her father leave just before midnight and knew by now he would be asleep in bed—she invited Billy to come in for coffee.

At first, they sat in the kitchen and wound down, talking about what a fun time they'd had at the Elks Club party. I had promised myself that, as Billy's GA, I would steer him as best I could away from the sinful joys of *dallying*—but in this endeavor, in this instance, I was useless. Both of them being in a romantic mood, it was no surprise when Anna said, "Let's go into Dad's den. It's more comfortable than these kitchen chairs."

Seated close to Billy, Anna let her head droop onto his

shoulder as they reveled in the events of the evening. Of course, it didn't take an engraved invitation for Billy to let his hands roam Anna's generous bosom. I won't say it didn't occur to me what Billy had in mind, but, drawing Anna to him and kissing her soulfully, she let his hand find its way too far up her thigh—to what I, euphemistically, refer to as the *danger zone*—while she put her hand on his bulging trousers.

It wasn't hard to guess what might have happened next, if her father hadn't yelled at her from the top of the stairwell on the second floor, "Annabelle! Tell your friend to go home and you come to bed. Right now!"

Neither *fate* nor *coincidence*, but I would take it!

Chapter 19

April 1955

Billy's amorous instincts worried me, and I did take some credit for helping him stay cool after his and Anna's impassioned postscript to the Elks Club Sweethearts' Ball. Even so, I only had so much influence over his God-given urge to procreate. The best means I had to combat it was to keep prompting Billy to practice, play the 151 Club with Moss on Saturday nights, prepare for the summer season at the Ruhl, and hope for playdates at the Ritz and the remote possibility of the occasional weekend gig at Stardust Ballroom when the big bands weren't booked.

Dr. Lea had his own way of keeping things from heating up too much between Anna and Billy. In short, he restricted their dating. How he planned on monitoring their romance, I didn't know, but Anna's respect for her father made this jail sentence both unbreakable and unbearable. To keep their hearts throbbing, Anna and Billy talked by phone two times a week and sent each other a postcard every Thursday to plan to meet at Percy's for a milkshake at noon on Saturday. At least they had this much contact.

###

I don't think Billy regretted dropping out of school, but it was not the magic solution for all the band's problems that he had hoped for. They spent most of the spring of '55 bickering endlessly about Billy's ill-advised promise—"Trust me, we'll make it"—with Billy wondering if he might have been better off staying in school, saving himself all the frustration of constantly disappointing the Swing Kings. The only gig they'd gotten so far that year was a school dance in April to celebrate the Bellefontaine High School basketball team's winning the 1954-55 Western Buckeye League Championship.

It didn't take long for Billy's doldrums to get percolating. The band had rehearsed only once before the playdate, and sounded ungodly rusty. Worse, his bandmates bitched about the tunes he called, and groused about the funky food served at the break called *pizza* (the high school team captain, Vinny Corrova, came from a family that owned a shoe repair store and a carry-out business specializing in Italian cuisine). Billy thought the pizza tasted like shoe leather with tomato sauce, but so what? He wasn't about to let things get to him—until several of the victory-dancers insisted the band play some rock 'n' roll tunes, specifically "Rock Around the Clock," popularized by Bill Haley & His Comets. Being a jazzman, what Billy knew about Bill Haley et al. wouldn't fill a thimble.

After the crowd's repeated badgering, Albert Martin said, "I know 'Rock Around the Clock,' I'll take the lead." But despite Albert's best efforts, the Swing Kings reached a new low that night, with Jay plunking out a few weak bass notes, Styx filling with several mis-timed drum licks, Ned secretly picking his nose, Ike excusing himself to go to the toilet, and Jack ignoring the *no smoking* rule and hiding under his coat to light up while Billy sat at the piano cringing at their butchered performance. The *best* thing that happened—if you could call it that—was the crowd disappearing like the proverbial rats leaving a sinking ship, so the band could cut the torture short. Still, Billy was insulted when the high school principal, Mr. Floyd Kemper, handed him an envelope with a hundred and forty dollars and said, "Billy—my advice is that you boys might be better off playing things people want to hear."

Packing up after the gig was like the Swing Kings' funeral, with Ike announcing that he wouldn't be available to play for a while due to a canker sore on his lip, Ned claiming he suffered from nasal congestion and couldn't hear, Jack saying he was *burned out*, Jay muttering something about going to college, and Styx working at DeLong's Record Store all summer. Only Albert, his oldest friend, offered anything close to comfort. "Sorry about tonight's gig being such a drag, man. I think I need to hole up at my dad's place, practice a little, maybe cool it with Helen for a while—dig?"

Poof! Rigor mortis! Adios! Fare-thee-well and fuck you!—all wrapped up in a tight little package of steaming horseshit. Suffice it to say—with the exception of Albert—Billy was ticked. *Don't let the door hit you in the ass on your way out!* he thought.

Willa Mae was still awake when Billy got home. "Oh, Billy, I wasn't expecting you back so soon. Didn't you have a gig, or whatever you call it?"

"A high school dance. We quit early. They didn't like our music."

"What didn't they like?"

"Jazz. They didn't like what we played. They wanted rock 'n' roll." He shook his head. "The Swing Kings don't play rock 'n' roll! The Swing Kings play jazz! If no one likes it, maybe it's time for me to give it up and...and..."

Willa Mae put a hand on her son's arm. "Billy," she said, warmly. "Your father and I have watched you grow, mature, and take responsibility for your own success. Playing jazz piano is all you've ever wanted to do. And you've proven that you're good at it. Now, just because you had one bad experience, here you are doubting yourself and telling me you want to quit your passion?"

Billy could not muster a response. He sat down heavily on the sofa while Willa Mae continued.

"I've never told you much about gypsy philosophy because I worried that your friends would ridicule you if they knew you were part gypsy. People don't like gypsies. They don't trust gypsies. They think gypsies are dishonest. A lot of that is true about some gypsies— it's rooted in their culture of survival. But now I'll tell you what a good gypsy knows about a person like you and your affliction."

"Affliction?"

"Yes," said Willa Mae. "An affliction is infecting you, and it's called *self-pity*."

I had to agree with Willa Mae's assessment. I had never seen Billy quite so down-and-out, though I had worried he had this negative potential for years, ever since he'd started high school. Willa Mae was right: it did seem like a sort of sickness.

It bears mentioning that, from the very beginning, I had admired Willa Mae and her philosophy. True, unlike Christianity, which is written—or, I should say, *recorded*—in the Bible, the

Romani Code is kept alive in the oral tradition. And while my own makeup is rooted in the Judeo-Christian teachings, it was clear that Willa Mae's Romani Code embraced the broader principles of Judeo-Christian ethics, such as the dignity of human life, adherence to the Abrahamic Covenant (Genesis 12:1-3), common decency, and support of the principles of honesty. Willa Mae operated under the credo of *Pax et Bonum,* as in the motto of St. Francis of Assisi—I think the two of them would've been great friends.

"You are a Pisces," Willa Mae explained now. "You are supposed to be particularly artistic—and selfless. Be true to your sign: be helpful, not selfish. Pisces are naturally open and friendly—easygoing, with a genial, expansive character. You have all those traits, Billy, but you don't realize it. You get too focused on pleasing others and forget your own well-being."

"That's all well and good, Mom, but what can I do about it?"

"You haven't set your sights high enough. You're willing to be defeated because you think no one cares. My son—here is the truth of this world we are living in today: There is no reason for anyone to worry about who you are or what you do or why they should care, if you yourself don't care. Set your sights higher instead of lowering your expectations. And talk with Dukie Kincaid. He's been such a great mentor to you so far—he'll help you."

It was good advice, Billy had to admit. Dukie had never steered him wrong—and, he realized as he sat there with Willa Mae, neither had his mother.

"Remember this ancient gypsy proverb," she said in parting. "*Go in God's name—so you ride no witches.*"

Chapter 20

Friday, June 10, 1955

You may already know this, but in case you don't, GAs are free from sin. Unless, of course, one thinks he should be running the BIG show—but that would get into the whole imbroglio between the Archangels Lucifer and Michael, which, at the moment, is pointless to dissect. What I mean by GAs being free from sin is that we express our emotions in pure ways. For example, we feel sorrow or remorse without the taint of guilt or the ambiguity of a hidden agenda, as often happens with humans. When GAs speak and act sorrowfully or angrily, believe it, we really do feel that way.

Given that, I have to say I was highly incensed with the unconscionable treatment dished out to the Swing Kings by one Maurice "Mutt" Pickering and his money-grubbing associate, Johnny Mocha. I couldn't figure why they hadn't booked Billy and his band into a little classier venue than the Spinnaker Room. By comparison, the worst nightmare jazz club was a palace.

But I'm getting ahead of myself. It all started when Dukie

took Billy to Mutt's office at Stardust Ballroom and asked for an audition. After Mutt heard Billy play, Dukie was certain Mutt would agree to book the Swing Kings for a gig at the Ritz Club.

By sheer coincidence, the day Dukie and Billy walked into Mutt's office, Mutt was meeting with Stan Kenton to iron out a few wrinkles in his contract. Dukie had worked for Stan before, auditioning vocalist prospects (including the famous vocalist June Christy, though she'd been known as Shirley Luster at the time). Stan and Dukie embraced, their raucous greeting ending with Dukie introducing Billy as "The *best* young pianist I've ever coached!" With Dukie's shining endorsement, Stan immediately commissioned Billy for an impromptu audition on Mutt's office piano.

Billy's compelling version of "Take the 'A' Train" prompted Stan to insist that Mutt book the Swing Kings—if not at the Ritz, then somewhere else. I sensed some reluctance in Mutt's demeanor, but still he pumped Stan's hand in tacit agreement. On his way out the door, Stan clapped Billy on the back and said, "Keep it tight, man!"

After Stan's departure, Dukie turned to Mutt, pointed to the phone, and said, "If it's cool with you, Mutt, we'll wait while you call Johnny Mocha."

Which brings us back to the night of Friday, June 10th, 1955.

Billy and the Swing Kings arrived at the Spinnaker Room in the old Lakeview Inn at 7 p.m. They unloaded their gear and soon discovered that the Spinnaker Room was on the basement level, in the old section of the hotel's lower lounge. Billy went ahead of the band to check and be sure they were in the right place. Inside the lounge entryway, just off a side street, long strands of queer plastic beads hung from the ceiling, forming a ridiculous faux barricade.

As Billy entered, he squinted through the beads. The room was a tacky, rundown, out-of-date nightclub. Billy brushed the fake beads aside and sauntered into the inner room, holding his breath against the musty air's rancid aroma. The room reeked of stale beer and vomit. A dingy, dimly-lit bar sat against the far wall, and behind that was a cluttered, elevated stage. As Billy weaved between the sparsely occupied tables, he heard a voice behind him and turned to see a thirtysomething man dressed in slouchy attire.

"I'm Monk," he said. "I run this joint. You Billy with that swing outfit?"

"The Swing Kings," Billy corrected. "Johnny Mocha booked us."

"Yeah, little Johnny. He keeps me in good weed."

As Billy reached to shake Monk's hand, Monk produced a

pint bottle of Thunderbird wine from inside his baggy side pocket and offered it to Billy. "Better have a little snap of this—it's a long night."

After declining the offer, Billy watched Monk take a long pull on the bottle and tuck it back into his pocket.

"My band is coming in to set up. Do you mind if I check out the piano?"

"Follow me," Monk said, and pointed to the stage.

After showing Billy the worst, most broken-down piano he'd ever seen sitting cockeyed on the stage, Monk turned to leave. "It's a piece of shit," he said, "but who cares?"

As the Swing Kings set up to play, Billy plunked a few random notes on the yellowed, cracked keys in the all-important middle-register, and frowned as they pinged off-key. Turning away from the piano, Billy watched quietly as Styx set up his drums; Jack, Ned, and Ike warmed up; and Albert assembled his clarinet. None of them said anything, but I could tell by their faces they thought Billy was nuts for dragging them into this God-forsaken joint. When Jay asked Billy to hit his bass tune-up notes, the piano was so out of tune it didn't matter what notes Billy played.

Ike was the most critical. "Billy, I can't believe you talked us into playing this dump. What the hell is the deal?"

I felt frustrated for Billy. He didn't have anything near a reasonable answer, so he said what his temper allowed. "Ike, if you or anyone else has a better gig, just say so and we'll split."

As the grumbling died down, Monk approached with a woman who looked like a streetwalker wrapped in a swath of ratty-looking, gauzy pink veils.

Billy gazed at the vision of the aging woman—old enough to be his grandmother. As she approached, he couldn't help but wonder if he'd misunderstood Johnny Mocha's reference to the Swing Kings playing for a *very cool vaudeville act*: this appeared to be a down-and-out comedy act.

"This is Lady Sylvia," Monk said, handing Billy a dog-eared file of a few worn music charts. "And here's her book of tunes."

Billy studied the hand-scrawled inscription on the file cover: *Sylvia of the Seven Veils*. Trying his best to keep a straight face, he opened the file and turned to Monk.

"Is this the order of play?"

Ignoring his question, Monk turned to the woman and said, "Say hi to Lady Sylvia."

"Pleased to meetcha," Lady Sylvia extended a bony hand.

With Sylvia standing this close, Billy changed his mind about her. Despite the crone-like voice, she had a face that clearly had once been very pretty. He took her hand and felt an unexpected softness to her thinning, waxy skin. Her long fingernails were nicely manicured, and she had a firm but gentle grip. She drew back her hand and gave Billy a cordial but fatigued smile as he said, "Likewise."

I felt a pang of sorrow for her, and couldn't begrudge her for just trying to make a living by performing at the Lakeview Hotel— my poor impression of its management notwithstanding.

"It's all *bump-and-grind*, sonny," Sylvia said. "Ya ever play a burlesque joint?"

"I play...mostly jazz...and some blues," Billy said.

"Then ya know 'Night Train,'" said Lady Sylvia.

"We're on in ten minutes," Monk declared, and escorted Lady Sylvia offstage.

Turning to his band, Billy hoped he could depend on them to make the best of the scene. "It's not my idea, but the lady wants bump-and-grind blues in B-flat like we played before we knew any better."

The stage lights dimmed. A weirdly glowing, spooky violet

light washed over the performance area as Lady Sylvia made a sylph-like entrance from stage left. She moved with the grace of a thirty-year-old dancer and, over the rising chatter from the now-filled barroom, Billy yelled at his players: "Hit it!"

Nearly blowing out Billy's eardrums, Styx slammed his nineteen-inch Zildjian brass crash cymbal and frantically beat an increasingly deafening drum roll. When Lady Sylvia reached center stage, she turned to Billy. I now understood why the piano sat cockeyed on the stage: Lady Sylvia could make easy eye contact.

"Let's hear that piano, sonny!" Lady Sylvia shrieked.

Though he was pounding out "Night Train" as loud as he could, Sylvia paused in her routine, turned to Billy, and fired another vocal salvo. "Louder, goddammit!" she bellowed.

Mesmerized by the macabre scene unfolding before them, the Swing Kings watched Sylvia of the Seven Veils work the stage from left to right. Despite her age, Sylvia was agile and poised, and she had good rhythm. With each seductive body move, every twist and turn, Lady Sylvia teased the audience by gradually removing one of her seven veils and flinging it into the bar area. At every propitious moment, Styx slammed his crash cymbal as hard as he could. Jack played a few funky riffs and Jay slapped his bass with alacrity.

Surprisingly, when she was down to her last veil, it was apparent that Lady Sylvia was still quite voluptuous. Never having seen a *professional* burlesque show, Billy assumed that Lady Sylvia's swishing her seventh veil back and forth—never totally revealing her bodily assets—was her titillating finale. As she was about to doff her final veil, Styx smashed on his piercing brass cymbal. In a blinding finale, the overhead stage lights flashed on, then off, as Lady Sylvia exited stage left and disappeared behind a tattered velvet stage curtain. To sparse applause, the Swing Kings reprised the last few bars of "Night Train" as Lady Sylvia came back onstage for a final bow.

Afterward, Lady Sylvia appeared at the bar to mix with the wino-type older men crowding around her. After ordering champagne, she yelled at Billy: "Next set, sonny, ya gotta play louder!"

When the gig ended at midnight, Monk handed Billy an envelope. He looked inside to check if Johnny had payed what he'd promised and was shocked to see four dog-eared fifty-dollar bills and a new tenner. He was about to say something to Monk, but Monk swigged on his Thunderbird, grinned, and said, "The extra bread is from Lady Sylvia. She likes you and wants you to work her next gig in Detroit."

Their equipment trailer loaded, Billy handed each of the Swing Kings thirty dollars. He knew they appreciated the little extra bonus, but in the back of his mind, he also knew that a trip to Detroit to perform with Lady Sylvia was not in his future.

In the end, I was proud of Billy. He was starting to focus—narrowing his career playing field and thinking about doing what was important now: excelling in his own backyard and worrying about the Detroits of the world when he had truly honed his craft and felt fully equipped to take his show on the road.

Chapter 21

About a mile west of Lake Ridge High School, just off Marina Way, sits the once prosperous Shawnee trading post now known as Flourish. Flourish is currently populated by ten American Indian families, including one in particular: patriarch Red Dog 1, his wife Singing Crow, and their twin sons Bear Fat and Big Eagle.

After switching allegiances between the British and French throughout the late eighteenth century—and facing the disappointment of broken treaty after broken treaty in the nineteenth century—the Shawnee attempted to ingratiate themselves to the colonists by adopting their customs. It was the hope of Shawnees like Chief Black Hoof—and, later, Red Dog 1's father, Chief Red Horse—that these efforts might further ensure the tribe's rights to land ostensibly protected by the Treaty of Fort Meigs.

Recognizing the fickle nature of the white settlers, however, Chief Red Horse pursued additional assurance that at least some part of Ohio would remain in Shawnee hands—namely, by staking out a five-acre tract of land in the center of the triangular reservation formed by the lines drawn by the original three Shawnee reservations. In 1914, on his self-granted five-acre tract, Chief Red Horse's only son—the enterprising Red Dog 1—constructed a six thousand square-foot, three-story arts-and-crafts house he named Woodland Cottage Sporting Club.

In keeping with his belief that the white man's customary appetites for whiskey, women, and gambling were insatiable, Red Dog 1 assigned complementary floors to Woodland Cottage Sporting Club. The first floor was dedicated to "refreshments and socializing," the second floor to "games of chance," and the third floor to "other pleasures." Each floor had its own manager. Affable son Bear Fat oversaw the social parlors serving booze and food on the first floor; combative son Big Eagle took charge of the gambling rooms on the second floor; and ebullient wife Singing Crow supervised the third floor, where a staff of eight service ladies dispensed carnal favors for various prices based on the clientele's ever-changing predilections. A monthly rotation of third-floor service staff, managed by Johnny Mocha in Lima—who also supervised three other similar operations, most notably Lima's Chicken Shack—virtually assured patrons the pleasure of regular *fresh talent*.

Red Dog 1's pièce de résistance was agreeing—albeit

reluctantly—with alleged Black Hand capo Angelo "The Fish" Bronzini to lease space in the sporting club to one friendly French restaurateur: Eugène François Martin. The agreed-to space would accommodate a cozy piano bar featuring wine, whiskey, and a bistro-style menu. And, as a tip-of-the-hat to his French culture, Eugène François Martin named this spot *Café des Amis*.

Tuesday, June 14, 1955

Despite Billy's positive takeaway from the whole Spinnaker disaster, I was still disturbed by it and suspicious of the "gentlemen" who had arranged it—which is why I used my powers of *Penso Appositus* to sit in on a meeting between Mutt Pickering and Johnny Mocha a few days later. At Johnny's invitation, the two met for lunch at the Alpine Grotto in Lima, compliments of Angelo "The Fish" Bronzini, a.k.a. Little Angelo-B. Mutt knew Little Angelo-B only indirectly: Bronzini and a man named Vincenzo "Whitey" Bianco were the off-the-books "owners" of Danceland, and had hired Mutt as an assistant bookkeeper at the behest of his father, Ralph Shanahan. The givens of Mutt's situation being very clear, he had no choice but to accept Mocha's lunch invitation, which Johnny claimed was to discuss "bidness."

In the nicely appointed Sorrento Room, Johnny introduced Mutt to JoJo "The Gardener" Gardini, the sleaze ball known to do anything to make a buck. It was common knowledge that he set up Herman "The Mouse" Forghett's gambling operation, where high stakes poker games were held from time to time in a private suite behind the Spinnaker Room in the old Lakeview Hotel. Mouse was also the reigning dimwit of dope, working the Spinnaker Room during the Swing Kings' appearance, not to mention the Ritz all those years ago during Billy's first performance there.

They took their seats, and as JoJo poured each a glass of wine, an older, squat, swarthy-looking man with a large belly and unruly white hair ambled into the room: Little Angelo-B, or "Angie" as his friends sometimes called him.

For nearly half an hour, they ate in virtual silence—clam sauce, linguine, and garlic bread—until Little Angelo-B shoved his plate aside and made it very clear how much he would appreciate Mutt Pickering's help with a sales opportunity—from which, of course, Mutt would derive significant benefit.

"We're all friends here, Mr. Pickering," Bronzini said. "So, I want to assure you that we all will hold you in the highest respect if you would agree to my simple request."

"More than happy to help," Mutt said, with little enthusiasm. "What can I do?"

"Our organization has several sales representatives who provide a much-needed service to those who care to participate in the joys of smoking—how shall I say—a special herbal blend?"

"I understand," said Mutt.

"Excellent. Then my simple request is that you are *otherwise occupied* when any of my sales associates seek entrance to your Danceland venues to accommodate the travelling musicians' medicinal needs."

Of course, Mutt's answer had already been decided for him. Still, he thought to push for a favor in return from Little Angelo-B. He knew that Stardust Ballroom would be dark over the July Fourth holiday, allegedly due to a plumbing problem in the ladies' restroom. True to his deity complex, Johnny Mocha had saved the summer season at Danceland by signing exclusive contracts for Moonlight Terrace with the bands of Billy May, Ralph Flanagan, Charlie Barnett, and Les Brown—impressive, but still not enough to carry the season. Knowing the big band of Karl Beach had recently parted ways, Mutt had Bronzini and Mocha where he wanted them.

"I don't foresee a problem," Mutt said. "But if there could be a way for the ladies' restroom plumbing to be repaired in time for the July Fourth weekend, I would like to book a promising group of young musicians called Billy Barnes & the Swing Kings. Mr. Mocha is familiar with them, having recently booked them into the Lakeview Hotel's Spinnaker Room."

I could see Johnny's face flush crimson as Mutt continued.

"And, since we're all friends, Dukie Kincaid will manage the band. In addition to the July Fourth weekend gig, I would also like for Mr. Mocha—with all his connections—to agree to book the Swing Kings for a tour of at least ten days of college jazz festivals in the fall."

Bronzini turned to Mocha, nodded, then turned back to Mutt.

"I'm certain Mr. Mocha can put his best people on the plumbing problem—and, well, in exchange for your assistance with our sales force, I will personally see to it that we reach out to our many associates to arrange your requested tour. As you said: 'I don't foresee a problem.'"

As Mutt stood to depart, Little Angelo-B signaled for him to remain seated.

"One more thing," he said. "You know my goombah—let's just call him *Whitey*—has invested a lot of green in our Flourish property. He set up Woodland Cottage Sporting Club a while ago, with a variety of pleasant diversions. You know, some socializing with a staff of very accommodating lady entertainers, beverages, games of chance—all very professionally run. Besides that, I leased the fancy restaurant..." He turned to Johnny Mocha. "Moko, what's the name of that frog joint?"

"Café des Amis."

"Yeah," Bronzini affirmed. "High priced and classy. The guy I leased it to is a *Frog*...knows his wines but plays loose with the *scharole.*"

"The what?" Mutt asked.

"'Scusa. Money. Moolah. Loot. Gelt."

Little Angelo-B lifted a gold-rimmed cordial glass to his lips and tossed off a few fingers of greenish colored liquor, wiped his lips, and bore in on Mutt.

"If he doesn't play ball with us, he's gonna be sorry. *Capisce?*"

"Where do I fit in?" Mutt asked.

"You remember that kitchen fire at the Golden Ruhl a few years back...shut 'em down for the season?"

"I remember it well."

"Shit like that happens when you don't pay attention, you know? The Frog owes me and Whitey ten big for the last remodel. Whitey don't like to wait. You see the Frog, put in a good word for me and Whitey. If he don't cough up pretty soon, I'm going to ask Moko"—Bronzini nodded his head toward Johnny Mocha—"to pay him a visit when no one's home. *Capisce?*"

Little Angelo-B extended his hand to Mutt, pulled him up off his chair, bear-hugged him, and whispered, *"Arivederci. Vaya con Dios."*

Following the meeting with his so-called *management team*, Mutt told Dukie about his luncheon agreement with Little Angelo-B and asked him if the Swing Kings could be in shape to play the Stardust over the July Fourth weekend.

Though I was exceptionally pleased by the deal Mutt had struck with Little Angelo-B, I must admit that his motives eluded me. Accordingly, I decided to do a bit more research into what, exactly, made Maurice "Mutt" Pickering tick.

I learned that he was not raised in the customary fashion, by parents who loved and cared for him. Mutt came of age in the post-Depression era. The rough-and-tumble culture of the 1940s was a brutally frank testament to the hardship of the times. In fact, Mutt was proud to be the bastard child of a *gandy dancer*—a tough breed of railroad worker who laid and maintained railroad track—and a woman named Iris Pickering. Iris died giving birth to Mutt in a railroad boxcar, but his father—Jocko "Tuffy" Nash—gave Mutt her name on the birth certificate he had to fill out when the health department caught up with him.

As with his father, Tuffy, Mutt was a product of the tough neighborhood around South High School in Lima. He was famous for instigating playground trouble with a long list of local toughs who occasionally tested Mutt and—much to their regret—learned that he was an expert knife fighter who showed no mercy. His oft-repeated mantra? "Cut the motherfuckers first, ask questions later."

Everyone in Allen County knew Mutt was not one to cross. Johnny Mocha—a local loudmouth and underclassman to Mutt at Lima South—nearly paid with his life when he challenged Mutt for the right to sample one of Mutt's girlfriend's sexual talents. There was very little made of the *incident* after Mutt—to his credit—agreed with the juvenile delinquency judge to turn himself over to Allen County Children's Services. Luckily, he was placed in a foster home with a family who was glad to have him. The family—Ralph and

Diane Shanahan—raised him in the Catholic Church, St. Rita's to be exact. Foster father Ralph taught Mutt the ins-and-outs of the bookkeeping business and got him a job at one of his clients, Danceland, at Sandy Beach Amusement Park.

Mutt adopted his given name of Maurice and showed his exceptional intelligence and accounting skills, working long hours. Within two years, Bronzini and Bianco promoted Maurice to senior bookkeeper and assistant general manager for big band contracts. Ironically, those same owners introduced Johnny Mocha to Maurice as their main man for talent booking in Northwest Ohio and parts of Michigan and Indiana.

Knowing Johnny Mocha from their past association at Lima South High School, Mutt thought Johnny was a low-class numb-skull adept only at bullying people to his advantage. Still, Mutt's boss encouraged him to work with Johnny on several of the big band booking contracts and learn what he could about Johnny's game: Get someone obligated, then take advantage of them by forcing unfavorable terms on them—which he could later retract, as though he were the original gift horse looking for a face to kick. In fact, Mutt was wrangling with Stan Kenton that day he met Billy Barnes because of Johnny Mocha, whom he knew had purposely written the bogus language into the Kenton contract just so Johnny could haggle with him later and eventually agree to what the standard terms were, as if he were a martyr.

In Mutt's mind, not much had changed since Johnny's high school days as a bully and general "jerk-wit." The contract Johnny negotiated with the Swing Kings was no different. Not only did he book the band into the trashy Spinnaker Room, the dummy also asked his moron dope peddler Forghett to sell weed to some of Billy Barnes's Swing Kings. Or at least this was the complaint lodged by Dukie Kincaid a few days later, when he relayed to Mutt that Billy had seen his guitarist Jack Roush exchanging money with the Mouse. That being the case, Dukie asked Mutt to inform Johnny Mocha that he, Dukie, wouldn't be available to fill in as Johnny's house pianist-on-call—not unless he agreed to book the Swing Kings for the weekend of July Fourth, plus a jazz festival tour in the fall.

All the facts laid out, I could easily see the forces that had led to Mutt's meeting with Angelo-B at the Alpine Grotto.

At the time, though I was disturbed by the proceedings at Alpine Grotto, I foolishly thought that Mutt's business with Johnny Mocha and Little Angelo-B would have little negative effect on Billy. After all, Mutt had finagled the Swing Kings' biggest break yet: a gig at Indian Lake's premier jazz venue, plus a multi-state tour in the fall. In short, though I disapproved of Mutt's methods, I could overlook them in light of their positive results.

Now, of course, this all seems like one more instance of me failing to fully protect Billy. It strikes me that whoever shot Billy could easily have been one of the hoods I observed at Bronizini's lunch meeting: Small-time gambler JoJo "The Gardener" Gardini; Herman "The Dope-Rodent" Forghett; or the bone-headed booking agent, Johnny Mocha. As for Mutt himself—my intuition takes him off the suspect list.

Chapter 22

<u>Friday, June 24, 1955</u>

Anna's father-imposed exile from Billy did have a serendipitous effect, in that it was easier for her to focus on school. In exchange, her father didn't say anything derogatory about Billy. After all, Anna had done her part: she graduated high school with honors, was nominated to be class salutatorian at graduation, and went to work as the full-time receptionist for her father's medical practice.

But, when Billy told Anna that the Swing Kings were scheduled to perform the weekend of July Fourth at Danceland's Stardust Ballroom, she couldn't wait to go see them. The only problem? Her father's recalcitrance. On a hunch, at Anna's graduation dinner party, she approached her father's lady friend, Juliette.

In my nearly six millennia of guardian angel duties, I've never known a more cordial, sincere, genial, or persuasive female than Juliette Barlow. I say that because, when Anna explained her father's putting the brakes on her relationship with Billy—a rule under which Anna had begun to seriously chafe—it was Juliette who went to bat for her. *Clever* is not the right word—it's close—but the word *innovative* speaks more to Juliette's talent.

Realizing that Arthur Lea was no pushover when it came to discipline, Juliette's imagination went to work. She decided to pluck Arthur's guilt-strings: she told him that it was time for him to recognize that his daughter was a mature woman and should be treated as such; moreover, he, Arthur—while being a physician and well intentioned did not have the wiring to deal with the feminine psyche, especially in matters of the heart and hormones.

This argument proved convincing—the next time Anna asked permission to see Billy, Arthur acquiesced without the slightest protest.

July was Billy's month to rejoice. Dukie brought him a contract for the ten-day Swing Kings tour of one-nighter clubs and college jazz festivals, all ending with an incredible weekend in Chicago.

"Check it out, Billy," Dukie said as he handed over the contract. "The fun starts on September eighth at Suttmiller's Supper Club in Dayton. The college circuit kicks off the next day at Butler University, followed by Indiana University, Notre Dame's Annual

Jazz Showcase, Valparaiso College, Northwestern, and Loyola. After an overnight at the Erie St. Arms on the North Side, you can sleep in and go sightseeing in Chicago.

"Everyone gets twelve dollars a day for food and expenses, so it's tight. The rooms at the Erie are cheap doubles—five bucks a person for the one night. But I have a little bread stashed away for emergencies." Dukie grinned. "By the way, you and I are roommates."

"You're going with us?"

"Since you aren't twenty-one, I'm the co-signer on the contract and the vehicle insurance."

"What vehicle are you talking about? We don't have—"

"Calm down. I'm working on that." Dukie was trying to get Billy to see the big picture. "The tour ends in Chicago at Mr. Kelly's on Rush Street for a two-night stand as the warm up band for Anita O'Day and the Chet Baker Trio. We come back home on Sunday the eighteenth."

The day following that hallelujah bulletin—which is how Billy had come to think of Dukie's announcement—he laid the good news on the rest of the Swing Kings. The road tour couldn't have inspired greater appreciation, and Billy took the opportunity to remind them that he had finally fulfilled his promise: *Trust me...we'll make it.* Not even Ike had a negative comment, other than wondering out loud if the sleeping rooms Dukie had booked at the Erie Arms included an alarm clock.

After their Golden Ruhl gig the weekend following their Stardust Ballroom appearance, Karl offered Billy a small but comfortable, nicely-furnished apartment behind his office in exchange for him mopping the floors, washing down the booths and tables, and caretaking the Golden Ruhl property Mondays and Tuesdays during the season and once a month in the off-season. For the first time, Billy felt as though good fortune had finally discovered him.

He couldn't have been more blessed when, after the band's first week working for Karl, playing their hearts out for huge crowds, Billy was beckoned into his office.

"I'm proud of you, Billy-boy," he said. "I like your attitude and your good work. The bar's never been cleaner and your band is bringing in more customers that we've ever seen."

That chapter in Billy's good fortune was like a gentle breeze enfolding him. He stood to shake Karl's hand and said, "Thanks, Mr.

Ruhl, it's been—"

"Don't thank me yet," he said. "The season isn't over. But, since you and your band are getting good results, I'm booking the Swing Kings every weekend through Labor Day Saturday. I'm closing up the next day." Karl paused, as if uncertain what to say, then continued. "I might as well tell you this now instead of waiting."

"Tell me what?"

"My wife isn't well—you remember we spent all of last winter in Florida?"

"Right," he said. "I drove you down there."

"Yeah, you did—it's 'cause you're a good kid. But here's the thing, Billy: my wife's health is only going downhill. The doc thinks we need to start spending a lot of the summer down south, too.

"Like you can imagine, it's hard for me to run my business when I'm spending the better part of the year down in Florida." Karl sighed, pinching his brow. "So, here's my offer for when I reopen in the spring: I'll give you a twenty-percent share in the Ruhl and the big apartment in the back for free, if you'll manage the business full-time over the summers. Meantime, you and the Kings can have a night off Sunday, August twenty-eighth. I'm closing for a private party, so feel free to take off a few days."

###

Sunday, August 28, 1955

For the first time in his life, Billy felt overwhelmed with blessings. Nevertheless, working for Karl in this capacity was quite an adjustment, even after all the work he'd done for him the previous off-season. Since he had to write new arrangements for the road trip, rehearse the group, and manage his gradually improving bank account, he barely had time for socializing. He hadn't seen Anna in weeks, and he knew he had to wait until he saw her in person to tell her how he felt—how he truly loved her, sincerely wanted her to be his steady sweetheart.

And so—since the Swing Kings would be off that night—Billy decided to invite Anna to meet him at Moonlight Gardens on August twenty-eighth to dance to the music of Les Brown and his Band of Renown. Their vocalist that night would be Lucy Ann Polk, whose version of "Just When We're Falling in Love" had always been one of Billy's favorites.

As he dressed very *cool* for that balmy Sunday night—pegged pants, pinch-collar French-cuff pink shirt, black knit tie, and new penny loafers—Billy wasn't sure how he would pull things off with Anna. He jumped into his parents' new used '49 Ford Fairlane, which they had lent him for the night, and, heading for Orchard Island, an inspiration struck. As a surprise for Anna, he would ask the band to dedicate their rendition of "Just When We're Falling in Love" to the two of them as they danced.

When they arrived at Moonlight Terrace Gardens, Billy's bandmate Jay Walter sidled up to them in the parking lot. Jay was attired in his usual sartorial splendor, as if having just stepped out of the first-edition pages of *Playboy*, with Marilyn Monroe on the cover—plush-red velvet vest, hair slicked back in ducktails, white silk shirt, sharply creased slacks, and blue suede shoes.

"You're both looking pretty spiffed-up," Jay said. "You planning to get lucky tonight?"

Anna let out a small gasp, and Billy gave Jay a quick punch in the arm. In his head, though, he was thinking, *That's* Mister *Lucky to you, Jay-boy. Keep your eyes peeled.*

When they walked inside, the first set had already kicked off with the band's hit recording, "Sentimental Journey." As couples moved to the center of the dance floor, Billy scanned the crowd seated at cocktail tables around the perimeter of the pavilion until his eyes came to rest on Helen and Albert, sipping their drinks in the balmy calm. "Why don't you go catch up with the two lovebirds?" he said to Anna. "I have to take care of something real quick."

"I hope you don't plan on getting into it with Jay," she said. "What he said was...well, you know. Boys being boys."

Billy shook his head—though Anna's response provided him with a handy excuse. He kissed her on the cheek and sent her off in the direction of Helen and Albert.

When he was sure Anna wouldn't be able to see him, Billy pushed through the crowd toward the bandstand. He managed to make eye contact with Lucy Ann Polk just as she finished singing "Sentimental Journey." When Billy beckoned her, Lucy stepped to the foot of the stage and leaned down to hear Billy's voice over the crowd noise. In his most persuasive manner, Billy cupped his hands to his mouth and spoke in a loud but distinct tone: "I've always really dug your version of 'Just When We're Falling in Love.' My girlfriend and I are...well...let's just say that song fits. Would you consider doing 'Just When We're Falling in Love,' and dedicating it to us?"

Lucy signaled for Billy to stand by while she approached Les Brown. Les grinned, then said something to Lucy. Stepping back to where Billy waited, Lucy leaned down and said, "Les is cool. What are you and your girlfriend's names?"

Armed with his surprise for Anna, Billy walked back toward

her to see her whispering to Helen. From the way Helen grinned, he felt that their whispers must be about him. Putting on his best smile, he stepped up to their table, leaned forward, and extended his hand to Anna.

"May I have this dance?"

They walked out to the dancefloor and moved in sync with Les Brown's next tune, "I've Got My Love to Keep Me Warm."

Midway through the song, Billy whispered to Anna, "Say, I have to ask you a question."

"Oh no," she joked. "Not another one of those patented Billy Barnes questions."

He ignored the gentle jibe. "I don't know how to say this, exactly…"

"See?" She smirked. "You shouldn't have dropped out of school."

Billy held Anna at arms' length as he said, softly, "Anna…I didn't have to graduate from high school to know that I love you."

He felt Anna's body tremble. She cleared her throat and, in a far more business-like tone than Billy's, she said, "If you're just saying all this because you want me to sing with your band…"

Billy chuckled and held her tighter. "Of course, I want you to sing with my band. In fact, once we're back from our college tour, I thought you and I could start practicing more songs." His voice grew gentler as he said, "But right now, I just want you to know that I love you. Will you be my steady girlfriend?"

As if on cue, Lucy Ann Polk's voice rang out from the bandstand: "Ladies and gentlemen, please join us in wishing our very best to one of our special couples tonight. Say hey to Billy and Anna! Les Brown, the band, and I want to dedicate this next song to them— enjoy dancing to 'Just When We're Falling in Love!'"

As the first few lyrics echoed over the crowd, Billy knew there would be no better time. He pulled Anna close to him and whispered in her ear:

I was a child and she was a child,

In this kingdom by the sea,

But we loved with a love that was more than love—

I and my Annabel Lee—

With a love that the wingèd seraphs of Heaven

Coveted her and me.

###

Later that night, as Billy and Anna walked to Jupie's barbecue tent—"So my father can meet my steady girlfriend," he said—Anna asked him a question he hadn't expected.

"Have you ever thought about doing anything other than playing piano?" she said.

The question surprised him, but he had a ready answer. "I have," he said, "and I do. I work for Karl Ruhl during the day. I've played his club every weekend this summer—and Thursday after next is the start of the Swing Kings' road trip." He breathed in and out. "So, will you be my steady girlfriend right now—and my vocalist for the Swing Kings starting as soon as we get back from Chicago?"

"We'll see, Billy." Anna sighed. Her voice quieter, more thoughtful, she added, "Of all the people out there, I never thought I'd find someone like you."

Though Billy didn't need to hear the words themselves to know she had agreed to be his girl, he savored Anna's remark and held her a bit more tightly as they continued their walk to Jupie's.

The air was unusually mild that August evening, and Jupie's BBQ was more crowded than usual, and louder than the typical Sunday. As Anna and Billy entered the tent, a burst of applause greeted them. Not for them, it turned out, but for a man sitting at the piano keyboard, with Dukie Kincaid standing by. He was about to speak into the microphone.

"Ladies and gentlemen," Dukie announced. "Here with me on the stage is one of my best friends, a fellow musician and our featured performer this weekend at the Ritz Club. His name is Frankie Carle." Dukie let the applause die down and continued, "As a personal favor to me, he's here to sample some of Jupie's fine barbecue and treat us to a performance of his popular theme song, 'Sunrise Serenade.'"

Scanning to his left, Dukie spotted Billy and Anna.

"And to add to tonight's entertainment," he said, without missing a beat, "please give a hand for my best piano student, Billy Barnes. And he has a guest with him." Dukie put his hand over the microphone and yelled to them. "Billy! You and your friend come on up here to the piano so everyone can see you."

Standing at the foot of the piano platform, Billy introduced Anna and Dukie, the latter of whom turned to Frankie Carle and yelled: "Please, maestro, do us the honor of gracing this young couple with your theme song."

When he had finished playing "Sunrise Serenade," Frankie smiled at Dukie and said, "I hope you'll be getting a new axe pretty soon to replace this relic."

Dukie leaned toward Frankie. "Will you do me one more favor? Ask Billy to play something. He'll be gassed for a week."

Grabbing the microphone from Dukie, Frankie gestured to Billy and Anna and addressed the crowd. "I'd like for you all to join me and welcome my friend Dukie's hotshot piano prodigy, Mr. Billy—I'll just call him Billy-the-Kid—and his sidekick, Lady Lovely." Frankie Carle leaned down close to Anna and said, "Lady Lovely? By any chance do you sing?"

Anna didn't have a chance to reply before Dukie informed Frankie, "Anna beat Billy in a talent contest last year by singing 'Too Young.'"

Frankie stood, raising his arms to exhort the crowd. "Ladies and gentlemen, allow me to present a rising young couple to perform that famous Nat King Cole song, 'Too Young.'"

I will say this: Anna and Billy were as natural a pair of performers as anyone in that barbecue tent could imagine.

Later, as Billy was preparing to leave, Anna tugged on his shirt sleeve. "I don't want to leave until I've said hello to your father."

Scanning over the top of the crowd, Billy spotted Jupie at the barbecue oven making sandwiches. Turning back to Anna, he yelled over the crowd noise, "C'mon...he's back here."

Wending through the crowd, Anna and Billy caught up with Jupie. "Dad," yelled Billy, "wait up! I want you to meet my girlfriend, Anna."

As the three of them mashed together, Jupie took Anna's hand, laughed, and said, "I'll want to meet you again sometime when I'm not so preoccupied with impatient customers and my hands aren't covered with barbecue sauce."

"Anna is coming over to the house Labor Day weekend," Billy said.

"And don't you forget," replied Jupie, "I'm paying you to help me close down the park that Wednesday."

Outside, the warm twilight beckoned.

"Let's go back over Dreamland Bridge to Paradise Island and go swimming," Billy suggested.

"My dad will expect me home soon," Anna said.

"It'll be fun," he said. "C'mon."

"I don't have a swimsuit."

"Anna." Billy grinned. "Have you ever heard the word *improvise*?"

###

Sandy Beach's swimming area was virtually deserted.

"Follow me," said Billy. "There's a bathhouse around the corner where we can leave our clothes."

A serene silence surrounded them as they stood together in the dusky twilight of the bathhouse. Billy enfolded Anna in his arms and whispered, "Did you know that *the moon never beams without bringing me dreams of the beautiful Annabel Lee*?"

"Someone's in a poetic mood," Anna said. She grasped his head and pulled it over her shoulder, his ear to her lips. "Do you think you can unbutton your steady girlfriend's blouse?" she whispered.

Billy's hands trembled as he lowered them from button to button. As her blouse drifted to the floor, Anna kicked off her saddle shoes, then stepped out of her poodle skirt and panties. She reached behind her back, unfastened her bra, and turned around to face Billy. Taking his hands in hers, she placed them on her generous breasts. His breathing virtually stopped as he gently massaged her firm nipples.

"Hurry and undress before it gets so dark I can't see you," she said.

Seconds later, he dropped his jeans to the floor and pushed

his erection against Anna. She reached down and caressed him, then put her hands inside his shorts, fondled him, and pushed his shorts to the floor. Clinging together, their mutual excitement brought sighs of passion as beads of sweat trickled off their bodies in small rivulets.

Billy pulled the dressing room bench away from the wall to the center of the small room and rolled up his jeans into a makeshift pillow. Anna sat down. As though arranging a plush quilt, she spread her poodle skirt over the bench and lowered her back onto it as she pulled Billy to her.

Sitting astride Anna, Billy stared into her deep dark eyes for a moment. Then, leaning over, he kissed her, stretched out on top of her, and—with her help—gently penetrated her moist warmth.

Chapter 23

I've seen it before.

Not often, but often enough for any GA to be alert to the possibility of being called upon for help. It's called the *Corona of Portent*, or, in the German gypsy culture, *Tiara auf Weltschmerz*. The phenomenon involves a visible aura of energy—considered to be preternatural—occasionally surrounding the entire person, but predominantly the person's head. You can see something similar in portraits depicting the saints with halos.

It was part of daily life with my former ward, Catherine of Aragon. In fact, her premonitions of disappointing Henry VIII by not conceiving a male heir with him were so powerful that they actually suppressed her ability to ovulate. Even after that most rigorous copulatory regimen demanded by Henry during the Windsor Castle feast of Michaelmas in 1549, Catherine's onset of menses revealed that, despite her best efforts, hopes, and prayers, she had likely accomplished nothing other than the thing she feared most: driving Henry into the arms of his paramour, Anne Boleyn.

We know the rest of the story of that schism...and, I have to say, King Henry's infatuation with Anne Boleyn—not to mention the gruesome fashion in which he ultimately ended their union—didn't sit well with the Big Boss.

Though rare, I would also sometimes see the *Corona of Portent* in Willa Mae, usually when she and Billy were alone together talking about his worries, fears, and hopes. Though I didn't dwell on it at the time, I saw it when Billy came home early from that disastrous high school victory dance and announced he might quit playing jazz—and Willa Mae talked him out of his self-pitying stupor.

And I saw it again as Billy and Willa Mae discussed his upcoming road trip with the Swing Kings. The *Corona of Portent* surrounded Willa Mae's head in waxing and waning intensities—more intense when Jupie's name was mentioned, less so whenever another name was mentioned. Oddly enough, when Dukie Kincaid stopped by to discuss the final tour itinerary with Billy, Willa Mae's crown of light morphed into what appeared to be an image of St. Christopher.

"Everything's set," said Dukie. "We have Fr. Stenz's permission to use the school bus, as long as I drive. There's plenty of room for everyone. The storage area is huge for luggage and instruments, and the padre will donate the first tank of gas and give us an advance of two hundred dollars—repayable on our return."

"Tell me again the schedule," said Willa Mae. "I'll write it down."

Dukie handed an envelope to Willa Mae, which contained a list of the band's shows. "It'll be a gas," he said to Billy. "I can't wait to lead you cats to the promised land."

After Dukie left, Willa Mae nodded for Billy to sit down.

"You're very lucky to have someone like Dukie to mentor you," she said. "I see you've taken my advice and set your sights higher."

Billy smiled. "It's been my lucky few weeks. And I'll learn a lot on this tour—you'll be proud of me. I just wish that you could see some of our shows. Maybe Dukie can get a camera for us to take some pictures."

"Well, your mother has already thought of that." Willa Mae reached under her chair and produced a brightly-wrapped package. "Your papa and I bought this Kodak Hawkeye flash model for you," she said, as Billy ripped through the gift paper. "I expect to see you and your band in some of those fancy venues where you're performing. And, if you can, get a picture of the Mills Brothers. I love their singing, especially 'Glow Worm.'"

"Sure thing, Mom."

As Billy turned to leave, Willa Mae put a hand on his arm. "There's one last thing you father wants of you," she said.

"Of course," said Billy.

"Your father is a very wise person. He wants your success as much as I do. But he thinks your future as a musician is far from assured. It's a beautiful wish, but also a potentially foolish one. He believes it's wise to make extra plans, in case playing piano doesn't go as well as we all hope it will."

Billy remembered the talk they'd had when he decided to drop out of school. "Yeah, he wants me to work at the park and the barbecue tent, just like him." Billy couldn't keep the irritation out of his voice when he added, "That's not what *I* want, though, Mom."

Seeing the beginnings of disappointment on Willa Mae's face, Billy softened his tone. He put his hand over hers. "Don't get me wrong, I'm happy to help out. I owe you both so much. But music has to come first."

Willa Mae knew better than to argue with Billy on this point. Instead, she took him into her arms. As she hugged him, she whispered the traditional Romani wish for good luck and health into his ear: "*Baxt hai sastimos tiri patragi.*"

Wednesday, September 7, 1955

The winter closing of Sandy Beach Amusement Park after Labor Day meant back-breaking labor for Jupie. Every ride needed maintenance, upkeep, repair, and repainting, and all the food operators and relief stations needed sanitation service. Power scaled back to the minimum necessary for safety illumination and emergency power in case of fire; the grounds were swept and the varmint traps set. The bandstands at Stardust Ballroom and Moonlight Terrace were protected with swaths of Visqueen plastic sheeting to prevent vermin from taking up residence in those hallowed structures. Pianos for all the entertainment venues, rented from Johnny Mocha via his "special" connections in Lima with Luigi Martinelli, were returned for safekeeping to Martinelli Music On The Square.

For the week following Labor Day, Jupie hired more than twenty spot laborers to help with the routine upkeep, such as washing and wiping down surfaces in picnic areas—trash containers, water fountains—and all ride seats. Jupie handled the more difficult tasks himself, with Billy along this year to learn the basic maintenance tasks, the most important of which was closing down the Silver Streak roller coaster and the larger power rides.

In the kitchen, as Jupie checked his tool kit, Billy studied a list of the larger, more difficult maintenance jobs to be completed:

1. DODGEM CARS – replace worn electrical contact pads

2. THE WHIP – install new passenger restraints and tension bars

3. LOOP-DE-LOOP – tighten/replace all rotating gears and replace worn passenger seating pads

4. TILT-A-WHIRL – lubricate swivel joints and motor bearings and reset ride timer to allow ten seconds more per ride

5. BUBBLE BOUNCE – clean agitator engine and propulsion gears

6. MERRY-GO-ROUND – tighten all seating rods, re-align offset crank rods, and lubricate rotating cams

7. SILVER STREAK – lubricate metal tracks, all chain drives, chain dogs, & braking fins, & check all passenger restraints

At the door, Willa Mae handed Jupie a bag of her famous gypsy tarts. Exchanging parting hugs, Willa Mae put her hand on Jupie's shoulder as she said, *"Dza devlesa."* She turned to Billy. "That means 'Go with God.' Be careful. I'll have a fine dinner for you two at sunset. It's bad luck to spoil a gypsy feast by being late."

I've told you that, as a guardian angel, I have many resources to call on when necessary—and, while a crystal ball is not one of them, GAs have a clairvoyance that gives us the ability to perceive events in the near term beyond normal sensory contact. And so I stayed alert to the possibility that Billy could need help if Jupie encountered any issues with the rides, particularly the aging Silver Streak roller coaster, now nearly thirty years old. But nothing had ever happened to complicate the procedure Jupie had depended on time and again for lubricating the tracks and the chain drive mechanism that hoisted the coaster cars up the lift hill, to be picked up by a chain dog and carried to the top, where gravity took over at the beginning of the ride.

I couldn't be sure of my suspicions, but I sensed that Billy was preoccupied with something on their way to the park, or was so enthralled with the Swing Kings' road trip that he lacked focus.

When Jupie said to him, "I know you need to get back home and prepare for your road trip," Billy's mind seemed a thousand miles away. Jupie stopped and turned to him. "The main thing for you is to watch me and be ready with the braking mechanism if one of those chain dogs acts up and we need to shut it down fast."

With little more than a vague nod of assent from Billy, Jupie asked, "Do you feel alright?"

"I feel fine. I was just thinking about the night we brought Anna over to your barbecue place. She really enjoyed it, seeing Dukic and his piano friend—and you, of course."

"I'll say this to you, Billy." Jupie smiled. "I was impressed with your girlfriend's singing. You should be nice to her. She looked good onstage, and not bad up close. Now, let's get to work."

At first glance, the Silver Streak, much like other roller coasters, was something like a passenger train with a series of cars that moved on fixed steel tracks. The obvious difference between a passenger train is that a roller coaster has no engine or power source of its own. For most of the ride, the train moves by gravitational momentum. Building up this momentum requires getting the train to the top of the first hill, the *lift* hill. On the Silver Streak, the traditional lifting mechanism was a long length of heavy-duty chain running up the lift hill under the track, fastened in a loop wound around gears at the top and bottom of the hill. The gear at the bottom of the hill was turned by a simple motor, which turned the chain loop like a long conveyor belt, continually moving up the hill. Several chain dogs—sturdy hinged hooks—gripped the chain and caught on to the chain links when the train rolled to the bottom of the hill.

Of course, like any train, a roller coaster also needs a brake system, so it can stop precisely at the end of the ride or in an emergency. These brakes aren't built into the train itself, but the track. A series of clamps, operated by a central hydraulic system, close in on vertical metal fins running under the train, creating the friction needed to gradually slow the train down.

The dangerous variable in Jupie's maintenance procedure was the starting and stopping of the chain drive. As Jupie cat-walked up the tracks, applying the grease to lubricate the track and moving chain, his helper would pause the drive motor, only resuming when Jupie was clear of the train. In this stop-and-go way, Jupie would lubricate each subsequent link of the chain as it moved beneath him.

This day, Billy was in charge of stopping and starting the coaster motor. The first three cycles went smoothly, so smoothly that Billy felt confident just going through the motions as his mind was on other things. But then, on the fourth cycle, an ear-splitting crack pierced the air. Startled, Billy looked up to see that the chain drive had broken halfway up the track, preventing the chain dogs from gripping the car to pull it all the way up the lift hill.

Panic stricken, Billy watched the passenger car stop, drift back, and gain reverse momentum down the track—with Jupie crouched between the car and the metal housing over the start of the car queue.

Instantly aware of what was happening, Jupie screamed at Billy: "Brake it! Brake it!"

But Billy's attempt to stop the renegade car was fruitless—it had rolled too far past the friction plates for them to be effective. Through astonished tears, Billy could only watch helplessly as Jupie scrambled to crawl over the coaster's wooden framework and drop to the ground. Within seconds, the loose car smashed into Jupie's leg, twisting it, and dragged Jupie foot-first to the metal housing before Billy could re-engage the emergency braking system.

Through Jupie's blood-curdling screams, Billy composed himself enough to race to the park's emergency phone and dial the operator.

###

The emergency medical team at Mary Rutan Hospital, led by Dr. Arthur Lea, discussed the option of repairing Jupie's right leg—crushed below the knee—or amputating it. After completing the traumatic injury assessment, Dr. Lea met Willa Mae and Billy in the waiting room.

"We've examined Jupie's—Mr. Barnes's—extensive injury. His lower leg is significantly damaged. The bone is virtually destroyed. The neurological fragments could, perhaps, be reconstructed, but it's highly doubtful his neuro-network—excuse me—his nerve network will ever function effectively. In all likelihood, it will never function at all. The vascular network—that's the channel for blood flow to and from his leg—is so disrupted, it's highly likely that his defense mechanism won't be able to withstand the assault of frequent, if not chronic, severe infections which eventually lead to…"

Dr. Lea paused, took Willa Mae's hand, and exhaled a deep breath. "What I'm saying is that, in our considered opinion…the medical team's decision is to amputate Mr. Barnes's leg immediately. With a properly-fit prosthesis, we believe Mr. Barnes will regain a full measure of functionality that will allow him to be productive and employable. However," he added, "it will take time."

"When will you operate?" asked Willa Mae.

"We'd like to begin right away." Dr. Lea put a hand on Willa Mae's shoulder. "I know this is difficult. I'm going to ask Annabelle to come stay with you both for a while later today. You shouldn't be alone."

Willa Mae thanked Dr. Lea as he departed. But Billy was still stuck on Anna's name. He couldn't shake the feeling that his preoccupation with his new girlfriend was at fault for his father's crippling injury. If he had been able to focus on the task at hand, his father's accident may never have happened, and none of them would be in this emergency room right now.

Chapter 24

I have to say that I was impressed with Anna. In fact, of all Billy's friends, she had become my favorite. Her personality, intelligence, and common sense—not to mention her softening opinion on Billy's career in jazz—made her a most compatible partner for my ward.

So, despite my concerns that he might fall victim to his own human nature (that is, be distracted by the specter of love from his goal of becoming a jazz pianist of prominence), I subscribed to the tenets of St. Paul: *Omnia Vincit Amor*. Beyond that pithy aphorism, I've always treasured Paul's Old Testament writings while imprisoned, particularly his exhortations to the Corinthians. These days, it's virtually an article of faith for couples celebrating the sacrament of marriage to include one of Paul's most popular passages in their ceremony:

> *Love is patient, love is kind. It does not envy, it does*
> *not boast, it is not proud. It does not dishonor*
> *others, it is not self-seeking, it is not easily angered,*
> *it keeps no record of wrongs. Love does not delight*

in evil but rejoices with the truth. It always protects,

always trusts, always hopes, always perseveres.

I have always been taken by the life of Paul, a.k.a. Saul of Tarsus; his was a profound journey from doubt to belief. In the hours following Jupie's accident, I wished for Billy to undergo a similar transformation: from guilt over his perceived culpability in Jupie's accident to forgiveness of himself—and, more importantly, forgiveness of Annabelle

From Anna's standpoint, it was unlike Billy not to have called her on his break at the amusement park. Still having not heard from Billy by late afternoon that Wednesday, Anna left work to go home. As she entered their kitchen from the garage, she was puzzled to find her father on the phone, and—from all his medical jargon—knew he was engaged in a serious problem at the hospital. After her father finished the phone call, he turned to Anna. "I'm glad you're home," he said, his voice stressed. "I was just going to call you."

"What is it?" she asked.

"Trouble at the hospital. Billy's dad suffered a catastrophic injury to his leg. I've been with him all day."

Anna put her hand to her heart. "What about Billy? Is he...?"

"Billy wasn't injured, but he was there when the accident happened. Billy was helping his father work on the roller coaster when a car dislodged and crushed Mr. Barnes's leg. There was no one else around. I don't know exactly what happened but, if it weren't for Billy, his father would have died from blood loss. Thank God for Billy—for all anyone knows, if he hadn't been there, his dad could've lain under the coaster for hours."

I know what you're thinking: *fate.* Me, I was just wishing that Dr. Lea could share this assessment of the day's events with Billy, in the hope that it might assuage some of his guilt.

Panicked, Anna could barely breathe as she clung to the back of the kitchen chair.

"Dad, please, how can I help? What can I do?"

"You can't help Mr. Barnes right now, but it would be good if you looked in on Billy and his mother. They're frantic. Mrs. Barnes couldn't stop crying, and Billy is so distraught that I'm worried about him slipping into a state of depression. My attending nurse told me he muttered your name—at least she thinks he's saying 'Annabelle.' She said it sounds like he's reciting some sort of poem, something about his beautiful Annabelle Lee. Does that sound familiar?"

"It's a poem we learned in school." Anna shook her head,

trying to clear it. "When can I see them?"

"Billy went home right after his father went into surgery. There wasn't anything his mother could do, so I sent her home just before three o'clock. You should be fine going over in a half-hour or so."

As she showered and changed, her heart aching, Anna brooded over what she could do to help Billy and his mother. In truth, she didn't know what to think when, at 5:30 that evening, she stopped by Billy's home. Willa Mae greeted Anna at the door and invited her in to the kitchen for some tea.

It was hard to know exactly what Anna felt, but I inferred from her fidgety shifting in her chair that she was worried. At first, I thought the worry was over her awkward intrusion on the Barnes's privacy. But it wasn't that at all. Anna wasn't worried—she was in awe. You see, Willa Mae's presence radiated a mystical spirit. A spirit born of hope. A spirit that—in the worst of times—quenched the hurt that comes with fear, worry, and the unexpected pain of traumatic news. Listening to Willa Mae's calm, candid discussion of her husband, his injury, and Billy's retreat into despair, Anna renewed her resolve to emulate Willa Mae's determination and help the Barnes family in any way she could.

Willa Mae looked into Anna's misting eyes and said, "Billy hasn't said one word. Not since before they took Jupie to surgery." Willa Mae shook her head. "And since I've been home, he hasn't come out of his room. He's refused to leave with his band for their road trip tomorrow."

"Can he do that?" Anna said.

Willa Mae sighed deeply. "Dukie and the rest of the band have to leave without him to avoid breaking the contracts."

Anna knew things had to be serious for Billy to so blithely abandon the Swing Kings. She told Will Mae as much.

"That's not even the half of it," said Willa Mae. "Three times this afternoon, I took a plate of food to Billy's door and knocked. He refused to answer. I called to him through the door. He still wouldn't answer. I hear music from his record player, but it's always the same song. I don't know what it is—a woman singing something about falling in love. Do you know what it might be?"

"I have an idea," said Anna.

"Will you talk with him?"

"If you think it will help," she said. "If he'll let me."

"I'm sure it will help——me as much as him."

"Why do you say that?"

"I am a gypsy. I try to live by the gypsy *way*, a way that springs from true love: the deepest, most primitive instincts of man. No matter what happens, it respects nature and man's place in nature. It teaches gypsies to take joy in the moment. Your visiting Billy will bring great joy to me this very moment."

Willa Mae reached across the table to take Anna's hand as she continued.

"I am the cause of my husband's injury, not Billy. A gypsy believes that arrogance is penalized by injury to a loved one. I have been prideful and self-important. I have been selfish and uncaring about those less fortunate. I have failed to repent in the gypsy tradition of showing dignity and respect to all."

Willa Mae paused to dry her eyes—the first time, since Anna's arrival, that she had allowed her tears to fall—and sip from her teacup. In my view, Willa Mae's mea culpa was too generous. True, sparing Billy the angst of taking most of the blame for Jupie's accident was in the tradition of gypsy filial love, but it couldn't change the fact that Billy would eventually need to confront his own culpability in what had transpired and admit that he had been delinquent in his responsibilities. Only by such honest reflection would he ultimately be able to heal.

Willa Mae continued: "Annabelle, I am not religious. But Jupie is, and I have asked his God for mercy. I believe he has heard my prayers. This afternoon, I saw two crows on our windowsill. To see one crow is sorrow. Two together means joy. Later, the two crows stood in the road in front of our house for several minutes. When one of them flew away, it was a sign of a joyful journey."

Willa Mae paused, withdrawing her hand from Anna's.

"I believe these good fortune signs—occurring right here, in our home, where Billy is lamenting his father's misfortune—are encouraging. And my fear is, if we don't help Billy, he will begin to feel sorry for himself—and that, too, is a form of gypsy arrogance. We must help him. You...you are the only one I know for certain Billy has strong feelings about. He talks about you. He speaks your name with love on his tongue. You are the one I believe will change his grief to joy. I believe that can happen."

And despite myself, I believed it, too.

Annabelle tapped lightly on the doorjamb of Billy's bedroom door. No response. She tapped louder. Nothing. Pounding hard now, she yelled at the top of her lungs: "Billy! It's me, Anna! "A long pause. Anna tried to steady her breathing.

"It's open," Billy finally mumbled. "Just push on it."

As she slowly entered his room, Billy made no attempt to greet her.

"Are you awake?" she whispered.

Through a rustle of bed sheets, a voice muttered, "Go away."

"Not until we talk."

"Go. Away."

"Are you feeling sorry for yourself?"

Billy sat upright in his bed wearing only a pair of shorts and a sweat-stained t-shirt.

"Take your self-righteous crap and *go home.*"

Deciding to ignore him, Anna meandered around his room, stopping at the window to look out on the evening shadows. Turning back to him, she was determined to make something out of her visit, even if he was going to be rude.

"What are you doing in here all alone?" she asked.

"What's it look like I'm doing?"

"I'd say you're imitating a thankless smart-ass."

Billy flopped back on the bed.

"Why are you here? Are you feeling horny?"

Anna put her hands on her hips, frowned. "If it makes you

feel better to belittle me, go ahead."

"I don't get it. You thought I was fun in the bathhouse the other night, so why not today?"

Anna shook her head, refusing to give up ground. "Make fun of me if that helps. I know your father's injury was horrible. I know you feel terrible about it. I know…"

Billy's ears reddened. He sat up, full height, and poked his finger at Anna.

"You don't know beans. You weren't there. You didn't see his crushed leg. You didn't hear him begging for help."

Anna softened a bit at the obvious pain in Billy's voice. She sat lightly at the foot of his bed, her body not quite touching his. "I love you, Billy," she said.

"Great." Billy snorted. "But I'm not really in the mood right now, darlin'."

"This isn't you." I had to give Anna credit. She kept her voice even, calm. "But I still won't let you treat me this way. If you want to see me again, you need to decide if you can be civil. Your mother is sitting out there alone and you ignore her. She adores you. Don't you know she has feelings, too? Or are your feelings the only ones that matter? Are you dead set on just crawling into a hole somewhere and drowning yourself in self-pity?"

Pausing for a moment to catch her breath, Anna hoped she'd stirred some response from Billy. But he just sat there, smirking.

"I came over here tonight to see you and your mother in the hope of helping," Anna said. "My father thought you would appreciate my visit, since he knows how devastated you are by Jupie's injury."

"Ah, yes!" Billy laughed. "Your father. I wonder what he would think if he knew his little girl had been intimate with a jazz musician?"

"Stop right there, Billy—I'm leaving. And I won't be back until you decide to leave your insults in that hole—you know, the one where you can moan about how you're the only person to ever suffer a tragedy."

Turning on her heel, Anna stalked out of Billy's bedroom and slammed the door. As she stopped to dry the tears she had managed to hold back until now, she heard one last withering insult from Billy. While clapping his hands, he yelled at the top of his lungs: "Hey, Anna! Great performance. First place, for sure! You could be your own vaudeville act. People would come from miles around to admire your big boobs...oops, sorry if I offended you! Ha!"

###

In spite of Billy's insults—especially the last one, which outright crushed her—leaving his bedroom was almost impossible for Anna to do. Whether he chose to believe her or not, she loved him. But not like this.

Willa Mae was still sitting in the kitchen sipping stale tea when Anna returned. She looked up as Anna approached and nodded to her, as though she knew all about what had happened in the past twenty minutes. She stood, embraced Anna, and whispered the gypsy blessing, *"Baxt hai sastimos tiri patragi."*

Driving home, the lyrics of "Just When We're Falling in Love" taunted Anna: this anger and misunderstanding between her and Billy might just put an end to their romance before it had truly begun.

Chapter 25

<u>Saturday, September 17, 1955</u>

You'll recall that, as a GA, I have many resources to call on when necessary—including the gift of clairvoyance, which gives me the ability to perceive events in the near term beyond normal sensory capability. You'll also recall that GAs can "nudge" their wards or those close to them when the situation warrants it. Billy's emotional floundering in the wake of Jupie's accident was one such situation.

However, nudging someone toward self-transformation entails a delicate process. It can backfire—and in this case, could possibly end Billy's budding relationship with his beautiful Annabelle Lea, forever. Still, I'm confident that my colleagues would agree with me that, even though there is a risk involved with so-called "nudging," the potential positive outcome makes the risk bearable.

Given that, the customary method is for the GA to prompt his ward to intuit something in order to stimulate a desired action. I didn't rush into this, spending over a week watching Billy's caveman behavior of starving, sulking, and insulting everyone within earshot. Finally, I hit upon what I thought would be the perfect, albeit inelegant, plan. I believed I needed to nudge Billy to a higher resolve of forgiving himself for his culpability in Jupie's accident; this would be the stimulus needed to break his emotional logjam and soothe his sense of guilt. It would begin by delivering a sincere apology to his father, thus accepting responsibility for what he had done without vilifying himself for what ultimately amounted to simple human carelessness.

Watching him that Saturday morning—as he physically struggled to get out of bed—I saw the dark anxiety clouding his face. Fumbling with the covers, he wrenched back and covered his head with the bedspread. Writhing in angst, he mumbled: "She said I'm dying—how does she know? I didn't hurt him, an evil spirit hurt him?"

He shook his head, as if discarding Willa Mae's explanation. "Dear God," he choked, "I'm sorry I've sinned. Help me, Mother Mary...Willa Mae...Anna." His eyes widened. "Where's Anna?"

Suddenly resolute on finding Anna, Billy began to dress. He almost immediately lost his balance, falling against the dresser as he put one leg into his pants. Righting himself, he stumbled headlong into the nightstand, pushed off, and lurched his way through his bedroom door, through the living room and into the kitchen. Wobbling precariously and trying to clear his head, he washed his face at the kitchen sink and reeled back across the living room to the front door.

Opening it, he took in a deep breath. He floundered out the door, down the steps, and staggered toward Jupie's car.

At this point, I began to worry about Billy's well-being and my overly-zealous nudging. I never thought I would so willingly accept it, but there's that word *fate* again—and, as *fate* would have it, Billy collapsed on the front seat of Jupie's car before he could get the key in the ignition.

Sunday, September 18, 1955

"Well, kid, you took your good old time waking up. I'm off duty in ten minutes, so I might not be here when Dr. Lea comes in to check on you."

"Who..." Billy cleared his raspy throat. "Who are you? Where am I?"

"I'm your day nurse. You're in the hospital. Your mama found you passed out in your driveway and brought you here."

The nurse cranked Billy's bed up higher and handed him a glass of water as two men in white coats entered. As they approached, Billy's foggy brain recognized Dr. Lea's voice.

"Mr. Barnes—Billy—this is Dr. Devoe. You took a nasty fall. He's here to examine you for a possible concussion."

"Examine me? I'm...I feel fine."

"It will only take a few minutes," said Dr. Devoe.

Dr. Lea put his hand on Billy's arm.

"Your mother is with your father in the physical therapy lab. She'll bring him back here to be with you when he's finished with his treatment."

"My father...is staying here? In this same room?"

"Right here," said the nurse, "I'll bet you'll be glad to see him."

"Dr. Lea," Billy said. "How...how is he?"

"Your father is an amazing man. He has more courage than any five patients I've ever treated."

"His leg...what about walking..."

Suddenly the curtain between Billy's bed and the next flung open as his father's voice rang out.

"I am walking. I just took a stroll on a pair of crutches with a very cute nurse...and your mother."

As Willa Mae wheeled Jupie into the room, he tossed his leg covers aside, revealing the amputated limb. He nodded to Dr. Lea and pointed to his heavily bandaged stump.

"Now I know why they call the docs *sawbones*," Jupie quipped.

"I'll be going now," said Dr. Lea. "Meanwhile, Billy, Nurse Busch will remove your IVs. You're hydrated well enough for now. I'll be back after lunch to check in."

Dr. Lea turned to Willa Mae. "Before Nurse Busch goes off duty, she'll also help get your husband back in bed."

Nurse Busch helped Willa Mae get Jupie situated in bed while Dr. Devoe pronounced Billy sound, and then they both left the room. It was as if they didn't want to interfere in Billy's quandary over what to say to his parents, especially his father. My heart went out to Billy when a sudden onrush of guilt swept over him: all at once, he felt the weight of all that selfishness and self-pity. And Jupie's spirit—his buoyant coping, his joking—where was that in himself, Billy wondered? With no reason to harbor fear, he feared being there that moment, in his father's presence. What would he say? What *could* he say? Could he ask his forgiveness, or was it too late now? For what Billy had done, would God punish him by making his dreams of a successful jazz career dissolve in futility? Had he used up his welcome at home? Would Anna ever forgive him...?

A gentle, fatigued voice interrupted Billy's reverie.

"Billy," Jupie said. "If you're not going to talk to me, I'm going take a nap."

Free of the hydrating paraphernalia, Billy sat up, swung his legs out of bed, and reached for the privacy curtain. Pushing it aside, Billy inhaled sharply at the sight of his mother lying next to his father in the tiny hospital bed. That image only exacerbated his anxiety.

His eyes tearing, he stepped across the narrow space between their beds, bent down, and put his lips on his father's fevered forehead. His outing down the hospital corridor had clearly taken a toll on him.

Pain-filled and soaked with perspiration, Jupie turned to Billy and spoke in a halting, hushed, tone. "I'm glad you're here," he said. "Sorry I was so...I should have been more worried about your safety...and...I shouldn't have been so clumsy."

Billy clutched Jupie's hand. "It wasn't your fault. I...I..." Billy's eyes welled at the thought of his own negligence. "I should have been paying better attention."

For one of the few times in my tenure as a guardian angel, I felt a special glow of attachment to my ward's parentage which, normally, is incidental. But, with the help of *Penso Appositus*, I had become privy to Jupie's efforts to strengthen his bond with Billy—and this was at the heart of my growing affection for him. This was especially true when Jupie turned to Billy and said, "I tried to be the best father I could be, but I never really had a father of my own to show me how. He was killed in the Great War."

"Your father had to help his mother raise his brothers and little sister," added Willa Mae, stroking Jupie's cheek.

Jupie shrugged. "It's no excuse, but I'd like to think that having my old man around when I was your age, and younger—well, that it might have made me a better father to my own son."

I was impressed with Jupie's ability to admit his failings and provide context for them without *blaming* them for whatever missteps he may have taken as a father. In fact, this provided a fine model for how I hoped Billy might cope with his own feelings of responsibility over Jupie's accident.

Jupie squeezed Billy's hand and forced a pained smile. "You know I've... in a way, I've been very selfish about your piano playing. In fact, I've resented it. Now, I see that I've offended God by my selfishness...and I—"

"Dad. Please don't think that. I've been selfish, too, and I—"

"Don't give up your dream because of what's happened to me," Jupie interrupted. "Your mother knows a million gypsy proverbs. I like this one best: *God is good...and the Devil is not so bad to those whom he likes.*"

Love!

I don't want to get too far off track here, but I'm sure you've heard the tired adage—*it goes without saying*—which some writers and teachers lean on when their vocabulary abandons them. But, since I've brought it up, *it goes without saying* that *LOVE* has such a profound familial power that philosophers, saints, mystics, and poets have put in considerable effort pondering on it—in addition to such concepts as time, happiness, knowledge, God, and the meaning of life.

One of my favorite Indian philosophers is a Hindi named Kabir, whose writings influenced Hinduism's Bhakti movement. Many of his verses are found in Sikhism's scripture *Guru Granth Sahib*. My favorite quote: *Love does not grow on trees or bought in the market, but if one wants to be loved, one must first know how to give unconditional love.*

I couldn't say exactly how Jupie's accident triggered his family's outburst of profound filial love, but seeing the three of them sleeping in that cramped little hospital bed, I *can* say that Kabir's principle struck a resounding chord, one that very few of my past guardianships could match.

Reflecting on the moment, I barely heard Dr. Lea's voice addressing Billy: "Dr. Devoe has given you a clean bill of health," he said, standing at the open curtain. "Drink lots of fluids and take two aspirin twice a day. I don't want you to drive for two more days, so I've arranged a ride home for you. If you're ready to go, the driver is waiting for you at the main entrance. It's a green Ford station wagon."

Billy's parents were both asleep, so he left a note on Jupie's bedside table: *Love to you and Mom. Be back tomorrow. Billy.*

Though Billy's mood had swung from depressed to buoyant, he was totally unprepared to see Anna behind the wheel of her father's station wagon. The instant Billy stepped into the autumn sunlight, his thoughts ran together over what he could possibly say to make up for his unconscionable behavior toward her in his bedroom. Gripped by anxiety, Billy watched Anna back up and pull in front of the entrance, where he stood as though rooted in concrete sandals.

She rolled down the passenger side window, leaned over, and handed Billy a cold Dr. Pepper. I could read his thoughts: *Am I delusional? How can she be nice to me when I've been so horribly rude to her?*

"Dad said you should drink as much water and stuff as you can," she said. "Get in."

Dumbfounded, Billy backed away from the car.

"Hurry up and get in," she said, laughing. "I can't block the entrance all day."

Hesitating, Billy recalled how rude he'd been to Anna when she came to visit him just a few days ago.

"Billy, do you want me to pull over and park while you decide if you want me to take you home?"

"No, please, wait..." Billy opened the door and eased in. His mind a jumble, he tried to say something, but he couldn't speak. It was as though the words were glued to his tongue.

As Anna looked over her shoulder and turned the car toward the hospital exit, Billy tried to relax. But he could only purse his lips and exhale a long, slow breath. Turning left, they headed west on

Route 33 toward his parents' home on Indian Lake. It wasn't a long drive, but it would be an excruciating one unless Billy or Anna spoke up soon.

Finally, Anna broke the ice. "I know what you're thinking," she said. "You're thinking you need to say something clever, or apologize, or...whatever. Don't. I'll take you home and we can sit down and talk about how I can help you and your mother when Jupie gets home."

"You don't have to do that," Billy said, a hint of defensiveness creeping in to his voice. "We'll be fine, we just need—"

"Stop right there." Anna shook her head. "My dad says you are *not* fine—and, in fact, with Jupie getting out of the hospital soon, your lives are going to change dramatically."

In the back of his mind, of course, Billy recognized this. He thought back to the obvious pain on Jupie's face after just a brief stroll down the hospital corridor. He knew his father would need more help than Willa Mae or Billy alone could provide.

Anna went on. "You need me," she said, simply. "Or, well, you need *some*one, but why shouldn't it be someone who loves you and cares about your family?"

Billy was a little taken aback by that word, *love*. How could

Anna be so confident in her feelings for him after all that had happened between them in the past week?

"And, by the way," Anna added, "I know I don't *have* to do anything—I'm choosing to."

"But..." Billy frowned. "What about the way I treated you?"

"We don't need to talk about that. As far as I'm concerned, that's cold porridge."

Billy turned to her, shaking his head. "*You* may not need to talk about it, but *I* do. Anna, I feel like hell over the way I treated you last week. I have to...I mean, you have to *let* me..." He sighed. "Look, can you please pull over? There's a roadside picnic spot just ahead."

Slowly, silently, they eased off the highway, drifting to a stop under a weeping willow tree. Anna started to say something, but Billy reached over and touched his index finger to her lips.

"It's my turn to talk," he said. "I love you, too, but I regret being so selfish. I'm just trying to understand how this past week changed everything about my life, especially you—and what's going to happen now."

Anna smiled. "What's going to happen now is we're going to go to your house and I'm going to help you get organized and clean it up before your dear, sweet mother comes home."

"Do you think we'll ever—"

"We can do anything we want," Anna said. "By the way, I think your band is home from their road trip. I saw Dukie park the tour bus behind the church. I suppose you'll have to check in with him sooner or later."

"Man, I haven't thought about the band in...well, not since the day of Jupie's accident." Billy bit back the lingering feelings of guilt he had over his own distraction on that fateful day. "I'm not sure I'm going to be able to keep the band together."

"It's probably too soon to say."

"Maybe. It's just—with Jupie being so badly crippled...well, frankly, we don't have any savings. My parents depend on Jupie's job and the barbecue tent for their livelihood. There's no one but me now, and Willa Mae, to support us."

"And you're worried you won't be able to do it on a jazz musician's salary."

"Something like that." Billy shrugged. "I know most of what Jupie does at the park, so I can be ready in the spring to help him do what he can do, and follow his guidance on the rest. And Willa Mae knows everything about Jupie's barbecue tent—it's all her recipes. I'm sure she can run it, and I can help her, too. It's my..."

"Responsibility," Anna said. She touched her fingers to Billy's cheek. "I know what you mean."

Billy put his hand over Anna's on his face. "I owe it to both of them," he said.

And with that, Anna eased the station wagon out of the roadside park toward the highway and drove Billy home.

At home, Billy and Anna worked side-by-side to the music from his stack of 45-rpm records. The silence between them was composed of a most potent concoction of love, desire, trust, and allegiance. The more Billy watched Anna—her graceful movements, her giving of herself—the more he felt as though he could never again stand being separated from her.

When a GA has been with their ward long enough, there's rarely a doubt about the sentiments flooding his or her mind. In Billy's case, to me, there was no question about his feelings for Anna. He wanted her to be his forever.

As that thought consumed him, the song Billy had first taught Anna in anticipation of the Lakeview Country Club New Year's Eve Party, "Skylark," began to play—the Dinah Shore version. Billy didn't expect Anna to notice, but she came over to where he was vacuuming around the sofa. She put her arms around him and, to his complete surprise, sang softly in his ear:

Skylark...

Have you anything to say to me?

Won't you tell me where my love can be?

Is there a meadow in the mist

Where someone's waiting to be kissed?

Skylark...

Have you seen a valley green with spring

Where my heart can go a-journeying

Over the shadows and the rain

To a blossom-covered lane?

And in your lonely flight

Haven't you heard the music in the night?

Wonderful music, faint as a will o' the wisp

Crazy as a loon

Sad as a gypsy serenading the moon.

Anna embraced Billy tenderly, smothering him with affection as she sang the last verse in unison with Dinah:

Oh, Skylark

I don't know if you can find these things

But my heart is riding on your wings

So if you see them anywhere

Won't you lead me there?

As Billy lifted her head and kissed her passionately, a sharp knocking startled them both. Anna pulled away and stepped to the front door, opening it to reveal Dukie Kincaid.

"I won't stay long," Dukie said in a somber tone. "Heard from Willa Mae what happened to Jupie. I'm so sorry, Billy."

Billy motioned for Dukie to join him on the living room couch. "Thanks, Dukie, I appreciate it. What's up?"

"I just wanted to give you some news from the road trip."

"How did things go?" Billy asked.

"Mostly great," Dukie said. "Until we wrapped up at Mr. Kelly's."

"What? Who screwed up?"

"No one screwed up." Dukie shrugged. "At least not playin.

Jack played the best guitar he's ever played. Even Chet Baker

impressed. He invited Jack backstage to jam after hours."

"Sounds like a good time to me," Billy said.

Dukie stood, paced, and then flopped down in Jupie's easy-chair, covering his eyes and shaking his head.

Anna and Billy exchanged puzzled frowns.

"What...what happened?" Billy asked a second time.

Dukie leaned back. He looked up, as though pleading for help, then turned to Billy. "The next morning, I found a note from Jack under the wiper blade on the bus windshield. Just four words: *I'm staying in Chicago.* It hit me pretty hard. I know Jack was on dope, but I wasn't expecting this."

Billy shook his head. "I know he's been mixed up with one of Johnny Mocha's bags since we played the Spinnaker Room. I tried to convince him to see a doctor about it—like you did, for booze. I wanted him to see Anna's father, in fact. But, when I brought it up, Jack just blew it off like I was out of my mind."

"Billy," Anna said. "I had no idea."

"Me neither," said Dukie. "Your heart was in the right place, kid."

Billy waved off the platitude. "Anyway, Dukie, what happened in Chicago?"

"Chet Baker's piano man—Elmo Hope, old friend of mine— gave me the scoop. Believe me, Billy, Elmo knows the drug scene. Tells me Jack was doing LSD."

Billy rocked back on the sofa and drew a deep breath. "LSD? You're kidding. Really? Where would Jack get that stuff?"

Dukie wrinkled his brow, contorted his lips into a sarcastic frown. "Where did he get it? Billy! Where does the Pope get holy water? It's Chicago, man. Help yourself."

Dumbstruck, Billy sat there like a stone. He couldn't believe what had happened over the past few weeks—it felt as if bad news had been specially bundled and delivered to him by the god of triple whammy.

Dukie left soon after, with apologies and promises to find a replacement guitarist. His dispiriting visit left Anna and Billy in a state of shock. She kissed Billy gently, then turned for the door where her car keys hung on a hook. She grabbed them, opened the door, then turned back to Billy.

"I'll pick you up tomorrow morning for the hospital," she said.

"You sure you can't stay the night?" Billy said, with a weak grin, trying to lighten the mood.

Anna smiled at him softly. "Your steady girlfriend will be here at nine," she said, "so be ready."

Chapter 26

Over my centuries as a guardian angel sharing experiences with my compatriots, I can assure you that, as a group, one thing remains constant: We are able to easily notice and understand things that are not obvious. The word for this wherewithal is *perspicacity*. Here's an example of its usage: A perspicacious child can't be fooled when his parents try to keep a secret by talking in a foreign language or Pig Latin; a perspicacious lover knows when he or she is being intentionally misled to spare him or her embarrassment. Angst often follows, and blues songs are written to placate the troubled heart. You can get a better idea of what I'm saying by listening to the song "Dust My Broom" by Mississippi Delta blues singer Robert Johnson. The song was recorded by him in 1936—coincidently, the same year Billy Barnes was conceived. The lyrics tell a familiar story about troubles between men and women...

Where am I going with this thought?

Despite my many assignments, I've had very little experience with the brutal realities of limb amputation. And while frustration is not a situation GAs are drilled on by God the Son, it is part and parcel of "nudging" a ward into more productive emotions. In the case of the Barnes family, I hoped to grant them patience and calm during Jupie's long recovery.

And I did my own research, as well. Much has been written about limb amputation, and most of it is about physical pain—not the accompanying psychological trauma. Often during the period of recovery, people reach a plateau or find that when the enormity of the amputation sinks in, they suffer delayed shock or anxiety to varying degrees. In other words, even if the first few days following a limb amputation see the patient and his family in relatively good spirits, there is no guarantee the tide won't turn later on.

This was unfortunately the case with Jupie. In the days leading up to his discharge from the hospital—after nearly four weeks of recovery—his mood turned dark and full of angst. I happened to be present in the room on the day Dr. Lea visited Jupie in his hospital bed. It was the afternoon he was to return home; I was the sunlight peeking through half-open blinds.

"Mr. Barnes," Dr. Lea began, "I don't want to intrude, but might we visit a while before Willa Mae and Billy come to take you home?"

His gaze fixed out the window on the hospital parking lot below, Jupie acted as if he hadn't heard the doctor's request,

Pausing politely, Dr. Lea repeated, "Mr. Barnes, may I please—"

"I heard you," rasped Jupie. "As far as I'm concerned, everything's been said that's worth saying."

"Yes, but we're talking man-to-man now, so maybe I can—"

"My leg's gone, doc." Jupie's voice grew louder. "You're the one sawed it off, as I recall. What more is there to say?"

Dr. Lea reached out and touched Jupie's still heavily-bandaged stump. "Mr. Barnes—Jupie. You know I lost my wife many years ago, when my Annabelle was still a little girl."

"Oh," said Jupie, if not sympathetic then at least a hair abashed. "Billy never mentioned that."

Dr. Lea released a shaky breath. "I was so afraid, in those weeks after she died. I was afraid I'd never be enough—of a man, of a *father*—to keep Anna—to keep our home, and our life—*safe*."

Jupie said nothing. I could tell, though—much like that night all those years ago when he first met Willa Mae, recounting his father's sacrifice in World War I—that there were tears building behind his eyes, in his throat. Only time would tell if they would actually fall.

"I'm not saying I know what it's like to lose a leg," said Dr. Lea. "But I do know what it's like to feel as if you no longer measure up as a man—as a husband. As a father."

Jupie cleared his throat. His voice cracked only slightly when he said, "That assumes a fella's ever measured up at *all* on that score."

Dr. Lea flashed the smallest of smiles. "None of that, Mr. Barnes—*Jupie*. I've had the pleasure of knowing your son Billy for several years now, and he's a fine young man. You won't convince me that's an accident—I'm certain it has everything to do with the way you raised him."

"That's very true," said Willa Mae, now standing in the doorway.

Jupie wiped at his cheeks swiftly, embarrassed. "You're early," he said.

Willa Mae took a few steps into the room. "Don't worry, my love—Billy's down in the car. I won't say a word—and I wouldn't have to. He already knows how strong—how loving—you are."

"Good talk, Jupie." Dr. Lea gave Jupie a pat on the shoulder as he stood from his seat. "And listen to your wife," he said. "She's a wise woman."

###

At home, the days following Jupie's discharge from the hospital were difficult, but also full of true devotion and affection. Jupie made a point of thanking Billy when he helped move him in and out of his wheelchair, of telling Willa Mae he loved her as she fixed him breakfast each morning. Willa Mae and Jupie welcomed Anna into their home and expressed their gratitude each time she offered to take her car on an errand to pick up a carton of milk or a refill of Jupie's medication. And, of course, Billy took every opportunity to remind Anna of his love for her, to whisper a verse of a song in her ear or to kiss her softly on the cheek whenever they passed each other in the house.

With all that in mind, I was surprised that Billy's marriage proposal to Anna was anything but flowery. (If he had his way, their vows would be exchanged in the bathhouse where they first made love!) In fact, I would say his marriage proposal took a page from *A Working Man's Guide to Ho-Hum Betrothals*, as in: "Anna...what about us getting married?"

See what I mean? No *please*s, no *honey bunche*s, no *lamby-pie*s, no *macushla*s, and no *sugar bun*s.

Still, I was not at *all* surprised when Anna agreed to marry Billy by the end of 1955. Consequently, Billy promised to return to his music by the spring of 1956, when Jupie would be well enough to work part time with Billy's help—at least until the summer big band season at Stardust Ballroom and Moonlight Gardens, and the reopening of the Golden Ruhl.

Wednesday, October 5, 1955

I first learned of Ivey-Joe Priest after Billy and Albert posted flyers all over Danceland—plus marinas, parking lots, telephone poles, and payphone booths throughout Russells Point—announcing auditions for the Swing Kings' guitarist slot left vacant by the delinquent Jack Roush:

GUITARIST WANTED

Audition Saturday, October 15, 1:00 P.M. – St. Mary's Parish Hall

Immediate Opening for Talented Musician

Swing Kings Septet (Jazz–Blues–Swing)

By way of *Penso Appositus,* I learned that Ivey-Joe was born in Cincinnati, Ohio. Both parents played instruments, and Ivey-Joe began playing guitar at the age of twelve. At age fifteen, he won the annual WNOP Jazz-On-Fountain-Square radio contest, playing a memorable rendition of "My Funny Valentine," and was awarded a three-day gig with Benny Carter at the Beverley Hills Supper Club in Newport, Kentucky.

To say that Ivey-Joe had been deprived of a solid grounding in jazz performance, composition, ensemble arranging, and Kenny Burrell blues-style improvisations—*à la* T-Bone Walker and Blind Boy Fuller—would be like saying that Duke Ellington couldn't find middle-C on the piano.

By age twenty, Ivey-Joe had soloed with the Cincinnati Symphony, taught third-year music majors at the University of Cincinnati, and assisted various jazz guitarists in a series of master classes held at Central State University in Wilberforce, Ohio. It was there that Ivey-Joe met and married his sweetheart, Lola Brown, who eventually whisked him away to Russells Point, Ohio, where she had been hired by Sr. Maria Theresa Parks, O.P., to teach English, arithmetic, social studies, and hygiene to St. Mary's of the Woods's seventh and eighth graders.

The news of Ivey-Joe's successful audition for the Swing Kings' guitar job took up half of the *Indian Lake Weekly*'s back page, along with pictures of Lola and Sr. Theresa posing with Fr. Stenz, and Ivey-Joe posing with Billy in front of Jupie's—pictured sitting on a stool playing his Gibson L-5CES Electric Archtop guitar.

The other half of the weekly's back page announced a special attraction: The Swing Kings would play a fundraiser concert—for the benefit of Jupie Barnes's medical debts—in Jupie's barbecue tent, Sunday afternoon, October thirtieth.

At this point, there isn't any reason not to give credit where credit is due: it was Juliette and Anna, along with Willa Mae and Billy—working behind the scenes with Bernard Sweeney, chairman of the Sandy Beach Businessmen's Association—who devised this fundraiser. The goal: to prevent Jupie from feeling as though his injury had incapacitated him to the point that he wasn't capable of handling his indebtedness on his own. In my experience as a GA, I can't tell you how counterproductive self-pity is to a person's recovery. By celebrating Jupie's contributions to the park instead of lamenting his new limitations, this fundraiser was meant to elevate Jupie's spirits as much as possible.

As presented to Jupie by Mr. Sweeney, the fundraiser promised to be quite the spectacle. The ladies' arm of the Association would judge a children's Halloween costume competition and Billy's Swing Kings would provide the music for listening and dancing. Everyone in the community was invited to attend, provided they made a reservation, paid five dollars admission at the door, and pitched in by agreeing to bring a covered dish of a salad, vegetable, or dessert to complement Jupie's barbecued ribs, courtesy of the Knights of Columbus.

Ostensibly—and I mention this now only because of how profoundly this particular part of the plan was ultimately soured—the Halloween concert and fundraiser would also introduce Ivey-Joe and Lola to the Indian Lake community.

Saturday, October 22, 1955

Loving Anna was one thing, but I could see the differences between her and Billy's religious biases coming to a head when Anna insisted that they get married at her father's church—the Church of the Loving Brotherhood. When Billy pushed for an answer as to *why*, Anna repeated what her father had said: "Marrying a Catholic is very complicated. You'll have a lot of rules to explain to your kids."

Anna insisted that Billy accompany her to a prenuptial counseling session with the Loving Brotherhood rector, the Reverend Chester C. Chester. The meeting took place on a beautiful Indian summer day. The title of the counselling session: *The Role of Intimacy in Marriage.*

Arriving on the stroke of ten that Saturday, the Reverend Chester—a jowly man in his sixties, bald as an egg with mutton chop sideburns that tapered down to a scruffy goatee—met them at the door. He wore a white clerical collar, a purple vest, and a burgundy satin stole draped around his neck and resting on his bulbous stomach. He welcomed Billy and Anna into his study, a small but nicely-appointed room adjacent to the narthex of the church. After declining the good reverend's offer of coffee and frosted cookies, Billy announced their intended wedding date: "We would like to be married on Christmas Eve."

Stroking his beard, the Reverend considered, consulted a leather-bound calendar, drummed his fingers on the desk, puffed out his cheeks, and exhaled. "Christmas Eve is a no-no," he said. "We can't interfere with our holy Savior's birthday party."

Amid the silence of Billy and Anna's disappointment, the rector perked up and said, "Now, if I were you—silly to say—but with my demanding schedule, I'd jump on my ten o'clock morning date of Saturday, December thirty-first. Would that be simpatico?"

After twenty minutes of tedious discourse on everything from parking restrictions on the Loving Brotherhood's postage-stamp size lot, to proper etiquette for family and guests to observe during the ceremony—*No talking!*—the rector glanced at Billy, then turned a wry smile on Anna.

"Now tell me, Miss Lea—have you been living a chaste Christian life?"

I could see Anna's face flush as she started to reply, but Billy jumped in. "Reverend Chester, Anna and I aren't living together and we haven't engaged in premarital sex, if that's what you're asking."

A lie, of course, but one I was willing to grant Billy in this particular instance. As an emissary of God the Son, I might be expected to demonstrate a surplus of reverence for any man or woman of the cloth. But Reverend Chester's sanctimoniousness rubbed me the wrong way—I couldn't blame Billy and Anna for being bothered.

As Anna squirmed in annoyance, the good reverend continued. "Matters of marital coupling have to be discussed." He paused, then said, "Mr. Barnes are you aware of the role of the man's penis in marriage?"

Billy did his best to maintain a straight face. "As far as I know, Reverend, the role of his penis is to make itself happy."

Reverend Chester frowned, sighing deeply.

"Mr. Barnes, at the risk of sounding bourgeois, it's my duty to inform you that the role of your penis is *not* to make itself *happy,* as it were, but rather to procreate. As in populating our earth. Am I clear?"

"Very!" Billy folded his hands in his lap. "I'll keep that in mind."

Furrowing his brow, the Reverend turned to Anna.

"Now, Miss Lea. I'm sure you have several questions. But, to get the proverbial ball rolling, tell me about your sexual knowledge. Other than your monthly menses, are you aware of your vagina's function?"

Where is this going? I thought.

"No." Anna grinned. "Perhaps you should explain it."

The reverend beamed. "I appreciate your candor. As your conjugal activities evolve, it's very likely that one day you'll discover that the Holy Spirit has visited you and your husband, because your monthly menses will cease and you'll discover that you are bearing the fruits of connubial bliss. In plain English, as it were: you'll be pregnant. Do you understand?"

"Oh yes, Reverend. I read all about that in health class."

"Very good." The reverend cleared his throat. "Now, for the question regarding your vagina. It provides the passageway for your baby to emerge into God's light of day. From that point forward, your vagina should rest after being stressed. I would suggest that you and your husband"—Reverend Chester nodded to Billy, then back to Anna—"abstain from relations for a period of at least six months."

"Six months?" Anna said, plaintively.

"Remember: lust has no place in our modern Christian world."

Barely able to keep a straight face, Anna said, "Thank you, Reverend Chester, for your insights and valuable advice. We appreciate your time."

As Billy stood and motioned for Anna to follow him, the rector said, "By all means. Now, if either of you have any questions at all, don't hesitate to contact me."

As Billy shook the rector's hand, Anna couldn't resist his offer. "Reverend," she said, "it's very embarrassing for me to ask, but...what if Billy's penis is too large for me?"

Billy guffawed, then quickly covered it up with a cough.

Grinning, the rector replied, "A very important question. Let me know if that's the case and I'll be glad to recommend an experienced gynecologist. They have things that will enlarge you enough so that you'll be comfortable."

On their way to pick up cookies and coffee to take home to Jupie and Willa Mae, Billy put his fingers to his lips, kissed them, reached over, and touched Anna's cheek as he said, "If we stop by your father's on the way to my house, will it take you long to pack?"

"Where are we going?"

I had to admit, Billy's idea was brilliant. He and Anna would be married on Dreamland Bridge a week hence—the day before Jupie's Halloween fundraiser. His grandfather Yoska would perform the ceremony, which would be attended only by a handful of close friends and family: Willa Mae, Jupie, Dr. Lea, Juliette, Albert, Helen, and Dukie Kincaid. It would be the perfect prelude to the fundraiser, and a great way of keeping Jupie's mind preoccupied with joy—and therefore *off* the topic of his missing leg—for an entire weekend.

"Does that sound okay to you?" Billy asked, after unveiling his plan to Anna. And though it truly was more than okay with Anna, she could not resolve a few unanswered questions, most notably: "When we get married, what will we live on—and where will we live?"

"You know that Karl Ruhl hired me to manage his bar," said Billy. "The apartment in back is mine as long as I work for him."

"What about playing piano—with the new guitarist, won't the Swing Kings start booking performances soon?"

"Every summer weekend at the Ruhl starting Memorial Day. Meanwhile, I'll get back with Dukie and Johnny Mocha to book a couple of road trips for the fall and winter."

"I won't stay home if you go on tour," said Anna.

"Of course not," replied Billy. "You'll be travelling with the band as my wife—and, more importantly, our featured vocalist."

Saturday, October 29, 1955

I can only say that all went according to Billy's somewhat impulsive wedding plan. Annabelle's father beamed—Juliette, too—as they escorted Anna up the east ramp of Dreamland Bridge while Albert and Helen led Billy up the west ramp. Their marches were accompanied by Yoska on concertina and Willa Mae on violin. When Billy and Anna met in the middle, the strains of Pachelbel's "Canon in D" sounded throughout Sandy Beach Amusement Park as though performed on Padua's largest pipe organ by Bohuslav Matěj Černohorský, putting me in mind of when I was the guardian angel for František Xaver Brixi, the son of Šimon Brixi.

So, with nothing more than a marriage license, good will,

good weather, and good friends, Yoska Stanley pronounced Mr. Billy Barnes and Miss Annabelle Lea husband and wife, henceforth known as Mr. and Mrs. Willis "Billy" Barnes.

Despite forecasts of clear skies, autumn rain eventually drove the wedding party into Jupie's barbecue tent, where a feast awaited them that would rival the culinary talents of St. Hildegard—my favorite mystic nun. Hildegard was a German Benedictine abbess and a true Renaissance woman who dabbled in the arts and languages, philosophy, music—and, most relevant to the current discussion, fine cooking and baking.

In another time, she would have created Billy and Anna's wedding feast. As it was, the dinner was exceptionally elegant: Turkish chicken, Hungarian goulash, gruyere biscuits, wine punch, salmon with avocado, leek and watercress pudding, mojo lamb chops with pineapple-mint salsa, and double duck tourtière. These were topped with Willa Mae's homemade three-tier plum wedding cake, laced with Yoska's homemade *țuică*, *pălincă*—a strong aromatic alcoholic beverage made of distilled fermented plum juice and equal amounts pear and apricot liqueur—and complemented by Yoska's second homemade specialty, *Eirelikör*, a rich, creamy German egg liqueur, to be downed in one gulp from a standing position by snatching a filled shot glass off the table surface with one's mouth, and, head tilted back, downing the liquid and—not using one's hand— spitting the glass into a waste receptacle while shouting, "*Naz-drah vi!*"

One highlight of the gypsy wedding tradition—and to a single young woman's delight—was the successful pilfering of one of the bride's shoes. This honor—rightly so, in my mind—went to Helen, who brandished Anna's left shoe in Albert's face as if it were a court summons.

Capping off the ceremony, Dukie Kincaid surprised everyone by playing and singing Oscar Levant's super sentimental composition, "Blame It on My Youth"—a fitting close to Billy and Anna's special day.

Chapter 27

I didn't need a crystal ball to foretell one possible outcome to Jupie's fundraiser celebration. My intuition told me that Red Suggins's mentality was a custom-made wrecking-ball for befouling this cordial and friendly community occasion with the smut of racism, for which he was the self-appointed *Guardian Devil in Charge*.

Along with seven other racist townsfolk, Red Suggins protested the introduction of Ivey-Joe in Jupie's tent with placards that advertised such heinous vitriol as UNCLE TOM IS DEAD and NIGGERS GO HOME. As if the hate scrawled on the signs wasn't enough, Suggins and his gang shouted these same slogans at the top of their lungs as Ivey-Joe and his wife, Lola, joined Billy and his all-white Swing Kings on the bandstand.

Officer Joe Kuldau must have shared my instincts, for I noted his "on-duty" expression at what was nominally a social event: he was clearly suspicious that something might happen to foul up the proceedings. And, sure enough, midway through the fundraiser, a gunshot sounded from behind Jupie's tent, dispersing nearly half the crowd. Kuldau sprung in to action, promptly exiting the tent in the direction of the gunfire. Within minutes, he returned with a solemn frown, took the microphone, and assured the remaining party attendees that the gunshot was fired by a prankster, who was seen scampering over the Dreamland Bridge to disappear from sight.

Of course, there was little consolation to be found in this announcement, and I could sense that the remainder of the guests were unmoved by Kuldau's speech. Folks continued to disperse from the area surrounding Jupie's barbecue tent, and the crowd thinned away to nearly nothing.

Still, in a fine testament to the town's fondness for Jupie, Red Suggins and his racist attempts at violence couldn't put a total damper on things. To beat the rain, the remaining crowd moved inside, sampling Jupie's fare and listening to the Swing Kings' musical tribute to the man. A sense of anticipation ran through the crowd as Billy introduced Ivey-Joe and Lola.

"Ladies and gentlemen, I'm privileged to announce the recent addition"—Billy gestured to Ivey-Joe and Lola—"to the Swing Kings' ensemble: Mr. Ivey-Joe Priest, and his fabulous young bride, Lola, who will entertain us with their musical talents and tasty renditions of a few jazz classics. I'll let Ivey-Joe be his own emcee."

His arm around Lola, Ivey-Joe nudged her ahead of him, where Billy shoved the microphone into her hand. Looking surprised but happy, Lola held the mike to her mouth and said, "Hey y'all. Back in Cincinnati, I had fun singing at a place called The Casbah, famous for its 'Black Pearl'—a deadly concoction of two rums, pineapple juice, and apricot nectar, all garnished with an orchid petal. It was a cozy, romantic hideaway on the lower level of a big downtown hotel, the Terrace Plaza. Back then—before sweet Ivey-Joe caught my eye—they called me 'Downtown-Lola-Brown.'

"When Ivey-Joe found out I had a decent set of lungs"—Lola smirked and rubbed her right index finger over her left index finger in the traditional *shame-on-you* sign—"I'm referring to my vocal cords—he goaded me into singing a lot of songs he loved, featuring himself on guitar. I asked him one day if I was singing for him, or was he playing that *gih-tar* for me?"

Lola paused, pulled Ivey-Joe close to her, and continued. "Guess what his answer was?" Lola shuffled her feet as her audience whispered humorous conjectures among themselves. "He said, 'Girl, if I didn't know better, I'd swear you want to marry me.'"

As the crowd chuckled, Ivey-Joe took the microphone and said, "If Lola is finished fooling around"—he grinned at his blushing bride—"we'd like to entertain you with three of our favorite duets: 'My Funny Valentine,' 'Where or When,' and 'How Are Things in Glocca Morra?'"

Ivey-Joe's subtle arrangements—blending Lola's sulky voice with his intricate chord voicings, inversions, extensions, and counterpoint fills—captured my attention to the point that I wished Jack Roush well, but applauded Ivey-Joe's gifted complement to the Swing Kings.

I have to say that Ivey-Joe and Lola captivated the crowd that afternoon at Jupie's fundraiser. Still, I couldn't shake the image of Red Suggins and his band of degenerates almost scuttling the whole event. I was plenty heartened though, when——at the end of the day—Juliette, Anna, Willa Mae, and Billy presented Jupie with a brown paper bag filled with bills and coins.

"Don't count it now," said Willa Mae. "But don't lose the six hundred seventy-five dollars in that poke you're holdin'."

Jupie bowed his head in joyful gratitude. And this time, he was not embarrassed to let his son—nor the rest of his wonderful extended family—see him cry tears of joy.

###

Friday, July 7, 1961

I can't get that October day in 1955 out of my mind. After Jupie's fundraiser had wrapped up, Officer Kuldau—recently elevated to Assistant Chief of Police—grabbed hold of Bernard Sweeney to pick his brain on something. Kuldau disclosed that he had found a spent .357 magnum shell on the ground next to the boardwalk path.

Sweeney held the shell between his thumb and index finger. He nodded. "I've never seen it myself, but I've heard Red Suggins bragging about his .357 magnum before."

Suggins was never taken to task for the events of October 30th, 1955—Kuldau had insufficient evidence to pursue the matter further, there being no public record of a permit for a .357 magnum to anyone in Indian Lake, whether Red Suggins or another of his racist cronies, and Bud Sweeney's word not being enough to justify pressing formal charges.

Which brings me back to the most recent shooting at Indian Lake—the one that took Billy's life. The ballistics report still hasn't come in, but I wonder if the gun that killed Billy might just be the same gun that fired the shot outside Jupie's barbecue tent all those years ago—whether it belonged to Red Suggins or another powerful person on Indian Lake.

I sense Anna harbors similar suspicions. This morning, I am following her around the home she shared with Billy in what turned out to be the final few years of their marriage. After a limited breakfast of tea and half an English muffin, Anna walks into the bedroom and pulls a photo album from a box in the back corner of the closet. I can see from the handwritten note on the cover that this particular album spans the years 1955 to 1956—that is, the "honeymoon period" of Anna and Billy's marriage. She flips through pages until she lights on the spread she must have been looking for all along: Jupie's Halloween fundraiser. I remember Helen Gordon walking around that day, snapping pictures, wanting to chronicle the happy day.

I watch from over Anna's shoulder as she traces a loose path with her forefinger from one photo to the next. Here is a portrait of Jupie, Willa Mae, Anna, and Billy in front of the barbecue tent; next to that, a candid shot of Ivey-Joe and Lola Priest feeding just a bit of Jupie's famous barbecue to their young son, James. I watch Anna's jaw tighten at these happy memories, her mouth set in firm resolve not to cry at the thought of how horribly things have soured.

She snaps shut the album and closes her eyes. At first, I think she has surrendered herself to the inevitability of tears, but as quickly as they closed her eyes fly open again and she goes back to the closet.

From the same box where she'd taken the photo album, she pulls a tattered white envelope: the photo negatives from Jupie's fundraiser. The details in these darkened images are a bit harder for me to make out, but Anna seems to know exactly what she's looking for.

"Suggins," she mutters, squinting hard, reciting just as much from memory as from the silhouettes she can make out in the film "Farmer. Stevens. Murphy. Plank. Drummond. Keating. Johnson."

That makes eight—the cadre of racist protestors at Jupie's fundraiser. Helen wisely chose not to develop any photos of these godless men, but apparently couldn't resist the urge to capture the spectacle on film.

And, in so doing, she has given Anna—and myself—a handy supplemental suspect list for Billy's murder.

Chapter 28

Friday, January 6, 1956

It's uncanny. Until Billy and Anna's marriage, I'd had mixed feelings about Billy's friend Albert Martin. At first, I saw him as an immature little wisenheimer who was too smart for his own good. But, after years of observation, I've decided that my initial concerns about Albert's character flaws were misguided; his less-than-stellar attributes were simply the understandable failings of an immature young man who'd lacked the proper male parenting in a time when both bad and good habits are formed.

Eugène François's lackluster parenting aside, I was beyond pleased when Albert convinced his father to contract with Billy for regular off-season weekend appearances in the newly-remodeled Café des Amis lounge. The gig would begin in January and carry over to the reopening of the Ruhl on Memorial Day. Due to space restrictions, only a trio (Billy, Albert, and Ivey-Joe) and a vocalist (the newly-minted Annabelle Barnes) would play these shows.

(And here, I'll mention my surprise when Ivey-Joe asked Lola if she would sit in at the Café des Amis as a backup vocalist to

Anna. Lola's unequivocal answer left little room for negotiation: "If you want to hear me sing, you'll find me and our baby boy at Bountiful AME Church every Sunday morning. Pastor Sanders always asks about you!")

Upon returning from their brief honeymoon, Billy coached Anna to learn a few new songs in preparation for the upcoming gigs at Café des Amis. Annabelle kicked off Billy's downsized Swing Kings' performance with a rendition of "Darling, Je Vous Aime Beaucoup" so good that she might be confused for the composer herself, Anna Sosenko, performing it in a Paris bistro in 1935.

Three weekends in a row, the crowds filled the Café's lounge—all of them eager to hear what Annabelle Barnes would belt out next. Though Anna was proud of the work she did with the band, she also found it exhausting—not loving it as deeply as Billy and his bandmates, and therefore not as blindly committed to the task as they were. Accordingly, she requested a break after those first three madcap weekends.

Albert arranged for Lola Brown to sit in for Anna—despite her earlier, cheeky protestations to Ivey-Joe. With the help of a small leaflet distributed at the checkout counter of Lew Cost's IGA Grocery, the Swing Kings and guest vocalist Lola Brown invited everyone to *An Evening of Billie Holiday's Blues*, three nights' worth of performances in the final weekend of January.

Sunday, January 29, 1956

With everything seemingly lined up for the continuing success of the Café des Amis lounge gig, I have to say that the events on the final night of the *Holiday Blues* weekend were quite a jolt. After the first two sets played to standing room only, the third—and most popular—later set began with Lola singing "Tell Me More and Then Some." Just seconds into the second verse, inspired by a particular lyric, a raucous voice from the crowd bellowed, "You and your Black Sambo husband made a *real* mistake movin' to these parts, you silly bitch!"

In an instant, Billy descended the bandstand and collared Woody Plank—a thirtyish numbers runner with Angelo-B's crew and muscle-man/driver for Red Suggins—as he tried to escape through the shocked crowd. "Plank!" Billy yelled. "If I ever see you here again, you'll be sorry!"

As the crowd applauded Billy, Plank disappeared, not to be seen any more that night.

###

Friday, March 16, 1956

Jupie's first fundraiser had earned only about half the money they'd set out to make, courtesy of Red Suggins and his racist gang (including that numbskull Woody Plank) scaring a large portion of the crowd away. Thankfully, Billy and Anna's share of proceeds from the regular winter gigs at Café des Amis had put a modest dent in Jupie's medical bills.

Still, Jupie would be without work for several more months, and he and Willa Mae were struggling to stay whole financially. With this in mind, Anna and Juliette Barlow suggested a second fundraising effort that spring: the town would dedicate its annual May Day parade to Jupie and take up a collection to pay off his remaining debts. Included in this proposal was a stipulation that a small sum of money raised from Jupie's parade would go to Eugène François Martin, as modest compensation for providing Billy and his band with winter work. Of course, neither Anna nor Juliette knew how badly Eugène François needed the money, still owing quite a bundle to Little Angelo-B and his friend, Whitey...but I'm getting ahead of myself.

It was an ingenious plan that could very well settle Jupie's debts once and for all—provided Anna and Juliette could secure the approval of the mayor of Russells Point, Bunny-Sue Macrath.

At ten o'clock on that lionesque Friday morning, Mayor Macrath fixed herself a cup of viscous black liquid from her paper-cone pour-through coffeemaker, held up two stained-but-mostly-clean cups, and turned to her guests, Annabelle Lea and Juliette Barlow.

"How d'ya like your mud, ladies?"

"Mud? Oh, black is fine," Juliette said.

"None for me," said Anna.

Mayor Macrath plopped down a cracked ceramic mug in front of Juliette. A scratchy rendering of Russells Point City Hall reigned over the caption *Acta Non Verba!*

"Thanks for coming," Mayor Macrath said. "Hard to get anyone to volunteer for anything these days."

She paused, glanced from Juliette to Anna, sipped her odious black brew, looked over the cup rim, and said, "Now, which one of you two is the main flea on this parade dog?"

"Juliette and I have already discussed several ideas," Anna said, nodding to Juliette.

"Alright, Miss Anna," said the mayor. "I been over this ground a few times but I'm open to any fresh ideas. Whaddya thinkin'?"

Taking a deep breath, Anna glanced at her parade notes. Talking face-to face with the mayor was different from asking people *How do you feel?* when they departed her father's medical office.

"I...I was hoping...if you're not too busy..."

"Ya know the history of May Day?" Mayor Macrath interrupted.

Flustered, Anna paused, considered. "I...it's about May...and flowers...a Roman goddess and..."

"Goddess's name was *Maia*. People say the name stands for *elders*—word *June* means *youngsters*." Mayor Macrath bobbed her head and continued. "And it usually doesn't happen on May first. Like this year, May first is on a Tuesday. That means Saturday, April twenty-eighth, is our May Day parade."

"Why won't Sunday work? asked Juliette.

Mayor Macrath leaned forward and smirked.

"You been here as long as me, you learn a thing or two about Sundays. I call it the 'Ain't No Way' day." Mayor Macrath's face spread into a wry smile as she said, "Ain't no way this, ain't no way that, ain't no way, *no how*. Churches around here got everybody thumb-cocked to where you can't buy a liquor drink, can't buy a pack of smokes, can't make noise—and you sure as hell can't have anything but church music until afternoon, when all the preachers get burned out preachin' all that hellfire and damnation."

Anna and Juliette exchanged a slightly helpless look. Anna took a deep breath, then tried to redirect the conversation. "I know you're very busy, Mayor Macrath," she said, "so is it okay if we discuss the parade floats?"

"I know all about 'em," she said. "About three years ago, had one catch fire. Some jackass decided to have an American Indian teepee and a campfire on one of them long trailers. The morons started smokin' some kind of *peace pipe* and set the whole damn thing on fire. Had to stop the parade and get the fire department to bring an extinguisher and snuff the thing out."

"Gee," Anna stuttered. "Well...I don't think we'll have..."

"Still sticks in my craw," Mayor Macrath groused. "But whaddaya need from me, sweetheart?"

Anna produced a portfolio of parade-theme renderings she had drawn. Each one was in full color with hand-lettering. "Well, first, I was thinking about honoring local heroes—sort of patriotic," Anna said.

Mayor Macrath reached over and refilled her coffee mug, then pulled the plug on her dilapidated hot plate. Apparently thinking about Anna's theme, she adjusted her ample frame and squirmed forward to the front of her chair, leaned her Popeye forearms on her desk, took a sip of the steaming black liquid, and grinned through her thin wire-rimmed glasses at Anna. "Local heroes, huh?" She snickered. "Might be a damn short parade!"

"Well... I'm sure..."

"Just pullin' your chain, girl. I like the idea, go on."

"I'm not just thinking about individuals." Anna shook her head. "I also want the hero idea to be symbolic, like a goddess of flowers and things. And I want to have music, too."

"What kinda music ya thinkin' about? I hope it ain't any of that rock 'n' roll crap. We need some good old American stuff."

"Oh, I definitely agree," Anna said. "My husband Billy and I picked out a few songs—sort of like a *freedom* reminder. All very patriotic."

"Sounds good to me, girlie." Mayor Macrath smiled. "How many floats ya got lined up?"

Anna produced a two-page, typewritten and numbered list of parade participants.

"Would ya look at that," said Mayor Macrath, clearly

impressed. "Last year we were lucky if we had twenty-five entries all together. Might have to get you on city council someday."

"Oh, well...thanks. I love—"

"What about our local businesses?" Mayor Macrath asked. "Who's gettin' them lined up?"

"Well, the Chamber of Commerce and the Young Businessmen's Association are working on them," Juliette said.

"With your permission," Anna added, "we want to give Jupie a free float for his barbecue tent. Is that OK?"

"Damn right, girl—he's the big cheese! Put him near the front, close to me."

As Mayor Macrath stood to dismiss the meeting, she put her hands on her hips and, short of breath, huffed, "You tell whoever wants to be in the parade the entry deadline is two weeks from tomorrow, last day in March, so hurry up and send me your entry fee or don't squawk if you get dinged."

"I'll get all the details to you," Annabelle said, and placed a manila folder on the mayor's desk. "That's the fireworks budget. Lake Ridge High School said we can use their football field."

"Perfect size," said Mayor Macrath. "Everyone in the county turns out for the fireworks—long as it's free."

Anna glanced again at Juliette, as they watched Mayor Macrath scan the document.

"City council boys don't want to upstage the Fourth of July—we never spent this much on fireworks for May Day." Mayor Macrath frowned. "City might be able to help, but we don't have no twelve thousand dollars to just blow up."

"I know it sounds like a lot, but it has to be special," Juliette said.

"Where in the Sam Hill are you gonna find that kind of money?"

Anna paused, cleared her throat, and said, "My father is on the Board at Lakeview Savings and Loan. He and the President, Mr. Gross, have agreed to put up half of the fireworks cost, if the city will cover the other half."

"Hmmm—guess you about got things wrapped up," the mayor said. She arched her shoulders, pinched her eyebrows, squinted at the fireworks budget one more time, and sighed. "Get our share down to five thousand, and I'll push it past those old buzzards on city council. If they balk, I'll let the whole county know they're anti-American!"

Chapter 29

<u>**Saturday, March 31, 1956**</u>

Late that Saturday afternoon, while Billy tuned the Ruhl's studio Baldwin and fixed the spotlight focus to spread a wider beam on Anna's microphone position, Anna cleaned their borrowed apartment in the back of the bar, dusted, and made their bed.

As she fluffed the pillows, her attention was drawn to a picture hanging over their bed. It was a portrait of Billy and her, taken by Helen on their wedding day. They were standing in the middle of Dreamland Bridge, waving to the wedding guests assembled in front of Jupie's barbecue tent. Removing the picture from the wall, Anna sat on the edge of their bed to examine it more closely. A beautiful, hand scripted legend was scrawled across the bottom: *Remember... Children are the bridge to heaven! Love, Willa Mae, Jupie, Arthur & Juliette—October 29, 1955.*

Anna felt a void open in her heart, as if this message had been tailor-made to torment her. She pinched her brow, bowed her head, and sighed at the sound of Billy's voice as he entered their bedroom

"Albert's dad is making dinner for us before we play," he said.

"I don't want to be late, so let's get dressed and head over there."

Anna usually would have feigned interest, but tonight she just couldn't bring herself to enthuse over another gig at the Café. She needed a break. "Please forgive me," she told Billy, "but I just don't feel like I'm up for singing tonight. Do you mind asking Lola to sit in for me again?"

Billy's disappointment was betrayed only slightly be his tone when he said, "I'll try."

Aside from her anxiety, there were two reasons Anna didn't want to accompany Billy that night to the Café des Amis gig. First—a most difficult admission even to herself—was the reality that she had an increasing aversion to the whole club scene, the dark bars, the stale atmosphere, the noisy crowds, the aroma of alcohol and cigarette smoke. Second, Anna had already invited Willa Mae to stop by that night for a visit to get caught up—and, perhaps, to grant herself an excuse to miss that evening's Café performance.

Anna hoped to discuss Billy and his plans to become a successful jazz musician with Willa Mae. Specifically—and at the heart of Anna's anxiety—Anna needed advice on how she could possibly tell Billy that she no longer wanted to be the Swing Kings' vocalist. She didn't love it in the same way that he did, and she could no longer pretend as much just to make him happy.

Willa Mae arrived at 5:30—an hour after Billy departed for Café des Amis. Savoring one of Willa Mae's gypsy tartlets, Anna sat forward, leaning her elbows on the kitchen table.

"I know Billy desperately wants to be a professional jazz pianist," she said, without preamble. "But, frankly, I want to settle down and have a baby."

Willa Mae wiped at some crumbs at the corner of her mouth with a napkin. "Have you told him that?"

"I've tried. But it seems like he either doesn't hear me or doesn't believe me."

"Why do you say that?"

"If I try to discuss it with him, he changes the subject."

"Well, he'll certainly pay attention once you get pregnant."

"That's just the point. I've wanted to get pregnant, but..." Anna stopped, reached for Willa Mae's hand, clutched it. "I'm so exhausted singing with his band. I don't want to do it anymore, and I'm afraid...I'm afraid he'll hate me for quitting."

Willa Mae held Anna's hand tightly in her own.

"Back in the thirties," she said, "just before I married Jupie,

I traveled with a gypsy band. Django Reinhardt himself—after his horrible injury—played with our band on occasion and asked me to tour with him as his main violinist. I agreed to go, but had to cancel when Jupie asked me to marry him. I just loved him so—the answer seemed clear to me."

Anna bit down on her lip, reluctant to ask her next question. "Can you tell me if...I mean, did you ever regret not going on that tour?"

"Oh, yes." Willa Mae smiled warmly. "But I knew nothing would ever compare to getting married, having a family, and being home with Jupie—for me, at least."

"Do you think Billy will ever feel that way?"

"He might." Willa Mae paused. "I'll tell you this much: Billy would feel terribly alone if you weren't around—and I'm not sure how he could deal with loneliness like that."

Following Eugène François's light supper of frisée des œufs au bacon, Albert and Billy discussed the band's upcoming season. Albert offered to manage the Swing Kings while Billy helped Jupie open Sandy Beach Amusement Park in mid-May. Billy was always reluctant to cede control of his band, but he knew Albert's offer was made in good faith, and not some backdoor attempt at a coup.

As Billy and Albert ironed out the details, I followed Ivey-Joe into the bar. There, he set up his guitar, plugged it in, and strummed a test chord.

Listening to his virtuosity with every practice passage, I felt great happiness for him—weighted on the other side by a profound sense of fear for the safety of Ivey-Joe, Lola, and their son James. Red Suggins and the hatemongers he had assembled at Jupie's fundraiser were hardly representative of the town's feelings on race, but they were a loud—and violent—enough contingent that I believed my discomfiture to be justified.

Given that, I pledged to nudge Billy to always do whatever he could to protect Ivey-Joe and his family. Moreover, I decided to speak with Ivey-Joe's guardian angel, *Lassuarium*, who also ruled the tenth hour of the night—the peak time for musicians to begin their work day.

"He's my most interesting ward in years," Lassuarium told me. "Whenever people speak of Ivey-Joe, they tend to use the same words: *elegant*, *graceful*, *versatile*. More than that, he's a true virtuoso. The way he plays guitar, it's like poetry."

Lassuarium was clearly just as partial to his ward as I was to

Billy. I knew this was more than just chest-pumping—it was a genuine, pure love.

I began to feel a similar affection for Ivey-Joe the more I heard him play with the Swing Kings. That said, notwithstanding the band's swinging repertoire and loyal following, this particularly dreary Saturday night at the Café des Amis held little promise of anything special. As expected, the sparse crowd barely generated enough business to pay for the trio's soft drink consumption, let alone the thirty dollars per man that Eugène François had agreed to pay. Curiously, however, one raucous patron insisted on drinking shot after shot of whiskey and soon took to heckling Ivey-Joe with racist slurs.

"Hey git-fiddle boy!" the man jeered. "What word starts with 'N' and ends with 'R' that you never want to call a black man?" Slugging back another shot, the man mopped his slobbering mouth on his coat sleeve and hissed at Ivey-Joe: "Hey, boy! The word's *neighbor*! You get it? Ha!"

In less time than it took for the drunkard's insult to make the few other patrons cringe, Billy bounded off the bandstand, grabbed Woody Plank, and wrestled him out the entrance. Outside, Billy held Plank by the collar and hissed, "I told you the last time you came in here to get out and stay out if you know what's good for you!"

"Get your damn dirty hands off me, Barnes." Plank broke free of Billy's grasp, then immediately stumbled to his knees. From the ground, to Billy's already-turned back, Plank made a weak, whiskey-soaked threat, "You touch me again, you'll get what's comin' to ya."

Relieved that the nuisance was now long gone, Billy rejoined Albert and Ivey-Joe inside. They each imbibed a glass of Eugène's favorite aperitif, Lillet Blanc. Smiling, Eugène paid the trio the promised thirty dollars, and, without further mention of the incident, sent them home.

There, Billy found Anna already asleep—albeit, from the looks of it, restlessly.

Friday, April 20, 1956

After welcoming Anna and Juliette into her office to discuss the final May Day parade plans, Mayor Macrath scrunched into her swivel chair and scanned the list of floats Juliette had handed her.

"Looks like you got your homework done," Mayor Macrath said. "See some names on here never been in our May Day parade before."

"I volunteered to help Anna with the accounting," Juliette

said. "Everyone has already paid the entry fee."

Mayor Macrath slurped the dregs of her four-hour-old coffee and squinted at the list.

"See you got the Lions Club and the Masons," she said. "First time that Cadillac dealer ponied-up, too."

"I talked to the community relations person at First Lakeview Bank," Anna said. "They've agreed to contribute twenty-five hundred dollars to the fireworks."

"I thought Lakeview Savings and Loan wanted an exclusive deal," Mayor Macrath said.

"Mr. Gross was very nice when I asked him if it was okay for First Lakeview Bank to participate," Anna said. "As long as Lakeview Savings can have the only banners along the parade route and at the fireworks, he didn't object."

"We need to get you on city council," Mayor Macrath said. "Those old buzzards couldn't talk a starvin' coyote into a steak dinner."

"The only thing…" Anna paused. "It's the grand marshal."

"Who ya got lined up?"

Anna shuffled her feet

"I haven't asked anyone yet."

Mayor Macrath leaned her flabby arms on her desk. "Damn, girl. Gettin' pretty late, ain't it? How come?"

"I've been thinking. It's almost always a man, but maybe it could be a woman this year."

Mayor Macrath rocked back in her chair. "If you're thinkin' about me, forget it," she said. "I was the grand marshal a few years back. All I heard was a lotta damned catcalls about fixin' potholes."

Anna shook her head. "Juliette and I are thinking about a woman who teaches at St. Mary's grade school."

"Yes," Juliette said. "She's very talented and sings at Bountiful AME Church, too."

"They got a whole passel of ladies singin' every Sunday," said Mayor Macrath. "Who ya talking about?"

"Lola Brown," Anna said.

Mayor Macrath paused as in thought, then said, "Lola Brown, huh? What's her story?"

Anna nodded and said, "Lola is married to Billy's guitar player, Ivey-Joe Priest. Billy always invites her to sing with the Swing Kings whenever I'm busy or under the weather. Sometimes, we sing a duet just for fun."

Mayor Macrath tapped a chewed-up ballpoint pen on her

desk, glanced at Juliette, then turned back to Anna. "You gonna have her sing during the parade?"

"Billy has a portable sound system," Anna said. "He can set it up in her convertible."

The mayor nodded. "All that music he does, I guess he would know."

"May I ask Mrs. Brown?" Anna said.

"What kinda music is she gonna sing?"

"Mostly gospel. Patriotic songs. She can start the fireworks with the National Anthem."

"Some of the jokers in this town could use a good dose of gospel music..." Mayor Macrath paused. "Go ahead, sign her up."

Anna beamed. "I'll call her as soon as we wrap up here."

Plagued by arthritic joints, Mayor Macrath braced herself on her desk as she said, "Gotta get ready for the council meeting tonight. I'll ramrod your budget through so fast those bozos won't know what hit 'em. We'll make it one of the biggest fireworks shows this town has ever seen."

Outside city hall, Juliette turned to Anna, shook her head in admiration, and said, "I can see why the mayor wants you on city council—you did a great job in there."

"Thanks. I might like to take her up on it some time—but not now, with Billy working all the time."

"I think that's something you can expect if he's going to be a successful musician: the more successful he is, the more he'll be gone."

"I hope not." Anna took a seat on the bench outside city hall. "I want to have a baby."

Juliette's face betrayed only the slightest hint of surprise as she sat down next to Anna. "Does Billy know that?"

"With him working for Karl—not to mention trying to line up gigs for the Swing Kings, and helping Jupie get the rides ready at Sandy Beach—we haven't talked at all about our plans, let alone about having a baby."

Juliette nodded, a cynical smirk curling the corners of her mouth.

"I had a similar experience," she said. "I was engaged to be married to my college sweetheart. He was a very talented writer. We hadn't talked about our plans after our wedding, but at our rehearsal dinner, he announced that he would be leaving for Spain the day after our wedding to write a novel about Franco's reign as King. It was…"

Juliette turned her head and dropped her eyes. Looking up at

Anna, she continued, "I didn't have much of a choice. After sitting there with my family—all of us stunned by my fiancé's news—I stood up, took the microphone, and said, 'Thank you all for coming. Our wedding tomorrow is postponed—indefinitely.'"

"Oh my god, you...you actually canceled your wedding?"

"Anna, I learned from my mother that being married to an artist is very risky. She was married to a photographer who spent too much time away from home photographing pretty girls for men's magazines. It all ended on a very sour note."

"Did she have any helpful advice?"

"Well, yes. I think it was helpful." Juliette took Anna's hand. "She said that I should plan for the worst, and if it didn't happen, I'd be lucky."

"That's it?"

"No. She also said that if I *didn't* plan for the worst and it *did* happen, I'd be screwed."

"She actually said *screwed*?"

"My mother was not bashful—Mayor Macrath reminds me of my mother a little, in that respect." Juliette squeezed Anna's hand. "You're a lot like the both of them, too."

"How so?"

"You know what you want, and you know how to ask for it. All that's holding you back now is the fear of what Billy might think—but that's no reason to resign yourself to an unhappy marriage."

Chapter 30

Friday, April 27, 1956

Preparing for the Ruhl's season opening and Karl's return with his wife from Florida, Billy had the odious task of flushing and cleaning the water lines, sanitizing the bar and kitchen equipment, checking cooler and freezer temperatures, and wiping down the counter and table tops. Meanwhile, Anna cleaned the restrooms, restocked them, and mopped the floors. At three in the morning, Anna and Billy collapsed in each other's arms in their temporary home behind the Ruhl.

"I don't know about you, but I'm bushed," Anna said as she rolled over to her side of the bed.

"Ditto, for me," said Billy. "I wish we didn't have to get up so early." He leaned up on one elbow. "So what's the game plan for tomorrow?"

"Since Juliette and I have done most of the work getting the parade organized, Mayor Macrath asked us to have breakfast with her at city hall beforehand."

"What about me?" Billy asked.

"I assume since the grand marshal is using your sound system, you'll be sticking close by to her."

"When will I see you?" said Billy.

"Mayor Macrath asked Juliette and me to help her get some volunteers to clean up the parade route while it's still light."

"Will you be finished in time for the fireworks display?"

"For sure. We have reserved seats for your mom and dad, and my dad, too. Juliette and I will help Lola get set up to sing the National Anthem. After that, we'll find you in the grandstand."

"Are you leaving early in the...this morning?" asked Billy.

"Juliette and I are meeting the mayor at six o'clock, sharp. She and Dad want to treat us to a few drinks at Café des Amis after the fireworks. I told her we'd love to."

"Sounds like a long day," said Billy.

Anna nodded, and soon she was fast asleep. Still a bit restless, Billy got out of bed and treated himself to a most relaxing shower. Then he poured a glass of Ross's Sloe Gin and listened to the cassette he'd recorded of his favorites. As "Straight, No Chaser" by Thelonious Monk geared up, Billy refilled his glass with two fingers of Ross's. Sipping the sweet liquor, Billy thought over the plan he and Albert had made regarding management of the Swing Kings. He still didn't love handing over the reins, but it was that or disband the Kings indefinitely and hope for the best.

On that somewhat sour note, Billy ambled back to bed, and—with Anna sound asleep—pulled back the comforter, jumped in, and switched off the nightstand lamp.

Saturday, April 28, 1956

Startled by the jangling phone on the nightstand, Billy fumbled to find it, then snapped to attention as Annabelle's panicked voice screeched at him: "Billy! Everyone's waiting for you to set up the speaker system on Lola's float. The parade's ready to start."

Billy's daze clearing, he blurted, "I'm...I'm on my way..."

A sudden strong gust of wind buffeted Billy as he caught his breath, searching for the grand marshal's vehicle at the parade's starting point. Spotting Annabelle, he pushed through the assembled judges as they evaluated each float's decorations for the award ceremony. Without warning, the superstructure of Simpson Realty Company's float wavered in the wind, collapsed, and toppled over into the street. As his son tried to salvage it, Nelson Simpson gestured to the pile of debris and bellowed, "Forget about it! Too damned windy to worry about it now!"

Disheveled and hung over, Billy set up the speaker system on the back of Lola Brown's grand marshal Cadillac convertible loaner from Lewis Motors, and tested it: "One-two-three...this is a test...one-two-three." Annoyed by the interference of gusting wind crackling over the speaker, Billy snatched the foam wind-protector from the box, snugged it over the microphone, and retested the sound: "One...two...three." He handed the microphone to Lola. "Try it out," he yelled.

Grabbing the microphone from Billy—and in her sweet alto voice—Lola sang the opening to "Lift Me Up Above the Shadows," then nodded to Billy and yelled back at him: "Ready!"

Catching up with Anna and Juliette, Billy patted them both on the back. "First class," he said, squinting up at the blinding overhead sun. "Other than the wind, it's a gorgeous day."

"I hate to say it, but if it doesn't calm down some, the mayor might call off the fireworks tonight." Anna said.

As the parade passed by Lake Ridge High School and turned the lazy S-curve of Blue Jacket Bend in the direction of the old Shawnee site of Flourish, Juliette said, "I'm out of flyers. Is it okay if I walk with Billy and listen to Lola's beautiful voice?"

Anna nodded and gave Juliette a quick hug. "I'm going to trail behind a bit, make sure everything goes smoothly."

As they began walking in step, Juliette turned to Billy and said, "Your wife is very talented."

"You're telling me," said Billy.

As if shaping her thought, Juliette paused, then said, "I wouldn't be surprised if the mayor asks her to be on city council."

Taken aback, Billy said, "Anna? Working for the mayor?"

"The mayor, all of us. She'd be great for the city."

Billy had no set response to that, so he and Juliette continued their walk in silence. Following the parade as it inched lazily forward, Billy and Juliette took in the beauty and sweet aroma of the spring flowers and trees. Block after block, lampposts festooned with hanging flowerpots swayed in the wind. Long strands of spiraling azalea blooms cascaded halfway to the ground. They inhaled the scents of budding dogwood, magnolia, and redbud trees; viburnum hedges rustled in the wind.

Further west, Blue Jacket Bend passed by the turnoff to the community of Flourish and its main attraction, the Woodland Cottage Sporting Club and its recently remodeled Café des Amis. Distracted from the floral beauty of the Café's spring landscaping, Billy's eyes drifted to the parking lot to see only one car there—Johnny Mocha's dilapidated old four-door black Lincoln Zephyr. He was able to quiet the quick pang of anxiety that rollicked his gut, and continued to follow the parade route.

As the parade advanced, Billy waved at the people riding on the Lakeview Savings and Loan float—Anna's father and the bank president, J.G. Gross—cheering them on. First Lakeview Bank's Carter Duffy and his wife, Nadine, followed behind. Carter nodded at Billy in recognition and Nadine waved as they passed him.

At the screeching sound of a siren, Billy turned and saw a shiny new black-and-white 1955 Ford Fairlane police cruiser with newly-appointed Detective Joseph Kuldau tucked behind its steering wheel. A blast of wind kicked up as Detective Kuldau tooted the cruiser's horn and yelled out something. Though Kuldau's words were swallowed by the wind, Billy bowed in respectful acknowledgment.

Following behind Detective Kuldau in the Russells Point Volunteer Fire Department's 1929 vintage Seagrave fire engine, Chief Elwood "Sammy" Powers waved as he tossed packets of sparklers to the pleading children scrambling to retrieve them.

On the final approach to Indian Lake Roller Arena, Billy and Juliette stepped to the side of the roadway and scanned the array of floats, high school bands, and decorated bicycles; the strolling clowns throwing candy to eager squealing children; the collectors showing off their prized vintage Corvette convertibles; and the procession of members of the Lions Club, the Chamber of Commerce, Boy Scout Troop 55, Brownie and Girl Scout troops, and Lake Ridge High School's graduating class.

Billy turned to his left and saw the city hall float, festooned with the city council's slogan: *We Can Do It!* Seated on the float were six city councilmen and their wives. Spotting Juliette, they all waved. As Juliette waved back, a blast of swirling wind sent one of the wives' sun bonnets sailing into the street; Billy grabbed it and ran back to return it.

Winded from his quick sprint to retrieve the bonnet and still woozy from his early-morning bout with Ross's Sloe Gin, Billy watched the last three commercial floats––Karl's Golden Ruhl, Fern's Ritz Club, and Sutton's Ark Restaurant—teeter in the wind and move on.

In the Roller Arena parking lot, Anna said to Billy, "Juliette and I are going to help the mayor clean up the parade route. You should go back to the apartment and take a nap. I'll call you when it's time to meet for the fireworks."

###

Finally recovered from overindulging, Billy sat with Anna, Juliette, Arthur, Jupie, and Willa Mae in the high school grandstand and listened to Lola Brown's rendition of the National Anthem. They rocked back at the thunderous boom of an M-80 silver salute signaling the start of the May Day fireworks. Glancing at the sky, Billy saw the smoke and sparks from the M-80 drifting westward on the gusting wind.

Gasping at the assortment of aerial displays—bursting Roman candles, flaring color stars, horse tails, diadems, peony and spider patterns crackling, popping, and parachuting—even the most critical pyrotechnic aficionados sat transfixed.

After thirty minutes of the spectacular display, with the echo of the ear-splitting finale abating, Billy, Anna, Juliette, and Arthur parted company with Willa Mae and Jupie––the lattermost now in obvious discomfort from the long day. Turning to Anna and Billy, Juliette said, "Arthur has to stop at the hospital for a few minutes before we join you. You two go ahead and we'll catch up with you shortly."

As Billy and Anna made their way through the smoke still swirling above the football field and headed toward Café des Amis, Anna held a hand over her nose to guard against the smell of sulfur.

Walking side-by-side down Marina Way, Billy decided to broach the subject raised by Juliette earlier. "I hear you and the mayor really hit it off," he said. "Juliette thinks maybe the mayor wants to hire you."

"She's mentioned that."

"I had no idea you were so...civic-minded."

"Me neither, I guess—not until I really got in to planning this parade."

"Well, I think it's great." Billy took Anna's free hand as they continued their walk. "I just had no idea you were so good at all this...stuff. Would you take the job if she asked you?"

"I could be interested." Anna shrugged. "It would certainly help us out a lot financially."

"What about the Swing Kings?" said Billy.

I sensed that Anna wanted to say something more confrontational here, to point out to Billy that his earnings as a musician were enough to support the two of them, but would not be enough to provide for whatever children they might have in the future.

"We'll just have to wait and see," she said instead, somewhat cryptically.

Before Billy could press her on this further, they rounded Blue Jacket Bend. Billy lifted his eyes and saw the starry sky shimmering as if illuminated by a million candles. Ghostlike billows of smoke danced in the flickering overhead glow as the piercing sound of sirens punctuated the thick night air.

That wasn't fireworks, Billy realized. "Someone's house is burning!" he said, frantically.

Running to the corner of Woodland and Indian Acres—the Shawnee reservation—Anna and Billy stopped short and searched the street in the direction of Woodland Cottage. Jammed together and clogging the street in front of them, Billy could see the Russells Point Volunteer Fire Department's engine struggle to activate its power system to douse the blaze. Adding to the spectacle, Sheriff Williams's vehicle and Detective Kuldau's new police cruiser blocked the way, their red lights strobing through the smoky haze.

Anna and Billy ran toward them until they were abruptly intercepted by a fire department volunteer who yelled, "Stop right there!" The inferno engulfed the Inn as Anna held her hand up to defend against the fire's heat. Acrid smoke fouled the air. Chief Powers's voice blared orders from a bullhorn: "Ladders! West Portico! Now! West portico!"

Anna yelled at Billy, "I hope to God Albert got his father out of his restaurant."

"Me too," Billy yelled back. But he couldn't get the image of Johnny Mocha's car out of his head. Especially in light of his idiot associate Plank's racist heckling, Billy wouldn't trust Johnny Mocha with a five-cent ice cream cone.

The only two pressure hoses owned by the Russells Point Volunteer Fire Department were barely attached to the only fireplug when they split in two from dry rot. They had to be taped up to function even remotely effectively.

Suddenly, the Inn's lights went out as the only power line broke apart, sending a sparking, serpent-like tendril whipping to the ground. Once again, Powers's voice boomed over a bullhorn: "Get back! Move!"

Through the haze, flames licked the trees that stood in front of Woodland Cottage. The trees bent and broke, shedding charred leaves that danced in the wind as they found the ground.

Billy and Anna jockeyed through the chaos to get closer until another volunteer fireman stopped them. "Too dangerous to get any closer," he said. "Folks from the reservation already bollixed everything up."

Billy pleaded, "I work here!"

"I know you do, but—"

"Did everyone get out?" Anna asked, plaintively.

"Whoever sounded the alarm, I guess it was one of the two guys I saw leave in a beat-up old Lincoln." The fireman pointed to an elevated area across the street and shouted, "Go stand over there. You'll be safe there—you can see all you need."

As Billy and Anna crossed the street and stood on the small rise he had pointed to, a muffled sound of an ominous explosion rocked the ground. Turning toward the blast, Billy saw a burst of fire rupture out of the ground at the side of the Inn and—from his experience working for Karl—knew that Woodland Cottage's propane tank had exploded. Bullhorns exhorted the awestruck crowd: "Clear the area! Clear the area!"

By the time the third pump truck arrived from Lima, flames shot from the roof—higher than the spectacular fireworks at the high school—gutting the structure. Standing dumbstruck at the devastation, some shook their heads and gawked at the scene. Others shuddered as the fire's hypnotic effect dulled their sensibilities. Several couples embraced as they edged away from the calamity. Billy couldn't guess how many people still lingered, but however many, they stood in mute witness to the cataclysm.

From their safe distance, Billy and Anna watched the fire consume Woodland Cottage as strong winds wafted the smoke and embers up in swirling patterns, all of it vanishing into the eerie light of the night sky.

"I can't look at this any longer," Anna said.

"Me either," Billy said, and led Anna around the safety barrier to the front lawn of Woodland Cottage, where a fatigued squad of volunteer firefighters remained ready to respond to any sign of sparks hitting the structures. Peering through tear-filled eyes as they walked, Anna saw Juliette and Arthur up ahead.

As Anna pointed them out to Billy, the revered old Woodland Cottage collapsed in a God-forsaken, thunderous quagmire of black mud, slime-covered ash, smoldering embers, and hissing debris

Anna and Billy pushed their way through the crowd toward Juliette and Arthur. As Anna and Juliette embraced, Billy saw Albert and Helen standing nearby, both of them crying.

Easing through the remaining bystanders, Billy offered his condolences to his best friend.

"Albert, I can't...I'm so sorry," Billy said.

"My dad's whole life...gone," Albert moaned, shaking his head.

As Anna huddled with her father and Juliette, Mayor Macrath approached.

"In all my years," she said, "never had a disaster like this!"

"Do you know how it started?" Anna asked, her voice tearful.

"Fire Chief Powers said the damned fireworks did it. Sparks. He warned everyone it was too windy," Mayor Macrath said. "Likely the Cottage's wood shingles is where it started.

Sunday, April 29, 1956

Early Sunday morning—standing under their umbrellas in the misting rain—Anna, Billy, Helen, Albert, and Eugène François surveyed the still-steaming ruins of Woodland Cottage. The bitter odor of wet ashes and charred wood reeked from the pit of black rubble.

After scanning the disaster, Eugène François turned to Albert and said, "I promised that asshole, Johnny Mocha...I never thought those bastards would..." His voice trailed off in muffled tears.

"What's your dad saying?" asked Billy.

"He told me that creep Johnny Mocha tried to shake him down yesterday during the parade."

"Shake him down? Why?" said Anna.

"Dad owed some mafia cats a lot of bread for remodeling the Café," Albert said. "That's all I know."

In the end, the disastrous Woodland Cottage fire, and its devastating consumption of Café des Amis, was a major blow to Billy's dreams. He wondered if the places he loved for their good cheer, warmth, and good times—Karl's Golden Ruhl, Fern's Ritz Club, Danceland, Stardust Ballroom, Moonlight Terrace—would one day be swallowed up by greed and hatred, too.

Anna shared these fears—though she and Billy never spoke of them. Her pain was compounded by a sense of guilt for having arranged for so many fireworks to go off that night—for providing the cover story Johnny Mocha needed to set fire to the Café des Amis. If she never saw another jazz club again, Anna thought, it would be too soon.

Chapter 31

June 1956

At the same time, I began to consider the possibility that Anna was undeniably right: her dream of a career in public service and a growing family was as valid to her as Billy's dream of jazz stardom was to him. In some ways, Anna's dream was *more* valid, especially in the wake of the fire at Café des Amis: clearly there was some trouble in the town, and why couldn't Anna be part of the solution to fix it?

Further, though GAs observe our time-honored precept—*nudge-not-judge*—it is not unheard of for us to examine the obverse side of the "nudging coin." And, whether I liked it or not, the truth I came to recognize was this: my sense of Billy's talent was tantamount to St. Paul's epiphany, which profoundly changed Saul of Tarsus's journey from *doubt* to *belief*. Only, in my case, my journey was from *belief* to *doubt*.

But nudging Billy toward Anna's point-of-view was a delicate proposition. For, while I had come to believe that Billy's musical talent was not in the same league as his role models', I knew this would be a harsh truth for him to confront. It was difficult enough for me to accept.

While I hesitate to say anything derogatory about Billy's talent—or relative lack thereof—soon after the Café fire, I confirmed my thesis on the subject by comparing Billy's playing skills to that of the pros in his considerable music library. Accordingly, I listened to Dave Brubeck and his blocky chords; Oscar Peterson, a lyrical soloist with classical influences; Red Garland and his innovative left-hand chording; the dizzying speed of Art Tatum; the smooth and soft touch of Billy Taylor; the blues-based styling of Wynton Kelly; the masterful technique of Hank Jones; and Willie "The Lion" Smith and his stride playing style.

In fairness, I listened to all eight of Billy's favorite artists until I was satisfied that my own biases couldn't mask the underlying truth that there were inadequacies in Billy's executional prowess. Given that, I listened to the remainder of the artists in Billy's jazz collection. After considering their recordings versus my in-depth knowledge of Billy's repertoire, I had to admit that Billy's playing offered a satisfactory level of entertainment, consistent with the expectations of the audiences in the local venues where he usually performed, but that they were not in league with his role models.

As a final test on my hunch about Billy's musical fortunes, I considered the conversation I'd had with Ivey-Joe's GA, Lassuarium, all those months earlier. And, while there were many marvelous descriptors I could apply to my own ward—*kind, dedicated, responsible, loyal*—I had to admit that words like *genius, master,* and *virtuoso* were not a part of that lexicon.

My unfortunate thesis being sufficiently proved, and my commitment to the GA Code of Truth being unbreakable, I began nudging Billy toward accepting a version of his future that did not center on jazz music, but instead reaffirmed his commitment to Anna and their family.

November 1956

Johnny Mocha called Billy to tell him that there was a change in the contracts for the Swing Kings' 1957 play dates. According to Johnny, "All bets are off when the calendar turns. There'll be a ten percent upcharge over this year." When questioned by Billy, Johnny deferred. "It's the freaking union, man. With all the colored musicians now, the venues want insurance to cover the cost of extra security."

Security against idiots like your pal Woody Plank, Billy thought but didn't say. With Mocha proving himself useless—and with Billy looking for an excuse to disentangle himself from the clutches of a probable arsonist—Billy took Dukie Kincaid's advice and booked the Swing Kings into a *terms-as-usual* one-night stand at the Blue Moon Supper Club in Toledo, Ohio, for its annual Black-and-Tan Holiday Gala on Saturday, December eighth.

Sunday, December 2, 1956

The Sunday before the scheduled performance in Toledo, Willa Mae and Jupie hosted Billy and Annabelle for dinner to celebrate the beginning of the Christmas season.

As the family dinner took place, my circle of warm light shone on Willa Mae's shoulder. After a jubilant toast to everyone's health, Anna raised her hand and turned to Billy. "I have a surprise—for all of us, really." She smiled. "Mayor Macrath has invited me to join the city council, working on the planning committee and heading up volunteer recruiting for all major events. She was so enthusiastic—and, besides, I'll love doing it—that I couldn't say no!"

To a round of applause, Anna continued: "And Billy—the mayor has authorized me to engage you and the Swing Kings to play at the city hall Children's Christmas Party on December eighth."

In my time as a GA, I've witnessed many startling

predicaments, and recognize that the element of surprise can be a very potent agent of change—perhaps the most powerful weapon of all. One of my favorite examples of an epic surprise comes from Greek mythology, where Helen of Troy—who was said to have been the most beautiful woman in the world—was married to King Menelaus of Sparta but was abducted by Prince Paris of Troy. The Achaeans set out to reclaim her and bring her back to Sparta, and so began the Trojan War.

A captivating tale, except for the fact that there is no reason to think there was such a woman as Helen of Troy, or that a war was fought over the abduction of any woman—no less a great mind than Herodotus believed it was just plain absurd.

All that aside, the story of the Trojan Horse makes my point about surprises. In one version of the tale, the Greeks finagle a way to get a large wooden horse inside the City of Troy. Inside the horse, Greek warriors hide. They emerge and, in a surprise attack, defeat the Trojans.

Though not quite as dramatic, Anna's news bulletin to Billy about the Children's Christmas Party was as shocking to Billy as the Trojan Horse caper was to Prince Paris of Troy.

"But Anna..." Billy stopped, inhaled deeply, and tried again.

"Anna, I'm booked for an important gig that Saturday night, remember? Can't we—"

"Billy," Anna interjected. "This is the first project I've been given by the mayor. If I can't book my own *husband* for an event, how will I ever convince her that I'm able to organize anything else?"

I won't say that I saw it coming, but it didn't surprise me that, despite their external harmonic appearance, the internal makeup of Billy and Anna's personalities—their mutual low thresholds for playing second fiddle—would eventually lead to discord on something or other.

It was clear that Billy felt a significant measure of resentment toward Anna's surprise announcement of her commitment of *his* time, directly interfering with the Swing Kings' gig. His face turned crimson as he said, "I have to be in Toledo, Anna. The band and I have already made a commitment—which you *knew* about, by the way."

"Toledo is a long way to go for a one-night stand," Anna countered. "I thought you'd prefer something a bit closer to home."

"Gee, Anna, I didn't realize you'd taken over as my booking agent."

"I didn't say that—"

"Look, from now on, I'll make my own plans. And don't expect me to ask you for your approval, either."

"That's just it, Billy—you *never* take the time to consider how I might feel about what you do with the Swing Kings, whether I approve of it or not."

"Oh, so suddenly you don't approve of the band I've poured the last four years of my life into?"

Anna paused for a moment, and when she spoke again, it was in a smaller, wounded voice. "I want you to be successful," she said. "But I want you to care about *my* success, too. This job with the mayor's office *matters* to me, Billy."

"And what about being the band's vocalist? Doesn't that matter to you?"

Anna braced back. "Don't misunderstand me, Billy: I want to do things together. Of *course* that time we spend together matters to me. But I want to keep my job at city hall. I want to have a family, have a normal life like our parents." At this, Anna turned to the heretofore-silent Jupie and Willa Mae, and offered an apologetic grimace. Turning back to Billy, she said, "You can still play a few gigs—in fact, I'll help you book them. But right now, things have to change, or..."

As Anna struggled to bite back tears, Willa Mae took the opportunity to intercede. She whispered to Billy, "*Te aves yertime mander tai te yertil tut o Del!*"

"I don't understand. Why is this my fault?" Billy shook his head. "I'm only trying to do what I've dreamt of doing all my life: be the best jazz pianist possible so that I can support myself, and my family."

Expecting his mother to defend him, Billy was taken aback when she said, "You can do that by honoring your wife's wishes—by treating them with as much respect as she's treated yours all these years."

A better word for what Willa Mae was suggesting would be *compromise*, the cornerstone of any lasting relationship—and, to be fair, something that had been sorely lacking throughout Billy and Anna's marriage thus far.

Perhaps Billy was finally coming to the same, albeit reluctant, realization—thanks to Willa Mae's *nudging*. He shook his head and made his concession: "Fine," he said. "If that's what you want, I'll ask Dukie to sit in for me in Toledo."

Chapter 32

That winter, still chastened by their blowout at the holiday dinner, Billy was reluctant to book many gigs for the Swing Kings—and certainly not through Johnny-the-four-flusher-Mocha, who had already bungled the year's early bookings. Billy told himself he was content with the occasional gig Anna booked for the band at some municipal event or other, and he betrayed no disappointment when Albert, Ivey-Joe, and the rest of the band took out-of-town engagements without him. To keep his mind off music, Billy tried to focus on getting the Ruhl up and running for its summer season, though his heart wasn't much in it.

In March, when he expressed his woes to Albert—newly back from his honeymoon with Helen Martin *née* Gordon—Albert made an obvious suggestion. "Why not ask my old man for some help with the Ruhl? He's beside himself since everything went down with the Café."

And so began a fruitful partnership between Billy and Eugène François. It wasn't long before Eugène revealed his wish to add a food service component to the Ruhl, and when he and Billy presented their idea to Karl when he was back in town over the Easter holiday, the proposal was a hit. The Ruhl would open as usual for Memorial Day weekend—with a newly-installed kitchen and world-class nightclub menu.

"It's simple," Eugène François said at his first meeting with Billy post-anointing by Karl Ruhl. "If you can learn how to make a good club sandwich, you won't have to think too hard about anything except good service and a clean place."

Eugène François opened his date book and scratched his chin. Looking up, he said to Billy, "To get ready for a May opening, the first thing we do is get ourselves a new mop and mop bucket. If there's one thing I beat over my employee's heads at the Café, it's that you can't have a clean floor with a dirty mop bucket!"

"Makes sense," said Billy, struggling to match Eugène François's enthusiasm.

Eugène François drummed his fingers on the table. "Just remember this: the food brings 'em in the first time; A good experience brings 'em in after that. Hire good people, train them, and get out of their way!"

###

Tuesday, May 28, 1957

Jupie couldn't help but notice how enterprising his son had become. It filled him with great fatherly pride, but also a kind of wistfulness: this was the sort of elbows-deep food service work Jupie had always assumed Billy had no interest in. Still, two nights before the Ruhl's official reopening—during the dry run Billy and Eugène François had invited their closest friends to attend—Jupie asked the question he had been afraid to broach all these years.

"Billy," he said, during a moment later in the evening when he could be alone with his son, "I'm so impressed with everything you've done here, and I'm wondering—well, do you think you'd be interested in taking over the barbecue tent for me after this summer's season?"

Billy was speechless. Jupie assured him he didn't need an answer right away—"Just think about it," he said. And then, tilting his head toward Eugène François, who was happily making the rounds, refilling everyone's glasses with more whiskey, Jupie added, "You'd certainly be leaving this place in capable hands."

Later that night, Billy stepped out for some air. He paced the front sidewalk. Up and down, up and down, again and again. Then, ambling toward the parish hall, he wondered just how much he would sacrifice, if anything, by leaving the Ruhl to run the barbecue tent.

More importantly, what would happen to the Swing Kings? Would accepting his father's offer mean giving up on his dreams of true jazz stardom? That would be the life-changer. Was it something he could bear—or would he eventually regret it?

And what about Anna? She had made it clear what she wanted: *to have a normal life.*

He would talk with Anna. He needed her guidance now more than ever.

Just then, walking past St. Mary's, Billy saw a figure approaching: Dukie Kincaid. Quickly, he extended his hand and said, jokingly, "Don't you know this is a dangerous neighborhood? You could be mugged."

"No such luck," said Dukie. "Just finished cleaning the parish hall, and now I'm headed home. What are you doing?"

"Just taking a break from the dry run at the Ruhl—we added that kitchen, you know? And, uh, I guess I'm trying to avoid my dad. And Anna."

Dukie offered Billy a sympathetic, if bewildered, look. "Let's go to Percy's and get some ice cream," he said.

Tuesday night's after-dinner ice-cream crowd being sparse, Billy and Dukie took the back booth and ordered milkshakes.

"So," Dukie said, taking a sip. "What's on your mind, Billy?"

It seemed like the perfect time for me to nudge Billy again about the question of his career as a pianist.

"I'm...I feel like I'm wasting my time," he said. "Do you know what I mean? No matter what I do, I'm not getting any better. The gigs are the same old joints. Mocha is useless. You've been great about getting us regular gigs, but I know Anna gets antsy if I'm away too long. On top of that, the bread is lame, and I don't want to travel that much anymore—"

Dukie didn't wait for Billy to finish. "That's what has you and Anna...squabbling?"

"That's part of it. She wants to have a baby. I'd like that, too, but man—I'm not sure I'm cut out to be a daddy."

Dukie sat back and smiled. "That's the usual hang-up. Babies and bar gigs don't work too well together. I've been there myself and made the wrong decision."

Billy sat forward, his eyes wide. "You...have a baby?"

"No, I had a wife. She wanted a baby and I didn't, so she ran off with the Omar bread man, had a baby, and...well, you know the rest about me. A little too much booze and a little too much blues."

"What do you..." Billy sighed. "I know you aren't me,

but...what should I do?"

"Here's what, Billy." Dukie held up a hand for emphasis. "Don't be a fool like me. Even though you'll love jazz all your life, it's no substitute for loving Anna and making her the happiest mother on earth with as many babies as you can make."

Dukie shook his head, appearing suddenly pained. "Besides, man, it's time we talked. I hope you aren't in a hurry."

"What's happening, man?"

Dukie sat back, drew a deep breath.

"This is from me to you, Billy. From my heart."

Billy tapped his fingers on the table top. "Dukie, if this is a sob story about you and booze, I can't—"

"Don't cut me off, man. I wish it was about booze, but it ain't—it's about you."

"Me? Did I piss off someone else? Who? If it's that jackass Mocha, tell him to screw off--we're finished anyway."

"No, man—this goes back to you and me. I've been a little...well, I guess I missed a bunch of opportunities to just be straight with you about something."

"What are you talking about?"

Dukie put his elbows on the table and leaned forward. "I've

watched you grow for a lot of years. In all that time, I've encouraged you to work hard—and you have. But man, I've been where you want to be as a musician. It's hard for me to say this, but man...." Dukie squinted his eyes, then: "The truth is, man...I don't think you're ready yet for the big time."

Jolted, Billy frowned and wrinkled his brow as Dukie continued.

"Don't get me wrong, man—you're damn good. But there are a lot of solid piano cats in New York, and Chicago, any of the big cities—guys as good as you, or frankly even better—and *they're* having trouble finding gigs. I guess what I'm saying is that I just don't like your odds, man."

Clearly rattled, Billy said, "So you're saying I should quit."

"I'm just saying you should *think* about all this, man." He tried to break the tension with a trademark grin. "But don't think about it too long—that's how I became an alcoholic."

Beyond Jupie's invitation and Dukie's advice, Billy's future hinged most on his own admission: *no matter what I do, I'm not getting any better.* This was the inescapable truth he could no longer ignore.

It gripped Billy as he ran back to see Anna. Entering their cozy apartment, he found her snoozing on the sofa. Tip-toeing toward her, he puffed out a long, slow breath, snuggled next to her on the sofa, and put his arms around her.

Awake now, Anna burrowed into Billy's comforting arms.

"Where have you been?" she asked. "I lost you somewhere in the middle of the dry run."

"I needed some fresh air after Jupie asked me...uh...he wants me to run the barbecue tent next summer."

Anna sat upright and turned to Billy.

"Run it? You mean full time? What did you tell him?"

Billy put his hand under Anna's chin and kissed her on the forehead. "I want to know what you think about that," he whispered.

"I don't...I can't..." Anna sputtered. "What I think? You know what I think, Billy. It's up to you—I just want you to be happy."

Billy squeezed Anna tightly and whispered in a most intimate tone, "You know what would make me happiest?"

"I...no...what? And don't kid around, just tell me."

"Now that I'll be working for Jupie and you're working for the mayor, we'll be home together at night." Billy grinned. "So let's pick out some good jazz tunes to listen to when we make love."

###

Wednesday, January 22, 1958

Ten o'clock sharp, the Sandy Beach Businessmen's Association convened its year's first meeting at city hall—attended by Stump Brewster, Red Suggins, Alma Dinova, Mutt Pickering, Marge Costin, Babbs Donley, James Dressel, and Dr. Tommy Ryan—plus Billy Barnes and Eugène François Martin.

One minute past the hour, ceremonial chairperson Mayor Bunny-Sue Macrath slammed down her oversized gavel, nodded respectfully, pointed to the younger of the association's two new members, and said, "I think you all know Billy Barnes. You might have heard him plunking on the piano over at Karl's place. Well, now he's running Jupie's barbecue tent since Jupie says he's throwin' in the towel and retiring." The mayor paused, shot a smile at Billy, and continued, "You tell old Jupie not to be a stranger," she said.

After taking a sip of water, the mayor nodded coyly at the other new member sitting next to Billy. "Now unless I'm goin' blind, that good-looking hombre next to Billy-the-barbecue-mogul is Eugène François Martin. He's Karl's new manager over at the Golden Ruhl. By the way, Eugène whomps up one damn fine club sandwich."

Following the introductions, a round of head bobbing signaled the formal beginning of the meeting agenda.

"Last time we met," the Mayor continued, "someone—I think it was you, Red—had something stuck in your craw about...what was it?"

Red Suggins consulted a crumpled piece of paper from his pocket.

"I wrote it all down right here," said Red, tapping on the paper. "I'm getting sick and tired of a bunch of rowdies causing trouble over at my Dairy King store. We gotta do something about it or, frankly, we can kiss our business asses—excuse my French—goodbye."

"What kind of trouble are you having?" asked Mutt Pickering.

"What kind? Retard boys runnin' around pinching girls on the butt," he blurted. "Three times last week!"

"If you're all that hung up on it, why don't you call the police?" said Mayor Macrath.

"I did. Took 'em two hours to get there last Saturday."

Mayor Macrath pointed her gavel at Red. "I heard about that fiasco. Our police report said your so-called security guard—that Plank character—was bullying people, just itchin' for a fight."

"He does a helluva good job and by god, I got a right to kick those trouble-makin' white trash off my property if I want."

"Can we move on?" asked Dr. Ryan. "I've got three root canals staring me in the face over at my office."

"We'll be out of here by eleven, sharp." Mayor Macrath cleared her throat and addressed Red Suggins. "You got anything else on your mind, Red—or does your butt-pinching report cover it?"

"I got one more thing," said Red. "I plan on buying that bakery next to my beer hall, so—"

Alma Dinova jumped to her feet. "You can stop right there, Mr. Bigshot. I wouldn't sell my bakery to a cafone like you if I was on my deathbed!"

Red leaned across the table toward Alma and hissed, "I'll remember that, you dago bitch." He straightened himself back up, making a show of fluffing his shirt collar. "'Sides, from what I hear, it's your damn dago husband that's on his deathbed. You're not gonna be able to hold onto that bakery much longer."

Mayor Macrath slammed her gavel down and barked, "That's enough, Red!"

Order was restored quickly as the mayor scanned the other meeting attendees, her eyes coming to rest on bookstore owner Babbs Donley. "Babbs, I see you sent a note to me complaining about the garbage people leaving the lids off your garbage cans after their pick up. What's that all about?"

As typical as any meeting I'd ever witnessed, the more trivial the problem, the more time spent on an equally trivial resolution. After answering everyone's written complaints, the subject of potholes took up a half-hour, leaving only the last ten minutes to the new members, Billy and Eugène François.

"Our food went like gangbusters last season," said Eugène François, "but I'm thinking about adding some more dishes to the menu—maybe drum up even more business."

Having sulked most of the meeting, Red Suggins leaned forward, cleared his throat, and addressed Billy and Eugène François as though they were defendants in a court hearing.

"Listen here, Frenchie—here's some *friendly* advice," Red growled. "You start foolin' around with food...if I was you, I'd be damned careful about puttin' anything out there expensive. Every bum in town will swamp the place—especially the coloreds—and heel out on the bill."

Shocked by the suggestion, the group sat mute as Suggins blabbed on. "And as for you, Barnes: I saw that colored guitar player of yours nosing around my place like he's fixin' to rob it." As if in warning, Red patted his bulging underarm coat-side and smirked at

Billy. "You get my meaning?"

I was more than pleased by Billy's prompt rejoinder. "Don't worry, Suggins, I got it. Ivey-Joe is a great friend of mine. So keep your bullshit threats to yourself or just name the time and place—"

"Now hold on just a daggone minute!" barked Mayor Macrath. "Before you two get lost in your underwear about who's gonna do what to who, I'm tabling this discussion until after the Park opens on Memorial Day. We'll straighten out what needs straightened out then."

Chapter 33

There's not much more I could tell you about the events leading up to Billy's demise. With my time in Russells Point running low and Billy's funeral only a day away, my obligation is to stick with the question at hand: *Who killed Billy?*

I'll offer just a brief summary of those intervening three years. First, the summer of '58 was a win for everyone. Jupie got the boardwalk attractions—rides, games, and food operations—running smoothly at full tilt. Mutt Pickering had a banner year of big band bookings at Stardust Ballroom, which frequently featured a few of the local Swing Kings filling in for vacationing or ill side men. First it was Georgie "Styx" Weaver for Ralph Flanagan's big band drummer at Moonlight Terrace; then, Ivey-Joe Priest sat in for Pete Rugolo at Stardust Ballroom in August; Albert Martin took the place of Artie Shaw's second clarinetist; and Jay Walter covered for Shorty Rogers's bassist, Curtis Counce.

Further, Eugène François Martin's always-evolving, innovative food service component at Karl's Golden Ruhl set impressive sales records, earning Eugène François the privilege of access to Karl's apartment behind the bar—formerly the domain of Anna and Billy. The two lovebirds moved into Anna's father's cottage on Orchard Island after his marriage to Juliette, and their subsequent move to Bellefontaine to be closer to the hospital where he served as Medical Director and she served as Chief of Nursing Service for Rehab and Physical Therapy.

Throughout 1959 and 1960, Billy and Anna thrived as never before in an atmosphere of cordiality, love, and togetherness. They remodeled *LeaWard Rest,* double-dated with co-newlyweds Albert and Helen, and stayed involved with the St. Mary's choir—which offered a perfect opportunity for Billy to keep at the piano, harkening back to his earliest days in the St. Mary's school basement, taking direction from Sr. Theresa.

Only one (considerable) ripple disrupted the couple's happiness, and it came in the early days of 1961. At its root, it was a microcosm of what's happened historically since the earliest conflicts going back to, let's say, about 2730 BC and the Set Rebellion during the Second Egyptian Dynasty. In all the hundreds of conflicts hence, there has been one common denominator: Someone takes a fancy to someone else's property or possessions. They express their abiding interest in the object of their affection, and are told in no uncertain terms to *get lost!* The ensuing enmity leads to an act of aggression by the covetous party and, accordingly, the violated party's response is a swift, crippling reprisal—and so on, until the last man standing claims the spoils of war.

Perhaps the allusion to history's greatest wars strikes you as extreme—but, had you been with me in those weeks and months leading up to this past Monday, July third, I feel certain that you would share my profound dismay over the depth and breadth of the stupefying injustices your human society tolerates.

Friday, March 17, 1961

Consider the events following the Sandy Beach Businessmen Association's March meeting. Call it what you will—*fate, luck, coincidence, pre-destination,* or *kismet*—but at that moment, the hand of God took an active role in shaping the outcome of Billy's demise.

To be more precise, it was the hand of Alma Dinova. At the meeting's conclusion, as everyone else dawdled out of the conference room, I saw Alma whisper something to Billy and surreptitiously slip a tightly-folded note into his hand.

Alma's note invited Billy, Jupie, Anna, and Arthur Lea to a

meeting at her home. Dr. Lea had been her husband's treating physician—as Red Suggins had cruelly (but correctly) noted several years earlier, Bruno Dinova was stricken with emphysema and had gradually been forced to reduce the time spent assisting his wife with the day-to-day operations of their bakery. The note hinted at the meeting's purpose without stating it outright: *Bruno and I would like to discuss the future of our business with people we trust.* The meeting was set for Sunday, April sixteenth.

It didn't take much convincing on the Dinovas' part to get Arthur to agree to purchase Alma's Patisserie on behalf of Billy and Anna. They had proven themselves effective co-owners of Jupie's barbecue tent over the past three seasons, and, in Dr. Lea's words, "this seems like the perfect time to expand your portfolio." Anna would learn to run the bakery every day under the tutelage of Alma, and would pass on her training to Willa Mae, who would then be on standby to help when the blessed event of a hoped-and-prayed-for grandchild arrived.

It all seemed perfect—and I didn't realize it at the time—but, in retrospect, Alma's note was the harbinger of Billy's death.

Upon Suggins's discovery of the sale of Alma's Patisserie, and recalling his earlier warning to her after her initial refusal to sell the bakery to him, Red concocted the whole scheme. Given his beer garden's adjacent location, he conscripted Woody Plank—his lamebrain muscle and nighttime bouncer at Suggins' Suds 'n' Grub—to make life difficult for Anna and Billy. Red's reasoning: enough trouble at their patisserie would dim their success, either driving them out of business or financially strapping them to the point of bankruptcy—at which point Red would swoop in, buy their whole operation, and leave them twisting in the wind.

Of course, Red Suggins being Red Suggins, there was little doubt that vengeance would be his. And, while *Penso Appositus* alerted me to the possibility of danger, I didn't fully appreciate that Red's raging temper would bring me to the most detestable, solemn, abject humiliation I was ever to experience in my entire existence as one of God the Son's guardian angels.

Chapter 34

<u>Saturday, July 8, 1961</u>

I know from past assignments that it would be off-base for me—actually, more like *insubordinate*—to question the timetable of God's will. And, no matter how many days—a hundred? A thousand? A million? Or just one—I can do very little to mitigate the pain of Anna's bitter purgatory. That would be the job of her own guardian angel, *Israfel*—who, ironically, is known for inspiring music and feelings of new hope. My suggestion to Israfel (never *advice,* only *suggestions* to a fellow GA) would be to resolve Anna's angst about her future alone by nurturing her recall of happier days, such as the Holland Theater Talent Contest seven years ago, when she knew she would love Billy Barnes forever.

Now, *forever* has come and gone in an instant.

Today, the day of Billy's funeral, Anna's grief is so profound she can barely get out of bed. She doesn't bother to get dressed until Fr. Stenz calls to say he'll be stopping by at 10 a.m. to visit and confirm the final arrangements for Billy's funeral mass at noon.

Crossing the threshold, he says, "I hope I'm not intruding."

Anna's voice virtually inaudible, she barely manages to say, "Come in...please...have a seat."

"Not to worry, my child. I won't stay long," says Fr. Stenz. "I just thought you might like to join me in a short prayer."

"Thanks, but I'd be surprised if God gives a hoot about me. I haven't exactly been one of his avid disciples."

"My dear young woman," he says, "there are no *ifs* or *maybes* in God's universe."

Shaking her head, Anna clears her throat and says, "I don't understand how a merciful God could let this happen to Billy. What did he do to deserve losing his life?"

"The center of His will is our only solace," the priest answers. "Let us pray that we may always know it."

Against her better judgment, Anna relents. "If you think it will help, go ahead."

Fr. Stenz pulls a booklet from his pocket, bows his head, and speaks in solemn tones:

"Dear God. Please take away Anna's pain and despair, along with any unpleasant memories, and replace them with Your glorious promise of new hope. I pray that her former doubts of Your infinite love will not color what she hears now. Help her to see all the choices she has ahead of her which can alter the direction of her life. I ask You to empower her to let go of the painful events and heartaches of these past few days. Comfort her and bless her with the knowledge that her grief is not about a lack of faith or a sign of weakness, but about the price of love."

Thinking Fr. Stenz has finished, Anna raises her eyes, only to see him offer her a holy card with the image of Christ crucified on it. He then turns the page in his booklet and continues reading:

"Help her to relinquish her pain, accept Your love, surrender to You her present, and move to the future You have prepared for her. I ask You to come into her heart and make her who You would have her be, so that she might do Your will here on earth. Together, we thank You Lord for all that's happened in her past and for all she has become through those experiences. I pray You will begin to gloriously renew her present."

Clearly touched by Fr. Stenz's soulful words, tears flow down Anna's cheeks as she mutters, "Thanks for coming to see me. I..."

"One more blessing, and I'll leave you to your thoughts," says Fr. Stenz.

Anna appears puzzled when he pulls a small leather pouch

from his inside coat pocket, opens it, and dips his thumb into it. As he touches his thumb to Anna's forehead and makes the sign of the cross with it, he whispers, "May this chrism of healing balm comfort you and blot out your sorrows."

Preparing to leave, Fr. Stenz hands Anna a typed page entitled "Order of Liturgy, Mass of Christian Burial." As Anna takes it from his hand, he says, "I'll see you at the church shortly."

After Fr. Stenz leaves, Anna's spirits have lifted enough for her to quit crying. Perhaps she's thinking that she must keep herself together: after all, she will be delivering the main eulogy at Billy's funeral.

She turns the holy card over to read the printed passage on the back:

Prayer of Redemption

Teach me O Father to fix my eyes on heaven

that I may generously trample under foot every

obstacle that presents itself in my path and attain

that degree of glory which You in Your mercy hold

out to me.

Anna must merely skim the prayer, for within seconds she puts the card aside on an end table. Then, she reaches for a brightly-embroidered pursette. From this, she extracts a small booklet and holds it to her lips, as if it contains a saint's relic: the book of Poe's poems Billy had given her at their lockers on that first day of school at Lake Ridge High.

Ignoring a tear trickling down Anna's cheek, I follow the words as she mouths them with quivering lips:

It was many and many a year ago,

In a kingdom by the sea,

That a maiden there lived whom you may know

By the name of Annabel Lee;

And this maiden she lived with no other thought

Than to love and be loved by me.

By poem's end, Anna's mouth has become a fixed line—determination, I think. I wonder what she'll choose to say at this afternoon's service.

###

Meanwhile, with a completed autopsy and an open investigation underway, the State of Ohio's "STAT" ballistics report arrives by courier at the Russells Point Police Department at 10:47 this morning. With my power of *Immunitas Temporalis* still within its grace period, I stand by as the report is delivered to Captain Joseph Kuldau, Chief of Police.

As Kuldau scans the report, I understand that—whatever answers are contained in this report—my assignment with Billy Barnes will still come to its official end tomorrow. And, while guardian angels don't speculate on what might become of God's privileged departed, my ongoing affection for Billy is a reminder that—while God's will can seem harsh—it *is* eternal and, in that sense, it *is* infinitely merciful.

And that's what I'm thinking as Captain Kuldau—in an act of professional courtesy—calls Bernard Sweeney and invites him to come to his office to review the details of the ballistics report on the bullet that killed Billy. Before handing the full report to Sweeney, Kuldau points to a typed summary below the forensic bullet chart. "I have something interesting to tell you after you read this," he says.

I watch Sweeney's eyes as he scans the letter:

Some common physical characteristics and performance parameters are on file for several .357 magnum loads, including—in this case—the projectile's unusual dull silver aluminum jacket. Therefore, I direct your attention to the load I've identified overwhelmingly as the fatal bullet—a Winchester Silvertip—typical of the loads mentioned above. Note: bullet weights ranging from 110 to 180 grains (7.1 to 11.7 g) are common for various applications based on desired use and risk assessments.

Accordingly, the weapon used to fire the aforementioned bullet was—in my opinion—a .357 Magnum Colt Python with a left-hand barrel-twist of six (6) rifling grooves, as opposed to five (5) for others. Consequently—in this examiner's opinion—the ballistics information points most certainly to the Colt Python as the weapon in question.

Signa a: Z.L. Bartlome, Ph.D.

Firearm Specialist,

Ohio Bureau of Criminal Investigation

Esse die: Friday, July 7, 1961

Captain Kuldau folds the report, hands it to one of his officers, and says, "File this and be sure you can find it later."

Turning to Sweeney, Kuldau smirks as though he's just cracked the code on who abducted the toddler son of aviator Charles Lindbergh in 1932.

For me, it feels as though God's team of mystery writers has finally given up toying with me. And Captain Kuldau will soon deliver similar closure to Anna—for, based on his analysis for Bud Sweeney, it is clear he knows now who killed Billy Barnes. "That Colt .357 magnum is the same shell I found outside Jupie's barbecue tent during the fundraiser a few years back." Kuldau pauses, scratches his head, and says, "Remember what you told me?"

Sweeney nods. "Red Suggins is the only fella in town I've ever seen with one of those."

"I couldn't get a warrant for the gun back then, but things are different when there's a death involved." Kuldau crosses his arms in front of his chest and smiles. "Officers are on their way to Red Suggins's place right now to collect the murder weapon."

From my vantage point in the choir loft at St. Mary's church, I watch as Anna Barnes takes the rector's podium, braces herself, and begins her heart-rending eulogy to her deceased husband. She wears a fashionable but conservative black requiem dress over a high-collared French-cuffed white blouse, with an antique broach once belonging to her mother fastened at the top.

As the crowd calms, Anna nods somberly and clears her throat. She dabs her eyes with a white linen handkerchief Willa Mae had given her, then blows a kiss to everyone assembled in the first pew: Jupie and Willa Mae, Helen and Albert, and Arthur and Juliette.

"Good afternoon," she says. "Some would say a funeral service rarely begins with a cheerful greeting, but this *is* a very good afternoon! Because I will reveal something which gladdens my heart. And"—Anna nods again to the first row—"I'm sure it will be a most joyful occasion for many."

Anna's eyes scan the church. Pew by pew, grim face by grim face. She flashes a small smile. "I have been given the greatest gift you can imagine. It's not that Billy's murderer is burning in hell—though, yes, that would be nice to know. No, the gift I've been given is from Billy himself. It's the ultimate gift of love. I'm..." Anna's voice falters. She dries her eyes and continues: "I'm carrying Billy's baby."

There is a shifting in the pews, people straightening in their seats at this unexpected (even to me) news. Anna's words—as though a canticle of hope calling all to rejoice—allay the spirit of regret, replacing the anxiety of remorse with the jubilance of God's blessing.

Anna pauses, inhaling deeply. "Regrettably, I decided to wait and tell Billy about our blessing until after the July Fourth holiday, when business would even out and we'd have some time to really cherish the news together."

When I catch the eye of Anna's GA, Israfel, she simply nods to me as though my days of influence on Billy Barnes are history. And...well...she's right. Her journey with her own ward, Annabelle Lea, will continue for years to come: my assignment with Billy Barnes, however, is over for good. Nevertheless, I've come this far in the life—now *death*—of Billy Barnes, and I've honored my vow to see it through to the exposure of his killer.

Hoping to close out this chapter in my guardian angel saga, my thoughts turn to one lingering question: *Should I just accept the fact that fate does exist—and that it usually leaves a trail of disaster no one can predict?* Maybe so.

But no! I've said it before—I don't like the word *fate*. There is a cruelty and hopelessness to the word and its variations—think *fatalistic*—and I refuse to accept such indifference to human suffering—and human *triumph*—is the true way of the world.

Listening to Anna's closing remarks, I'm gratified to hear her final thoughts: "And as for the so-called *accidental bullet wound to the chest* that took my Billy's life—well, I'm here to tell you that there's a bit more to it than that. You could call it greed, selfishness, indulgence, lust...I only began to recognize my *disease*"—Anna nods to Willa Mae and Jupie—"when I begrudged Billy the time he spent traveling and playing piano in those rundown, man-trap bars, instead of staying home with me. Yes, I admit I was selfish."

Anna pauses, dabs her eyes, and continues. "I can't help but wonder—if Billy had kept playing with his band, might they have found success on the road? Might he and I never have been here at all on that fateful July third night? In a way, isn't my own selfishness the root of the *accidental bullet wound* to Billy's chest?"

As the mourners lapse into an awe-struck silence, I can't recall anything from my past assignments more sobering than Anna's poignant comment.

How Anna will manage to go on from there, I can't say. But somehow, without hesitation, she continues: "In memory of Billy—and in lieu of flowers—Dukie Kincaid will now play Billy and my favorite song, Hoagy Carmichael's 'Skylark.' While he gets settled at the piano, I'd like to share a passage from the book of *Proverbs* that sums up my thoughts about Billy—and my resolve to raise our child in a way that honors the memory of their loving father and his world of jazz. I hope you'll forgive me for taking a few creative liberties."

Watching Dukie Kincaid slide onto the bench of St. Mary's recently restored Wurlitzer Spinet, it's clear he's doing his best to stifle his tears.

He plays the song's introduction as Anna delivers a most poignant elegy to the memory of her husband:

> *When one finds a worthy husband, his value is far beyond diamonds. His wife—entrusting her heart to him—has an unfailing prize.*
>
> *He brings her good, and not evil, all the days of his life. He works with loving hands to shear, plow, and render oil for cooking, warmth, and light. He puts his shoulder to the wheel, sorts the wheat from the chaff, and stores the best grapes for celebrating the return of a lost lamb. He reaches out his hands to the poor and extends his arms to the needy.*
>
> *Charm is deceptive and beauty fleeting, the man who honors his family is to be praised. Give him a reward for his labors. Listen to his music! Let his earthly works be*

celebrated in God's house of many mansions—the house of

the Lord—His house of music—His house of jazz, blues, and

gospel.

Some weeping silently, others sighing with joyful hearts, I wait and watch as Anna nods to Willa Mae and Jupie. "One last thought," she says, turning her attention back to the mourners.

"This morning, I was blessed with a visit from Billy's parish priest, Fr. George Stenz. I was grieving to the point that I could barely speak. No, I've never been a pious person—far from it. But I am spiritual enough to appreciate the padre's prayerful thoughts. As if he were standing here right next to me this minute, I clearly recall what he said that I will never forget: 'Grief is not about a lack of faith or a sign of weakness—but about the price of love.'"

Stepping away from the pulpit, Anna pauses, joins Jupie and Willa Mae, and exits St. Mary's Church. Outside, Anna hugs Dukie, Albert, and Helen, and—following Willa Mae and Jupie—they make their way slowly across the street to Billy's family residence.

In a bittersweet moment, Albert picks up a stone, turns, and hurls it at the funeral hearse bearing Billy's remains for burial in Calvary Cemetery.

Coda

It's tempting to gloat, but Luke 14:11 is a sobering reminder not to: *For everyone who exalts himself will be humbled.* Given that, I feel vindicated in my suspicions about Coroner Brown's slipshod conclusion regarding Billy's demise. I knew who killed Billy the moment the ballistics information was returned to Captain Kuldau from Columbus yesterday.

Given the whole disheartening situation, it's time for me to move on to my next assignment: the newborn English infant, Diana Frances Spencer. Looking ahead, I have to believe that my guardianship of her will pale in comparison to my time with Billy. I will always be faithful to his memory—and, in the end, I regret not having been more diligent when I was with him on the night of the riot. It was right there in front of my eyes! But, sometimes, God the Son reminds us guardian angels that we are *fallible.*

In that regard, I've quite relished the article written by Captain Joseph Kuldau and published in the *Indian Lake Weekly* the day of my departure for England: Woody Plank was arrested on a stolen gun charge filed by Red Suggins—a Colt Python .357

Magnum—which Woody claimed he had borrowed from Red to shoot rats at the county dump over the holiday weekend.

Preparing to leave for England, I am searching for an appropriate farewell. I feel the opening lyrics from Billy and Anna's favorite song, "Skylark," might serve as a touching, though bittersweet, summary of Billy's lifelong quest:

> *Skylark...*
>
> *Have you anything to say to me?*
>
> *Won't you tell me where my love can be?*
>
> *Is there a meadow in the mist*
>
> *Where someone's waiting to be kissed?*

And, for my own post-script, I choose the tune's final verse:

> *Oh, Skylark*
>
> *I don't know if you can find these things*
>
> *But my heart is riding on your wings*
>
> *So if you see them anywhere*
>
> *Won't you lead me there?*

OHIO HISTORICAL MARKER

SANDY BEACH AMUSEMENT PARK

Nicknamed "Ohio's Million Dollar Playground" or "Atlantic City of the Midwest," Sandy Beach Amusement Park opened here on May 29, 1924. The park at Indian Lake featured a 2,000-foot long roller coaster and other popular rides, a boardwalk, and the Minnewawa Dance Hall. The Minnewawa and its succeeding dance pavilions hosted the greatest names of the Big Band era, and thousands of people came from all over Ohio to listen and dance to these popular entertainers. Societal turmoil and rioting in the 1960s affected the popularity of the park. Diminishing crowds, plus competition from larger theme parks such as Cedar Point and Kings Island, led to the park closing in the early 1970s. The lone remnant of the park is the steel arch bridge that spans the harbor.

THE OHIO BICENTENNIAL COMMISSION, THE LONGABERGER COMPANY
LOGAN COUNTY HISTORICAL SOCIETY
THE OHIO HISTORICAL SOCIETY
2003

3-46

As America's amusement parks gradually closed in the 1960s, historical markers such as the one above spoke a somber requiem to the great era known as the "Nifty Fifties."

Afterword

It's been said that "Inside every older person is a younger person wondering what the hell happened!"

Perhaps this is true. In my case, however, the *younger* person lurking inside me for the past 83 years is my guardian angel. His name is *Anäel* (pronounced "Ann-yell"), meaning one who oversees all matters of the heart. Anäel has kept a record of all my blessings, good times, disappointments, and memorable occasions in a diary he's entitled:

FROM THE HEADWATERS OF POSSUM RUN:
A Brief Recap of the Events Leading up to the Demise of One
Charles W. Rath

(Anäel *does* have a sense of humor: Possum Run is an unnavigable little creek at the edge of my hometown of Bellefontaine, Ohio. And no, I'm not dead yet—just heading that direction.)

Now, to capture Anäel's precious memories and pass them along to others, I've recounted them in this novel. Many people have asked me what inspired this story. So let me share a short summary of my blessed life—all 80-plus years of which have formed the basis for *In Lieu of Flowers*.

During my childhood in Bellefontaine, Ohio, my mother and father gave me everything I ever needed and more. My mother was a loving, giving woman, dedicated to the art of homemaking (and I do call it an *art*). My father was a disciplined, hard-working salesman who took care of business and prided himself on never being on anyone else's payroll. He lived by his wits alone, prospering and growing through 100% commission-selling, pounding the west-central Ohio pavements selling groceries first, printing and business forms later—and providing everything for our family's needs and wants.

The truth about my life is that I always enjoyed what was going on at the moment and never spent much time worrying about what was around the bend or looming over the rise in the road. Interesting thing is, this attitude somehow managed to prepare me for what would come to pass, giving me the wits to recognize opportunities and take advantage of them. (Note: This is *good advice!*)

1948—my 12th year—began with my teachers' recognition that I had considerable musical talent. My grandmother had given us an old upright piano when she passed away, and we kept it in our basement. My mother eventually hired a woman to teach me *something* to play—

anything would be better than my incessant and mindless pounding on the keys.

That following summer, fate took an interest in me. Our trash man, Moss, always made our house the last stop on his weekly route. One Friday afternoon, I heard Moss ask my mother, "Who is that plinking on the piano I hear?" She brought Moss down the stairs into our basement where—over the next two years—he would teach me to play the blues.

Pretty soon, I had my own seven-piece jazz ensemble: The Swing Kings. We played for dances at our WeWantchaInn Youth Center; Victory celebrations at the American Legion Post 178 after our high school football and basketball games; and school events such as sock hops and high school proms. My experience was further enhanced and my skills strengthened by the Swing Kings' summer gigs at Indian Lake's nightclubs, such as the Golden Ruhl and the Ritz Club—plus Sutton's Ark Restaurant, picnics, lawn parties, and Fourth of July celebrations.

But the 1950s set the stage for my future—or at least what I thought would be my future—as a *famous* jazz musician. There was a magic quality to that time: World War II was a springboard to a new sense of freedom, legitimizing behavior that theretofore would have been considered "unacceptable." A feeling of permissiveness encouraged all of us to experiment with everything: sex, drugs, fast cars, fast food, loud music, revealing hemlines, and backseat romances at drive-in movie theaters. Beyond that, the icons of that time were so rich, vivid, and colorful. Indian Lake was like a gigantic electronic billboard; Russells Point was a flashing *come-hither* neon sign; Sandy Beach Amusement Park was rip-roaring and sexy!

And, in that milieu, I had fun bragging about my plans of becoming a famous jazz musician. It was true: right there in west-central Ohio, the *Nifty Fifties* grabbed everyone by the collar and spun them around until they were giddy and euphoric with newfound freedom and the certainty of success on what was generally thought to be *Easy Street*.

However, *thou shalt not survive by jazz alone.* Outside the music venues, I learned to earn my own keep by cooking in local restaurants (no fast food yet as we know it today) like Bob's Drive Thru and A&W Root Beer. Summer weeks were split between working on the boat docks and in the kitchen at O'Connor's Landing on Indian Lake, where Mrs. Tannehill taught me how to clean chickens, chop onions, peel potatoes, wash pots and pans, and scrub floors. Then, I'd embark for a piano gig at one of the summer-season clubs—or, in the winter, Bellefontaine night clubs such as the Elks, the Eagles, the 151 Club, the Hofbrau Haus, and the Rathskeller, or private events such as the Knights of Columbus parties at St.

Patrick's Parish Hall. After high school, there was the University of Notre Dame, where I played in a quintet headed by now world-famous New York-based jazz guitarist, Gene Bertoncini—now known as "The Segovia of Jazz."

Beyond that period circa 1959, another influence shaped my musical future: independent *"Show Biz"* venues like the Kirwan Hotel just off the square in Lima, Ohio. A friend arranged a gig for me at the Kirwan Hotel Lounge, playing piano for an act called *Vaudeville Memory*: a tired burlesque show featuring a worn-out performer who would later provide the inspiration for Lady Sylvia in Chapter 20 of this novel.

Regardless of repute, every musical outlet appealed to me: from school ensembles and local bars and clubs, to big-band venues in Youngstown, Cleveland, Cincinnati, and Buckeye Lake. I thrilled at playing music with my friends, all of us pressed as close to the bandstand as humanly possible—it was kindling for my desire to make music my life's work.

It all appeared to be a foregone conclusion until, *Bam!*—I realized, through trial and error, that my musical talents, though considerable, were a better fit for the local venues. Alas, the Big Apple was not in the picture. The final nail in the coffin came with the historical riot at Indian Lake over the weekend of July 4th, 1961. The crowds diminished, my former music venues dried up, and the big band era was over.

From then on, I embarked on a career in sales and marketing, courted my wife-to-be, got married, and raised our three children in the Buckeye State—where we've lived since 1964. Since that time, my lifelong goal has been to recount my life in the Nifty Fifties as an aspiring jazz pianist. Hence, *In Lieu of Flowers*. I hope you've enjoyed reading the novel as much as I enjoyed writing—and living—it.

-Charles W. Rath

March 18, 2019

Acknowledgments

My special thanks to the friends who helped me get this story out of my head and onto paper (well, into my computer): Msgr. David Sorohan; Stephen Devoe, M.D.; Alan Gregory; Matthew Dee; Trevor Torrence; Marge MacGillivray; James H. Gross; Jim Delong; Eric Rickstad; Dr. Mark Morton; David J. Shanahan; Tierney Sutton; Audrae Hughes; Bud and Pat Sweeney; Robert E. Byrnes; Daniel Rapp; Katie Talbott; Chas. A. Rath; Anne E. Lewis; John W. Guy; Clifford Williams; and Jim Merkel.

Many others along the way chipped in with various plot thoughts and suggestions. Collectively, I refer to this group as my fellow *Cascaders*: we would enjoy an occasional round of golf at The Homestead Cascades, followed by beverages and food at Woodland Cottage Sporting Club, and end the day on the veranda with cigars and discussion of odd topics—including what I was trying to accomplish with my writing. Thanks to all sixteen of them, as well as the occasional alternates.

Additionally, I'm indebted to my long-time friend and voracious reader, Robert E. Byrnes. Bob has always been supportive of my writing efforts and helpful with his ideas about plot and character, his significant knowledge of the culinary arts, and his insights as an accomplished jazz pianist.

Friends both past and present—in particular, professionals in the field of music, medicine, and culinary arts—have contributed so much value to this story.

Here's a word about my personal experience: From age fourteen, I've played piano, vibes, and bass in local jazz/blues clubs, bistros, bars, and ensemble workshops. I worked summers in a commercial kitchen at an Indian Lake resort—O'Connor's Landing— and as a short-order cook at different family restaurants around Logan County, where I benefitted from the counsel and guidance of those whose success and reputation were rooted in their dedication to good food, good service, and good value. I acquired my experience in marketing and advertising under the tutelage of Mr. Joseph Mack, Dancer Fitzgerald Sample (NYC); in public relations under Robert Dilenschneider, The Dilenschneider Group (NYC); and learned much more from many others through the day-to-day rigors of my fifteen years as Chief Marketing Officer for Wendy's International. Thanks to my close personal association with Wendy's founder, R. David Thomas, I grew to appreciate the role that dedication to quality and customer satisfaction plays in business, particularly in the food service industry.

My last—and, on many accounts—my most important acknowledgment and deepest debt of gratitude unquestionably belongs to a very talented and dedicated young woman named Jessica Rafalko. Not only has she been the eagle-eye of my novel's structure, grammar, accuracy, and good sense, but also an unerring compass by which my story finds its way to the reader's heart. Thanks, Jess!

CPSIA information can be obtained
at www.ICGtesting.com
Printed in the USA
FFHW020834100120
57631140-63012FF